THE KILLING STREET

Chris Ould has written more than eighty hours of television drama, including over fifty episodes of the hugely successful police series *The Bill*, one of which won a BAFTA in 2009. Chris lives in Dorset with his wife and son.

The Killing Street is the second book in the Street Duty series.

www.streetdutycasenotes.com

THE
KILLING
STREET

Chris Ould

USBORNE

For Siobhan – a little late, but with love

I would like to thank Keith Gausden for his endlessly helpful
and generous advice on police procedure. As ever, the credit for
accuracy is his and the fault for errors is mine.

First published in the UK in 2013 by Usborne Publishing Ltd., Usborne House,
83-85 Saffron Hill, London EC1N 8RT, England. www.usborne.com

Text copyright © Chris Ould, 2013

The right of Chris Ould to be identified as the author of this work has been asserted by
him in accordance with the Copyright, Designs and Patents Act, 1988.

Cover photography by Elisabetta Barbazza

The name Usborne and the devices ♀ 🌐 are Trade Marks of
Usborne Publishing Ltd.

A CIP catalogue record for this book is available from the British Library.

ISBN 9781409549499   JFM MJJASOND/13   02824/1

Printed in Reading, Berkshire, UK.

AUTHOR'S NOTE

The characters and events in this novel are fictitious. However, the law and police procedures – with the exception of the TPO training scheme – have been kept as close to reality as possible.

GLOSSARY

asp: an extendable telescopic baton

blues and twos: lights and siren (i.e. blue lights, two-tone siren)

a brief: a solicitor

CCTV: closed-circuit television

CHIS: Covert Human Intelligence Source, an informant

CID: Criminal Investigation Department (plain clothes)

civvies: civilians – members of the public or civilian members of police station staff. Also, civilian clothing

CPS: Crown Prosecution Service

CSE: Crime Scene Examiner

DC: Detective Constable (plain clothes)

Delta Mike: call sign for all officers and vehicles attached to Morningstar Road station

Delta Mike Five: call sign for IRV

DI: Detective Inspector (plain clothes)

DS: Detective Sergeant (plain clothes)

FME: Forensic Medical Examiner

IC1: white European person

IC3: African/Afro-Caribbean person

index (number): car registration number

IRV: Instant Response Vehicle

Misper: missing person

obbo: observation ("We're running an obbo")

OP: Observation Post

PC: Police Constable ("uniform")

PM: Post Mortem – forensic medical examination of a dead body

PNC: Police National Computer

reg: a regular, fully trained officer

Section House: residential accommodation for police officers

a shout: call to an emergency ("We attended a shout in the city centre")

SIO: Senior Investigating Officer

TOD: Time of Death

tom: a prostitute. Also, tart, prozzie, hooker

TPO: Trainee Police Officer

turn: a shift, e.g. early turn, late turn

writing room: office equipped with computer terminals for PCs to write up reports

POLICE RANKS
(IN ASCENDING ORDER)

Uniform

Trainee Police Officer

Police Constable

Sergeant

Inspector

Chief Inspector

CID

Detective Constable

Detective Sergeant

Detective Inspector

Detective Chief Inspector

HOME OFFICE PRESS RELEASE:

"The Trainee Police Officer programme is a pilot scheme which will enable the Police Service to enrol and train new recruits from the age of sixteen. Training will last two years, combining Academy study with Street Duty placement at selected operational stations.

On completion of the initial two-year training course, Trainee Police Officers will serve an additional year as Probationer PCs before joining their selected station as regular officers.

We anticipate that the TPO programme will enable the Police Service to more actively engage with younger elements of the community, as well as provide a fast-track entry to the Service for recruits demonstrating outstanding ability.

The TPO programme will be conducted on a trial basis in England and Wales and applicants will be chosen by selective interview. It is anticipated that the first intake of TPOs will number fifty, divided between three areas of the country: the South-west, North-east and the Midlands."

ENDS

FRIDAY

"Why don't you just go then? Go on – you're old enough, you know everything. Just go! Give us all some bloody peace and quiet for a change!"

So that's what she'd done, a couple of weeks after her sixteenth birthday – packed a bag and left.

She was sick of the rows anyway – on and on and on. Every time they were in a room together he was just looking for some reason to have a go at her. And her mum just let it happen, as useless and pathetic as ever. It was like he'd *wanted* her to leave, and now that she had she wouldn't go back – it would just be one more thing he'd use to rubbish her. He'd like that.

Dean was different though – the way he looked after her, right from that first time they'd met in the park. He'd asked if she was okay and she'd said that she was, even though she knew she probably didn't look it. She'd been sleeping rough for a few days by then, wearing the same clothes, wanting a shower.

Gemma knew enough to be wary when a bloke came up to her like that, but Dean wasn't creepy. He acted like he was genuine and he was decent-looking too – about thirty – so Gemma reckoned he'd probably got a girlfriend or a wife. He was just asking if she was okay, so she smiled at him and said *Thanks for asking* and that was how they got chatting – sitting on the steps of the bandstand in the park in the August sunshine.

Even after she went to stay with him at the flat she liked to go back to the park when the weather was nice. They'd just stroll together in the sun, holding hands, talking, making plans. When it was really hot they'd sunbathe on the grass and she'd lean her head on his chest, like a pillow. They'd share a can of lager, exchanging beery kisses, or get sticky from melting ice creams, bought from the kiosk by the gates.

Whatever they did, Dean made Gemma feel like she was special. He never treated her like she was only sixteen, but always like she was more his own age. He didn't make her feel like an idiot either, and he was always honest with her. Like when he told her that he'd had a girlfriend for three years, but she'd left him six months ago and it had taken him this long to get over it. He said Gemma was the first person he'd met in a long time who he knew he could trust. That was why he was telling her this. He *could* trust her, couldn't he? She *was* different.

And because of the look on his face and the need in his eyes, Gemma held him close then and said *Yes!* – meaning it and knowing, for the first time, that she was in love with him.

Of course, he wasn't perfect, she knew that. She knew the stuff he kept in the spare bedroom was nicked, but so what? It was like he said: *he* didn't nick it, he just sold it to people round the estates who couldn't afford to pay supermarket prices for vodka or fags.

And sometimes he did have a temper, but not often. And if he did lose it he always said sorry afterwards, making it up to her with kisses and presents. That was more than Gemma had ever seen her dad do with her mum, so this had to be better. It had only been a few weeks, but she knew that she loved Dean and that he loved her too.

She looked at him now, across the busy pub lounge, waiting for him to come back to the table. He was chatting with a guy in a denim jacket by the fruit machine, but every now and then he glanced over to her and smiled and she smiled back.

She didn't mind waiting. She knew he was probably talking business, doing a deal. It didn't matter. She always felt good when she went out with him like this. She liked it when he watched her get dressed up before they left the flat, like he was proud to be taking her out, like they were properly together: Gemma and Dean; Dean and Gemma – a real couple.

She was still thinking about that when she felt him sit down next to her again and put a hand on her arm. She hadn't realised that she'd gone off in a dream, staring blurrily at the tabletop and the glasses. She jerked her head up to look at him and smile, but it took her a few seconds to focus on his face. Maybe it was because of the rum-and-Cokes she'd been drinking, or the half an E from earlier. But it didn't usually make her feel this way. Could it have been something else…?

"All right, babe?"

Gemma nodded, smiled again. "Yeah."

Dean stroked her arm, then nodded away to the guy by the fruit machine.

"He fancies you."

"Get out."

"No, he does: he said."

"Get out."

Even so, she couldn't help looking towards the guy in the denim jacket. She was still having trouble focusing though. Everything more than a metre away was a kind of hazy blur – fuzzy and weird. And now her head felt heavy – disconnected, kind of unbalanced.

While she was thinking about that she lost interest in trying to see the guy by the fruit machine and instead pulled her gaze back to the table, refocusing with a kind of blink. Then she saw that Dean had been watching her – letting her look at the other guy, like he was waiting to see what she'd say.

"So?" he asked. "What d'you think?"

She smiled at him, even if it was a bit lopsided. By now she'd forgotten the question. Had there been one? – How pissed was she?

"'Bou wha'?"

That hadn't come out right, had it? She frowned and felt dazed.

"D'you fancy him?"

"Wha'? No! Get out!"

She tried to make a gesture so he'd know she really meant it, but her hand and arm didn't want to cooperate. It was odd, seeing them jerk around, all uncoordinated.

"I don' fancy nobody – nobody else – 'cept you. I love you."

She managed to find his hand on the table, grabbed hold of it, squeezing. He stroked her fingers.

"How much?"

"Wha'?"

"How much d'you love me?"

The question confused her. It was hard to work out what he meant. She wanted him to talk about something easier.

"Mass-es," she said. "You— Masses 'n'— massesnmasses…"

She lopsided-smiled again but then she felt her head loll downwards because she'd forgotten to keep it upright and when she tried to correct it it went too far the other way, backwards. Why was it so hard to get it to be in the right place? It wasn't usually this hard, was it?

"I love you masses too," he said.

She must have closed her eyes for a moment. Next thing she knew he was beside her, helping her stand, putting an arm round her waist. She giggled as she stood up. Giggled because it was funny, trying to stand when she felt all floaty and floppy and lovely and loving. She could just hug him, and she did, or at least tried to while he helped her towards the door on her uncoordinated feet.

Outside the fresh air felt good – cooler – and because it was dark she didn't bother to try and see where they were going as he supported her across the car park. She knew he'd be taking her to the van, to go home. She thought she heard him saying something but she wasn't sure. It didn't seem like he was talking to her.

"You got it, right?"

Who was he talking to?

She tried to look round but her head was too heavy to lift from her chest.

"Who— Where…goin'?"

"Shh-shh," he told her. "Not far. Just to the van. You need a lie-down, babe, that's all."

"Mmm… Lie down wi' you," she said, snuggling against him, feeling dreamy and lovey.

"Yeah, later," he said. "In a bit."

When they reached the van he held her up with one arm round her waist as he unlocked the doors. Through the heavy, warm cloud in her head she was vaguely aware that this was the back of the van, not the front, but it didn't seem to matter. Dean knew what was best. He must be doing something… Could she— What?

"There you go, all cosy – look."

Look at what? What was he showing her?

"Just climb in there. – Yeah, that's it. That's the way. Pull your legs in. – See? Nice and soft with that mattress, didn't I tell you? There you go."

Soft… It *was* soft. Like a bed… Like snuggling up on a bed in the back of the van. Lots of space… Dreamy, floaty space – like she was swimming…

Voices…somewhere…

"Come on then. Christ's sake…"

"No, man – she's out of it. I don't do…"

…Like she was swimming – floating – just on top of the water…rocking…rocking…

"Gem? Gemma?"

Something on her cheek. Harder. Sharp. Slapping. Try to look. Move.

"There. See? She's awake enough. Won't make no difference anyway. Do it in her sleep. I told you."

Rocking…rocking… She heard the van door close, tried to sit up, to see where he was. Dark – or were her eyes closed?

"Dea—?"

Then she felt him moving beside her.

"All right, sweetheart."

"Dea-n?"

No. No, it wasn't.

"It's okay. He's just outside. – Come on, turn this way…"

"Dean!"

She cried out but it was hardly a sound.

SATURDAY

SIX MONTHS LATER

1.

The room still felt chilly and damp despite the hiss of the gas fire – turned up full. Holly Blades kept her hands in the pockets of her jeans and looked out through the window at the winter-yellowed grass of the back lawn, untidy and strewn with last year's leaves.

It was March but the greyness of the sky showed no sign that spring was anywhere close yet. It was depressing, Holly thought. As depressing as the fact that Taz Powell was late – again.

In the kitchen DC Danny Simmons clattered a spoon into the sink and Holly turned away from the window. Like the rest of the house, the room was adequately furnished but empty of anything personal, anything that would have made it feel lived in – because it wasn't. It was a safe house and only occupied at times like this, for meetings with people who didn't want it known that they talked to the police.

"She's got till we've finished these," Danny said as he entered the room with two mugs of coffee. "Whatever the excuse, if she's not here by then we're leaving. She's taking the piss now."

"Okay," Holly said, accepting it.

He handed her a mug and sipped from his own, still looking hacked off. He was in his late twenties, taller than Holly by a head and he hadn't shaved for a couple of days.

"*And* the bloody pizza was a waste of money," Danny went on. "Bloody anchovies and chicken. Who eats those together anyway?"

This time Holly didn't bother to reply. A few weeks ago she'd have stuck up for Taz, maybe offered reasons why she might be late, but now she knew Danny was probably right – Taz *was* taking the piss.

It had taken a lot of time and paperwork to get Taz registered as a *Covert Human Intelligence Source* – in simpler language, an informant – and because of that effort Holly didn't want it to end up as a washout.

And at first it had seemed that Taz was just what they needed. She'd given Holly really useful information when Ashleigh Jarvis had been attacked on the Cadogan Estate six weeks ago, and after all that had died down she'd called Holly again with the name of someone who had done a couple of muggings.

That was when Danny Simmons had decided Taz might be useful as an official informant. Coppers weren't welcome on the Caddy, but because Taz lived on the estate no one questioned her right to come and go. Having someone like her – gobby, nosey and street-smart – as their eyes and ears should have been a real advantage. But with Taz's constant lateness

24

and two aborted meetings in as many weeks, it was becoming clear to everyone that she might be more trouble than she or her information was worth.

Then Holly heard the back door open and Taz's voice call out: "Hiya! It's me!"

"Just like she's popped round her nan's," Danny said acidly.

"In here," Holly called as Danny moved to check the street through the vertical blinds on the front windows.

"Hiya," Taz said again, upbeat and smiling as she entered the room. "All right?"

She'd just turned fifteen and even though Holly was eighteen months older and a Trainee Police Officer, Taz always acted as if they were equals. Her cheeks were glowing, as if she'd been running, and she had a scarf tucked inside the collar of a short leather jacket, which Holly knew was only a couple of weeks old.

"Hi," Holly said. "You okay? We were starting to wonder."

"Me? Yeah, I'm fine. Why, I'm not late am I? I thought I was early. Half twelve, right?"

"Twelve," Danny said pointedly, still looking out at the street.

"What? No."

"Let's just get on with it," Danny said, not bothering to argue any more. He came away from the front window, apparently satisfied that Taz hadn't been followed. He moved to the round pine table, sat down and opened a laptop.

"Listen, it's not my fault you got the time wrong," Taz said. "I can't help that, can I?"

That was one thing about Taz, Holly thought: she always managed to turn an accusation back on the person making it. You'd never get her to admit she was at fault even when there was no doubt about it. It was a good skill for an informant to have, but only if it helped them get useful information.

"Do you want pizza?" Holly asked her as a distraction. "It's keeping warm in the oven."

"Anchovies and chicken?"

"Yeah."

"Great," Taz said, unwrapping her scarf. "I'm starving."

"Okay," Holly said. "Two minutes."

"Sit down then," Danny gestured to Taz. "Let's go through the photos from last time."

In the spartan kitchen Holly took the pizza box out of the oven and a couple of boxed sandwiches from the fridge – hers and Danny's. She was hungry too, but they'd waited to eat because sharing a meal or drinks with an informant was supposed to help gain their trust and cooperation.

When Holly carried the food through to the other room, Danny was already directing Taz's attention to a series of grainy pictures on the laptop screen. They were all stills taken from CCTV footage of various suspects.

"I might've seen him," Taz was saying.

"Might have or did?"

"It looked like him. It's a crap picture though, innit?"

"Where was he?"

"In the precinct, on the estate."

"When?"

"Last week. Maybe Tuesday or Wednesday."

"Was he with anyone?"

"Nah, on his own," Taz said. Then: "Oh, ta," when Holly put the pizza box in front of her.

Danny made a note on a pad. "Anyone else?"

"Uh-uh," Taz said, biting into a pizza slice and shaking her head. She hardly glanced back at the screen.

Danny gave it a moment, then pulled the laptop back towards him so he could use the keyboard. Holly could tell by the look on his face that he already thought this was going to be a waste of time.

Holly took a seat next to Taz and opened her sandwich. "Have you seen anything of Drew Alford?" she asked, keeping it casual even though the fact that Alford was still walking around free continued to rankle with her.

"Nah, not much," Taz said. "He's still hanging out, you know. But I don't see him cos he's not with Bex any more."

"Has he got another girlfriend?"

"Dunno. Someone said he was with a girl from Haysden the other night, but I didn't see."

By now Danny had finished setting up the laptop again. He turned to Taz. "Okay, I want you to watch this," he said. "They're clips from CCTV cameras. Say if you think you recognise anyone. Look carefully."

He pushed the laptop back to the centre of the table and tapped a key to start the first of the clips running.

As Taz's co-handler Holly was required to be at any meeting with her, but because Holly was only a trainee, Danny and DS Ray Woods were the ones who prepared the briefings. This was the first time Holly had seen the images on the screen so she watched them with interest – perhaps more than Taz.

A lot of the pictures were similar to the footage you might see on *Crimewatch* or the news, although they lasted longer. They were often blurred and indistinct, almost always jerky and sometimes it was hard to tell who you were supposed to be looking at. The first clip was of two white guys in hoodies robbing an off-licence and threatening the owner with a baseball bat; the second was from a street camera, directed down on a mixed-race man dealing drugs; the next was of a fight outside a town centre pub.

For ten minutes they watched these and other clips while Taz ate her pizza. A few times she asked Danny to pause the video and then peered closely at the screen, frowning in concentration. To Holly it seemed a bit put on though – as if Taz was playing a role. And even when the girl did offer possible IDs on the figures she was looking at, she never fully committed herself. It was always *"Maybe that's…"* and *"He looks a bit like…"*

Finally Danny got to the last clip. It showed external and internal pictures of three men smashing their way into a warehouse through a roller door. They all wore beanie hats down to their eyebrows and had bandannas pulled up over their noses. They worked fast and efficiently as they robbed the place, quickly loading boxes into the back of a Transit van.

"They're taking laptops, hard drives and games consoles," Danny said. "We've heard some of the stuff's being flogged on the Caddy Estate." He gestured at the figures. "Recognise anyone?"

"Can't see 'em, can you?" Taz said, which was true.

"Wait a sec."

Danny hovered a finger over the keyboard. The view was of the warehouse door from outside. One of the raiders was hurrying to get into the driver's seat of the van and as he did so the bandanna over the bottom half of his face slipped. In the moment before he pulled it back into place, Danny hit pause.

Holly frowned, taken by surprise – squinted harder. The man frozen on the screen was white and looked as if he was in his mid-thirties, though it was hard to tell unless you knew him.

But if you *did* know him... Then you'd know that he was thirty-six, with dark, curly hair – *if* you knew him. *If* it was him.

"Seen him anywhere?" Danny asked Taz.

"Dunno," Taz said. "Maybe – or someone like him. I don't know. – Did they get a lot?"

"Enough."

"So there's a reward?"

"*If* we charge someone."

Holly realised the muscles in her shoulders had frozen up. She forced herself to shift, glancing at Danny to see if he'd noticed her stiffness; her sudden focussed interest. It didn't seem that he had.

"I'll listen out for anyone flogging laptops then," Taz said.

Danny nodded. "We're calling this one The Bandit cos of the bandanna. Got it?" When there was a particular suspect they were interested in they were given a nickname to make it easier for Taz to remember them.

"Yeah, The Bandit. I'll remember," Taz said. "I've got a good memory for faces, I told you."

Holly glanced at the screen again, still not certain if she was right. Was it – or not? She knew which answer she wanted, but before she could decide Danny shifted and closed the laptop.

"I know you said that," he told Taz. "But so far it hasn't helped much, has it?"

"What do you mean?" Taz asked, defensive.

"I mean, we need more than a few 'might-be's and 'maybe's," Danny told her. "And that's all you're giving us at the moment."

"I'm doing my best," Taz said, sounding hurt. "It's not easy, you know."

"It was easy enough to tell us which jacket you wanted though."

Suddenly angry – or making a good pretence of it – Taz pushed her chair back and stood up. "Okay, have it back then!" She unzipped the jacket with a ripping sound. "It makes me look fat anyway. Keep the stupid thing."

"Taz, come on," Holly said, standing up and putting a hand out to stop her. "That's not what— The jacket's yours, okay? But we *do* need your help. You're the only one who can tell us what's happening on the Cadogan Estate. That's why it's important for you to really try with this. We're relying on you."

For a moment Taz stood motionless and sulky, then she took her hand off the zip and shrugged her shoulders back.

"I can't just come out and ask, can I?" she said. "If they think I'm asking questions, if they think I'm a grass…"

"You don't have to ask, just watch," Holly said. "Like we told you at the start. Faces and names, that's all." She glanced at Danny. "Right?"

"Right," Danny said with a nod, though it sounded as if it was against his better judgement.

"So, can you do that?" Holly asked, turning back to Taz. "Anything you see. Anything at all that might be useful."

"I'll try," Taz replied, still a bit grudging and resentful, but calmer now.

"Fantastic," Holly told her. "Come on, sit down. We'll run through it again, yeah?"

When the back door closed behind Taz twenty minutes later, Danny Simmons leaned on the kitchen worktop and pursed his lips. "She's in the last-chance saloon," he said.

"I think she knows that," Holly told him. "You made it pretty clear."

Danny was unfazed. "Sometimes it needs to be. We're not here to be her mates – she's doing a job. That's what she's paid for, but if she's not going to deliver…"

"She might do better this time," Holly said. "Now she knows we're not happy."

"We'll see." Danny sounded unconvinced, but not so much that he was ready to call the whole thing off quite yet. "Let's get this place cleaned up and get gone."

Holly moved to the sink to wash their coffee mugs as Danny dumped the pizza box and crusts in a bin bag.

"That warehouse robbery," Holly said after a moment. "The last CCTV clip. When was that?"

"Week last Tuesday. Shenford. Why?"

"Just wondered." She made it sound like casual curiosity. "It looked more professional than the other stuff."

"It was. They must've set it up in advance. They knew what they were looking for and where to go in."

"Any suspects?"

"Not so far. Only thing we do know is the van was torched on Palman's Road two hours after the raid."

"That's why you think it could be linked to the Caddy?" Palman's Road was close to the Cadogan Estate.

"You don't have to be smart to be lazy. Short walk home."

"Right."

For a moment Holly thought back to the indistinct images of the warehouse raid and the man whose mask had slipped.

"Listen, if—" But as she looked up from the sink she saw that Danny had gone into the other room to tidy up.

"What did you say?" he called out.

"Nothing," Holly said.

2

At the end of the fourth-floor walkway Ryan Atkins couldn't keep from turning his head left and right every few moments, looking to see who else was on the landing, how far away, what they were doing. He'd have liked to move, to pace up and down maybe, but he couldn't as long as Drew Alford was inside the flat.

Ryan tried to look relaxed and innocent as he stood beside the railing. It was hard though. Even though he lived in the block he knew that when most people round here saw a teenager in a hoodie hanging about – especially a black teenager in a hoodie – they would come to the obvious conclusion: he was up to something.

Being stuck out here on lookout was the worst – not just because of what was inside the flat – that was risky enough – but because Ryan knew what Drew was doing.

"I'm just after two or three," Drew had said. "No one's gonna notice. Listen, trust me. I know, okay?"

Ryan hoped so. It was one thing to be involved with this flat in the first place, but it was another to be ripping off Tommy Vickers: a guy who'd reward that with broken legs – or worse – if he found out. No one stole from Tommy unless they had a death wish, but that was exactly what Drew was doing, and he'd made Ryan a part of it too.

Then the door opened in front of him and Drew stood in the hall of the flat, a tall, tightly muscled figure with a baseball cap pulled down to his eyebrows.

He didn't step out. Instead he looked at Ryan expectantly. Ryan glanced left and right. For the moment there was no one in sight and he nodded quickly to Drew.

As soon as he saw it Drew stepped out of the flat, pulling the door shut behind him. The Yale lock snicked closed and he twisted the second key in the mortise lock, withdrew it and moved away briskly, pushing the keys into his pocket.

Finally able to move, Ryan fell in beside him as they headed for the stairs. "You get them?" he asked, hoping the answer would be no.

"Yeah," Drew nodded. He reached into his pocket and pulled out a small plastic bag containing six E's embossed with the picture of a flower. He let Ryan see, then shoved them back.

"You said two or three," Ryan said.

"Yeah, well Riz wants some an' all, for tonight. What about you?"

Ryan shook his head. "You sure no one's gonna know?"

"Nah. I told you before. They're out of this big bag, no one's counted. It split open the other day when Malc had it. All over the floor. So if some got lost…" He grinned, tapped his forehead. "See? I've got it all figured out. You worry too much."

3.

"Pillock," PC Yvonne Dunlop said scathingly as a plumber's van pulled out and then stopped halfway across the junction ahead of them, blocking it. "Couldn't wait ten seconds, could you?"

She touched the brakes of the Instant Response Vehicle, knocked down from fourth into second gear and took a sharp left-hander, making Holly tighten her grip on the grab bar.

This was the first shout they'd had since Holly had changed back into uniform and rejoined Yvonne for the remainder of the shift. And although Yvonne hadn't said anything directly, Holly sensed that she was a bit cooler in her manner than she had been that morning. She wasn't sure, but she had a suspicion that Yvonne didn't approve of her going off cloak-and-dagger with DC Danny Simmons.

Once round the corner Yvonne punched the Beemer forward again, hands moving deftly between steering wheel and gear lever. They were on blue lights but no siren.

"Where are we?" Yvonne asked, not taking her eyes off the road.

"Wayland Street, going south. Junction with Clay Lane coming up."

As Observer and Radio Operator, Holly's job was to call out directions to get them to their shout as quickly as possible, but this role was almost redundant where Yvonne was concerned. The thirty-year-old PC had an intimate knowledge of the city streets, including the cut-throughs and quieter roads where she could ramp up their speed.

"Where next?"

"Right into Clay Lane to Albert Road. Right into Sandville Road?" Holly knew that Yvonne was just checking to see whether she was keeping up with their location on the satnav.

"Okay," Yvonne nodded. Nothing else.

Two turns and two minutes later Holly spotted their destination – a row of shops – up ahead, together with a knot of people gathered outside a hairdresser's. A gathering of spectators was usually a pretty good indication of where they needed to be.

Yvonne pulled the IRV in to the kerb and killed the engine as Holly keyed the radio.

"Delta Mike from Delta Mike Five, show us on scene and out of vehicle, Sandville Road."

"*Delta Mike Five, received.*"

As they left the car and crossed the pavement towards the hairdresser's Holly let Yvonne take the lead, not because she didn't know what to do, but because she had the feeling it would be better not to appear too cocky at the moment.

"Excuse me, please. Could you stand back? Thank you." Yvonne's tone made it clear that not doing so wasn't an option.

There were three or four people gathered at the entrance to the hair salon and when they moved aside Holly saw a man of about seventy sitting on the step, his hands turned palm-upwards so a middle-aged woman from the hairdresser's could dab at the grazed and bloody skin with an antiseptic wipe. The right knee of his trousers was torn, Holly saw, and the skin was scraped there too.

"How're you doing, sir?" Yvonne said as she squatted down in front of the old man. "I'm PC Dunlop, this is TPO Blades. Could you tell me your name?"

"Frank. Frank Chapman," the man said. He had a full head of grey hair and well defined features that would have been quite handsome when he was younger.

"Bit of trouble, was there then, Frank?" Yvonne asked.

"Would've been more than a bit if I'd caught them," Frank Chapman said bitterly. "I'd have clobbered the bastards – 'scuse my French."

"Reckon you might have," Yvonne said with a nod. She straightened up and glanced at Holly – wordless, but still an instruction – and Holly knew she'd been given her cue to take over.

"Have you got any other injuries, Mr Chapman?" Holly asked, looking at his hands. "Would you like us to get the paramedics to come in and check you over?"

"For this? Nah, I'm all right. It's only grazes. Bloody tripped, didn't I? That's the only reason I didn't catch them."

"There were two of them," the woman from the hairdresser's

cut in. "I heard Frank shout, then I saw them running – that way – so I dialled 999."

"Are you Mrs Clarke?" Yvonne asked.

"That's right. It's my shop."

"Okay. So would it be all right if we got Mr Chapman inside and had a chat with him there? You too."

"Course. I wanted him to come in before, but he wouldn't."

"Mr Chapman?" Holly asked. "Are you okay to go inside?"

"Yeah, yeah, I'm fine," Frank Chapman said, ignoring the hand Holly offered and pushing himself off the step with a grunt. "And call me Frank. Only people call me Mister is the doctor and bank manager."

Once they were inside the hairdresser's Frank Chapman took a seat near the window and refused to let the owner of the place do any more to his cuts and grazes. Instead he accepted the packet of antiseptic wipes and tended to them himself for a while as Holly took his statement. Yvonne was doing the same, getting descriptions from Mrs Clarke and another witness, but occasionally Holly felt Yvonne glance towards her and knew she'd better get this right. Yvonne's mood didn't seem to have thawed.

"So you came out of the newsagent's and you'd stopped to check your lottery ticket," Holly said, recapping what Frank Chapman had already told her. "You had your wallet in your hand. Then what happened?"

"I heard feet – you know, running," Frank said. "Didn't think anything of it for a few seconds cos I'm looking at my numbers. Then I realise they're running towards me and I look up. There's two of 'em – teenagers, almost on top of me. First one goes round the back, kind of brushes my shoulder, then the other one's going past in front, grabs the wallet right out of my hand and he's away. He calls out 'Gotcha, grandad!' and then they're both laughing."

"What direction were they going as they ran away?"

"That way." Frank gestured out of the window.

Holly looked. "Towards the Cadogan Estate?"

"Yeah. Where else?"

"Okay, and then what?"

Frank stiffened his chin. "I thought, *Sod that, I'm gonna get you*. I mean, what if I'd been some old lady and they'd just nicked my pension or given me a heart attack or something? So I went after them. And that's what they didn't expect, right? I mean, they were running, yeah, but not sprinting and they weren't looking back. And I'm still fast enough to catch up over a few yards, and I do – till they hear me and one of them looks round. He got a bloody shock, I'm telling you. Saw it on his face. That's when I called him a name – not something I'm gonna say to you – and I go to grab him. Only I kind of reached too far and next thing I'm going flying and end up down on the floor, hands and knees." He pulled a face. "Another foot and I'd've had him."

Holly made a couple of notes, then looked up. "Can you describe them at all?"

Frank nodded. "White, about my height. One had brown hair, the other one – the one who grabbed my wallet – he had one of those hats on, knitted thing. Blue maybe. One had a red jacket, the other was grey. I think it was grey."

"What sort of age?"

"Dunno. Hard to tell. Fifteen, sixteen."

"Would you recognise them again if you saw them?"

"One, yeah, for definite. The one in the hat."

"Okay, Frank, that's really helpful," Holly said and saw that Yvonne had finished with the other witnesses. "Could you wait there a sec while I talk to PC Dunlop?"

"She's the gaffer then, is she?"

"My training officer, yeah."

"Looks like a tough one to me," Frank said, giving Yvonne an appraising look.

"She can be. Depends which side you're on," Holly told him.

4

"Oi! Give it! – Give it, you tosser!"

Rizza, the older and harder of the two youths, plucked the lottery ticket from Skank's fingers and immediately turned away to examine it. Below his beanie hat he had strong cheekbones and a touch of stubble – he was shaving two or three times a week.

"It's not gonna win, is it?" Skank said, sulky. "Got more chance of…of…" He struggled for something there was more chance of and couldn't think of anything.

"Of what? Winning the lottery?" Rizza sneered.

"Anyway, they'd know," Skank said. He was skinny with lank hair and several angry zits round his nose.

"Know what?"

"That it was nicked. If it won and you went in to get the prize they'd know it was you who nicked it."

"Bollocks."

"It's on computer, innit?"

"Bollocks. A ticket's a ticket."

"Anyway, there's no chance."

Twenty metres away Taz had her hands in her jacket pockets as she sauntered along the elevated walkway, stepping round the litter-strewn puddles on the damp concrete. She couldn't hear what Skank and Rizza were arguing about, but she'd seen them running into the estate from the direction of Sandville Road a few minutes before so she knew they'd been up to something. No way Skank would run anywhere unless he had to, although Rizza was fit enough to play football when he wanted.

It was the suspicion that the two lads had been up to something that had made Taz head in their direction. After the way it had gone at the safe house – being late and everything – she'd only come away with ten quid to cover her expenses for getting there. What she'd really wanted was the pair of boots she'd seen in Shoe Zone, but she knew it would have been a waste of time to even ask for them. Danny Simmons had made it clear that she wasn't going to get any more rewards unless she came up with something useful, but that was easier said than done.

Truth was, the claims Taz made about knowing who was doing what on the estate and the gobby, self-assured front she put on was just that – a front. Sure, she did see and hear *some* things, but to get the sort of information Danny Simmons was looking for meant getting closer to people Taz would rather avoid – people like Drew Alford. On the other hand, if Skank and Rizza *had* been up to something maybe that would be worth finding out...

"All right?" Taz said when she was still a few paces from them. She made out that she wasn't going to pause, but she knew that just speaking to them would be enough to get a reaction – an excuse to stop.

"All right," Rizza said, looking away from Skank. "Where you going then?"

Taz shrugged. "Home," she said. "Nothing doing round here, is there? What you doing? What's that?"

She nodded to the lottery ticket Rizza was holding.

"My lucky lottery ticket for tonight," Rizza said. Skank giggled.

"What?" Taz asked him.

"Nothing," Skank said.

"No, go on, what?" Taz said. "What's funny?"

"Ask him where he got it."

"Where'd you get it?" Taz asked Rizza.

Rizza pursed his lips as if thinking about an answer, but Skank cut in before he could speak: "Nicked it, didn't he."

Rizza shot him a look. "Shut the fuck up."

"What? Straight?" Taz said, making sure she sounded impressed as she looked at Rizza for confirmation. "Where from?"

"Bloke on the street," Rizza said after a moment. "He's standing there with his wallet out, showing his wad. Too good not to, right?"

"Just steamed past him and snatched it," Skank said, not wanting to be left out. "Got the wallet right outta his hand."

"Cool," Taz said, but she was looking at Rizza. "Get anything else – any cash?"

"A bit."

"Cool. So, you buying then?"

"Buying what?"

Taz shrugged. "Dunno. Whatever."

"I'll buy you something," Skank said with a leer and a gesture at his crotch. "If you do something for me."

Taz rounded on him, thumping him hard in the chest before he had time to back away. "Piss off, creep."

"Jesus! All right!" Skank exclaimed seeing her raise her fist again.

Taz gave him a black look and held it for a moment before turning away.

"I'm gonna get some chips," she said, aimed at Rizza, and without waiting for a reply she moved away towards the steps.

She didn't look back, but a few seconds later she heard them following her, as she'd known they would.

"Hang on," Rizza said, catching up, and he fell into step beside her.

5.

In the entrance to the hairdresser's Holly waited silently while Yvonne scanned her notes. After a minute or so the PC tapped the bottom of the page with a pen. "What've you missed?" she said, looking up.

"Er…"

"Description of stolen property. The wallet."

"Oh, God. Yeah. Sorry."

"I'll get it," Yvonne told her. "Go and call in the descriptions."

"Right," Holly said.

Yvonne handed her the car keys and Holly headed across to the IRV. Yvonne never needed to say much when she wasn't impressed – it was always obvious.

In the front passenger seat Holly unhooked the radio mic and pressed the button on the side. "Delta Mike from Delta Mike Five, receiving?"

"Go ahead, Five."

"Re the robbery at my location, attention requested to two IC1 male suspects. Descriptions as follows…"

It didn't take long to list the descriptions Frank Chapman had given, but Holly knew it was already a long shot that any other patrols would spot the two youths. If they'd gone into the

Cadogan Estate – the most likely place – they were already beyond reach and they'd know it.

"*All received,*" the operator in the control room said when Holly had finished. "*Any idea when you'll be available?*"

Holly glanced at the hairdresser's. Inside she could see Yvonne talking to Frank and the shop's owner.

"Five or ten minutes, I think."

"*Received. Delta Mike out.*"

Holly turned in the seat and as she did so her attention was caught by the on-board computer screen set into the dashboard. A half-decided thought had been lodged in her head since she'd left the safe house earlier, and for a moment she hesitated to let it out.

She cast another glance at the hairdresser's. Nothing had changed. Yes or no?

Quickly she reached out and activated the touch screen, then tapped in her number and password. After a beat the screen changed and she had access to the PNC, the Police National Computer.

QUERY: NAME CHECK

SUBJECT: MASON, LIAM PAUL

She hit enter and there was a lag of several seconds before the screen refreshed and showed the details for Liam Paul Mason, from his date of birth and physical description to a list of his previous arrests.

It was more than three years since Holly had seen him and the sight of his details now felt like being dragged back through a time warp – as if nothing had changed. Except it had. In three years everything had changed, or so Holly had hoped.

Then there was a movement at the hairdresser's. Yvonne and Frank Chapman were coming out onto the pavement. Holly scrolled down the screen as fast as she could.

CURRENT STATUS: PAROLE

"I've circulated a description of the youths," Holly said as she crossed the pavement towards Yvonne and Frank Chapman. "One of our patrols might spot them."

"Better not hold my breath though, eh?" Frank said.

"Sometimes we get lucky," Yvonne told him.

"Can't do miracles though, can you?" he said philosophically.

"Unfortunately not. – Are you sure you don't need a lift home?"

"No, you get on. That's my car there." He gestured to a Rover saloon, at least ten years old but clean and well polished.

"Okay, if you're sure." Yvonne handed him a card. "That's my name and Force ID number, and the station phone number is there in case you want to contact us."

He looked at the card, then at Holly. "What's your ID number?" he asked.

"Seven-six-two," Holly told him, pointing the numbers out on her shoulder.

"Lovely, that'll do then," Frank said. He dug out some loose change from his pocket.

"For what?"

"They nicked my lottery ticket, right? And I'm not going to do the same numbers again, so I'll use yours instead, both of you. Bound to be lucky."

"That *would* be a miracle," Yvonne said, but she was smiling for the first time that afternoon. "So do we get a cut if you win?"

"Course. Fifty-fifty."

"I'll hold you to that."

"Better watch the draw tonight then. When they come up we're off to Acapulco. Buy yourself a new bikini."

Yvonne gave him a look that made him grin, then he shook hands with them both before heading back to the newsagent's. Holly saw he was limping a little on his injured knee but otherwise he kept himself straight.

"He's a tough one," Yvonne said approvingly, watching him go for a moment. "Okay, let's give it a turn round the Caddy, just in case they're more stupid than usual."

6.

It didn't surprise Holly when they failed to see any sign of the youths who'd robbed Frank Chapman. They drove round for ten minutes, then got a call to a shoplifter who couldn't or wouldn't speak English. By the time that had been dealt with, it was close to knock-off and Holly wrote up her notes quickly before heading away to get changed.

In the locker room she took off her uniform, keeping an eye on the time as she quickly squirted herself with body spray and got into her civvies. She knew she was purposely stopping herself thinking back to the pictures on Danny Simmons' laptop and hurrying helped that. She had enough time if she didn't hang around, but if she missed the 18:30 bus she'd have to wait an hour for the next one.

Outside in the corridor she was heading briskly towards the rear exit with her overnight bag on her shoulder when she saw Sam Marsden coming the other way. He was one of the other three TPOs who shared the Section House with Holly, but he was the only one assigned to Morningstar Road for Street Duty training with her.

"You off?" he asked, slowing down. Although he was a few months older than Holly he didn't look it.

"Yeah. See you tomorrow."

"Anything good?"

Glancing at her watch again, Holly paused. "Not much. Dangerous dog this morning, street robbery and shoplifter this afternoon."

"Bugger. I still need a dangerous dog."

The TPO training syllabus contained a list of offences and situations the trainees were expected to deal with during each stage of training and there was always some competition about who had ticked off the most, especially with Sam. It had put Holly off him for a while, but now she didn't take too much notice.

"Where was it – the dog?" Sam asked.

"Driffield Way. You'll have to find another one though. It's being put down. Listen, I've got to go or I'll miss my bus."

She left Sam heading towards the male locker room and was at the station's back door when Yvonne Dunlop came round the corner. She was still in half blues: uniform trousers and shirt, but with a red ski jacket over the top. Her hair was down, too.

"Going home?" she asked as Holly pushed the door open for them.

"Yeah."

"All right, come on, I'll give you a lift."

Yvonne lived in the flat above the Section House and had the responsibility of making sure the TPOs below were keeping to the rules.

"Oh. No, I meant I'm going *home*," Holly explained. "To see my mum."

"Where's that – your mum's place?"

"Collington. I'm going to the bus station."

"Okay, I'll drop you there then." And she took her car keys from her pocket as she started across the yard. It left Holly with little option other than to follow, and to hope that the unusual offer of a lift didn't mean Yvonne was looking for an opportunity to talk about anything serious.

Yvonne drove her own car – a red Alfa Romeo – the same way she drove the IRV: hard, fast and efficiently. She didn't say much until they'd pulled out of the yard and onto the main road towards Weston city centre. It was getting dark and most of the traffic had its lights on.

"So how did it go with the informant at lunchtime?" Yvonne asked conversationally.

"Oh, okay."

"Anything useful?"

"Not really." Holly hesitated. "I'm not supposed to talk about it."

"Good, don't. I just wondered if that was what had put you off your game this afternoon. You were thinking about something else half the time."

Holly knew that was true but she'd thought – hoped – it hadn't been so obvious.

"Sorry," she said lamely. "I think I'm just a bit tired."

Yvonne glanced at her briefly before looking back at the road. Holly held her breath, waiting to see if what came next was a question about the PNC check she'd run on Liam.

"Right," Yvonne said. "Is that all?"

"Yeah, I just need an early night, then I'll be fine," Holly said, as convincingly as she could. It seemed to be enough though, because after a brief pause Yvonne changed the subject.

"So is there any special reason for going home, or is it just to get out of the Section House for a bit?"

"It's my brother's birthday tomorrow," Holly said. "He's five."

"Yeah? That's a bit of a gap between you."

"I suppose." For a moment Holly hesitated, knowing that there was a hanging question but not anxious to say any more than she had to.

"He's really my half-brother," she said in the end. "His dad and my mum split up though."

"Oh. Right," Yvonne said. Holly couldn't tell what she was thinking, if anything. "So is he having a party?"

"Tomorrow afternoon, yeah. I'm on duty though. I'm just going back so I can give him his present in the morning."

"Lucky escape – from the party, I mean."

That surprised Holly, though she wasn't sure why. "Don't you like kids?"

"They're all right – as long as they're somebody else's. Wouldn't want any of my own."

"What, never?"

"Nope." Yvonne shook her head, definite. "I'll be out of the

Job before I'm fifty, with a full pension and no responsibilities. That's just the way I want it."

Holly couldn't get her head around the idea that anyone would be planning what they'd do in nearly twenty years' time. The furthest she could cast forward was just over a couple of years to when – if things went to plan – she'd be out of training and sworn in as a reg.

"I can't even imagine what I'll be doing when I'm your age," she said.

"Oh, thanks a bunch," Yvonne said, dryly. "That's really made my day, that has."

"No, I didn't mean— I just meant—"

"Yeah, yeah. Too late now," Yvonne said and pulled the car in beside the bus station. "Careful you don't trip over my Zimmer frame when you get out."

As usual she delivered it deadpan, but Holly was pretty sure she saw a hint of amusement on the older woman's face.

"I'll try not to," she said, taking hold of her bag. "Thanks for the lift."

7

"No, man, you go," Ryan said. "I'm gonna stay round here."

"Why? Fuck that." Drew made a contemptuous wave towards the estate blocks. "What's here? 'Less you want to start going to choir practice again with your brother. – Anyway, we need to see Madder: he owes us."

Without waiting for a reply, Drew set off towards the edge of the estate, walking quickly and with purpose. Behind him Ryan cursed under his breath for a moment, then finally shoved his hands in his pockets and jogged to catch up.

It was because Drew had mentioned Charlie – Ryan's brother – that Ryan knew he hadn't got a choice. It was Drew's way of reminding him about their deal to share control of the estate, which would never have happened if Charlie hadn't got himself on the wrong side of Drew's gang.

The price for Ryan to fix that was this "partnership" with Drew: combining their resources to take protection money from Madder and the other estate dealers; to do jobs for Tommy Vickers and make sure no one else tried to muscle in on the estate.

And at first Ryan had thought he could keep his involvement under control, but over the past few weeks

Drew had gradually been making more and more demands on him, wanting Ryan to go here, to watch that, to meet this guy or just to carry that.

On their own none of these things was a big deal, but bit by bit Ryan had come to realise that equal partners only meant equal when Drew decided it did and Ryan was starting to feel uneasy about that. Trouble was, he knew if he broke the partnership it could put Charlie back in the firing line, so – for the moment at least – he didn't have much choice: what Drew said went.

"So whose party is it anyway?" Ryan asked when he caught up with Drew and fell into step beside him.

Drew shrugged. "Fucked if I know," he said. "What's it matter?"

8

From the driver's seat of the dark blue van Dean Fuller watched the parked car while he talked on his mobile. He was about thirty, good-looking enough, although his hair was too long and he had two or three days' worth of stubble.

"*How long till it's ready?*" Vickers asked, on the other end of the line.

"A few more days. End of the week, tops," Fuller said. The car he was watching was about ten metres away and the street lights on the far side of the waste ground gave just enough illumination to silhouette two figures in the front seats.

"*What about the other place?*"

"Gonna be longer. A month maybe."

There was a pause, then Tommy Vickers said: "*Okay, let me know when you reckon you can cut the first lot. I'll get you some help.*"

"You want me to ask him about doing another grow after that?"

"*You reckon he will?*"

"Don't see why not."

"*Okay, ask him. Same deal as this time. – I've got to go. Let me know.*"

"Hang on," Fuller said. "What about that other stuff –

the Wiis, yeah? You said…"

There was a pause, then: "*You got a buyer?*"

"Yeah. Thirty. And I can do another ten on top, easy."

"*Okay. I'll get Malc to call you. Pick them up tomorrow.*"

"Right. Thanks, Tommy."

Vickers rang off and Fuller pushed the phone back in his pocket. He cast another look at the parked car near the waste ground, then took out a pack of cigarettes and lit one, opening the window a crack to blow out the smoke. When the cigarette was down to the filter he pushed the dog-end out of the van window. As he did so, the car's passenger door opened and a girl got out quickly.

Gemma took a second to get her balance before she closed the car door. Her heels made her a lot taller and she hated them. They made her legs ache because she had to stand for so long, and she hated the fact that they made her feel vulnerable, unable to run if she had to without fear of twisting her ankle. But like the skirt which barely reached her thighs and the shocking pink jacket over a low-cut T-shirt, Dean made her wear them. He didn't care that on a night like tonight she sometimes got so cold that she couldn't stop shaking. The clothes were "good for business", he said. That was the only thing he cared about, Gemma was under no illusion about that any more.

Behind her the car started up and its headlights came on as she reached the van. As the car pulled away she opened the van door and got in quickly next to Dean Fuller.

"Shit, it's cold," Gemma said. "Put the heater on."

He ignored her and held out his hand. "Give."

Gemma took a tenner from the pocket of her jacket and handed it to him. He took it, then immediately grabbed her wrist in one fast movement, twisting it hard.

She cried out. "Ow! Don't!"

"Give!" Fuller said again.

"It was only a tenner!" Gemma twisted in her seat, trying to ease the pressure of his grip.

"You think I'm stupid? I could see."

He forced her wrist further.

"Don't!" she cried out again.

"I'll fuckin' break it, you lie to me."

"All right! All right! Let go!"

She felt tears of pain in her eyes now and struggled to take another note from her pocket. "Here."

Dean let go of her wrist and snatched the money away. Gemma sobbed and held her arm. Dean took no notice. Apparently satisfied, he straightened in his seat. "You lie to me again you know what I'll do."

He looked out of the window, assessing. There were no other punters, no cars. He started the van.

"Are we packing it in?" Gemma asked, hoping it was true.

"For a bit. We'll come back later. Put your seat belt on."

Not wanting to delay in case he changed his mind,

Gemma tried to get the seat belt, but the pain in her wrist made it impossible to reach.

"I can't," she said. "I think you broke it."

"It's not broken," he told her, but he reached across and pulled the seat belt into place. Then he kissed her on the cheek. "Just don't lie to me," he said, almost an appeal. "I don't want to do stuff like that. You know I don't, right?"

For a moment Gemma said nothing, then she nodded because that was what he wanted. "Yeah," she said.

"Right. That's my girl."

He kissed her again on the cheek, then put the van into gear and pulled around in a tight U-turn, away from the cul-de-sac.

9.

There were five of them in the van, waiting in a side street till they got the call to move. In his waterproof jacket Sam Marsden felt bulky and overdressed but he didn't want to take it off in case they were called two minutes later.

"You know why it's called a red light district, right?" Mulvey said. "It's cos of the brake lights on the punters' cars when they're slowing down to look at the prozzies."

"Where'd you get that from?" Siobhan Kelly said scathingly. "Off a crisp packet?"

"Yeah, spicy tomato flavour," Vinny Appleby chipped in. "Get it? *Tom*-ato. Tom, right?"

"Jesus!"

The banter had been like that for the last half-hour, back and forth, killing time with gossip and arguments about anything and everything. It was all they could do until Inspector Moore, the officer in charge, decided the time was right to move. Somewhere on the main road he was in the OP – a van with one-way windows through which surveillance cameras and an automatic number-plate reader could record the cars that came kerb-crawling and the prostitutes who moved forward to show themselves.

Sam looked at his watch. This was his first operation of this sort and he wished they could get on with it. The waiting was just an opportunity for his mind to go over all the things he could do wrong to show himself up in front of the others.

Oz Sitwell must have seen him looking at his watch, even though he was tightening the laces on his DMs. He was Sam's Training Officer – "puppy walker" in police jargon.

"When we get out there they're going to tell you all sorts of sob stories – 'specially you," Oz said. "They owe money; the kiddies have got no food; they're going to be evicted; they've never done it before... Rule One: believe nothing. Rule Two: see Rule One."

Sam didn't need to ask why he'd be singled out for the sob stories. Even in the dark he knew there was no way he was going to look as if he'd been on the job for more than a few months. From what he'd heard, most of the prostitutes they'd be dealing with would have been on the game for years.

"Give 'em half a chance and they'll have you on toast," Bob Mulvey chipped in. He was enjoying it, Sam could tell.

"So *don't* give them the chance," Oz said, ignoring Mulvey. "And don't take any notice when they start making personal comments – which they will. Just keep your cool and stay in control."

"You think there'll be any trouble?" Sam asked.

"Nah," Mulvey said. "They'll just want to get it over and done so they can get back out again asap."

"What about the punters?"

"We won't get many." Oz finished his laces and straightened up. "The OP's logging their number plates so most of them are just going to get a letter in the post. Thing they'll be most worried about is stopping the wives or girlfriends finding out what they were up to."

"It's all a game anyway," Mulvey said, like he knew it all. He emptied his crisp packet into his mouth and screwed it up. "Politics. They did a big clean-up in Garston a few months ago, so the toms all moved here. Now we'll push them off to someone else's doorstep till *they* start complaining. Round and round."

"Over in Cardiff they let them use the trading estates," Siobhan Kelly said. "No one there to bother after half five. If they'd do that here…"

Then Inspector Moore's voice broke the radio silence: *"All Sierra units from Sierra One, stand by. Stand by."*

"That's us," Oz said. "Time to get an earful."

10

The place they were looking for was a few streets away from the estate and it wasn't hard to find even though Drew didn't know the exact address. You could hear the sound of the party halfway down the road and Ryan couldn't believe no one had called the police to complain.

Apparently no one had though, because the house was virtually throbbing with the amplified drum-and-bass beat and the ground-floor windows were lit up from inside by brightly-coloured strobes. There were at least a dozen people hanging around the low wall in front of the house – drinking, smoking weed and being lairy – and as Ryan and Drew turned in at the gate two lads were being refused entry to the open front door by a couple of bouncers.

Ryan hoped the door policy – whatever it was – might mean that they too were turned back. This whole thing made him uneasy, like he had a premonition that just by being here he would inevitably end up in the wrong place at the wrong time when the cops finally arrived – as they were bound to do eventually. He could see it now: Drew pushing something into his hand, telling him to hold onto it for a bit, just as the cops charged in, searched everyone, found him holding and then hauled him away, leaving Drew in the clear…

Drew clearly wasn't worried though. He walked up to the door as if he had every right to be there and when one of the bouncers moved to block the way Drew just gave him a nod.

"All right?" he shouted over the noise, as if he was on familiar terms with the man. "Seen Madder?"

The man looked him over, then jerked his head towards the door. "Inside. Try the kitchen."

"Right," Drew said, and then with a nod towards Ryan: "he's with me, yeah?"

Drew stepped inside and Ryan had no choice but to follow, pushing his way through the throng of drunken, yelling-over-the-music party-goers in the hall, all the time feeling his premonition getting stronger.

Taz was bored now and she knew she had to decide: drink some more – enough to take the boredom away – or get up and leave.

Beside her, Rizza was perched on the arm of the chair and she knew he thought he was in with a chance. Each time he offered her a drag on his fag or thought of something to yell in her ear it was an excuse to edge in a bit more. He hadn't tried it on or anything yet, but she knew she'd have to find a way of ditching him before she left or he'd want to go with her so he could try and cop off. No way that was going to happen.

They'd been there for an hour and although the kitchen was a bit quieter than the rest of the house the noise level still made it impossible to talk without yelling. Not that there was anything to talk about. The only thing to do was sit there, sipping her can of cider, and watch the various people at the makeshift bar or those yelling into Madder's ear, telling him whether they wanted speed or E or weed.

At first she'd been looking out for any one of the dozen or so faces Danny Simmons was interested in, but it wasn't as easy as you'd think. There were too many people coming and going, and trying to match anyone to the descriptions or photos she'd seen was impossible – they all seemed to blur together.

Then she did spot a face she knew, as Drew Alford elbowed his way into the kitchen with Ryan Atkins close behind him.

Drew looked round, the usual scowl on his face, and when his gaze came her way he made a gesture, but it was aimed at Rizza, not her.

She felt Rizza shift, then he put his head down by her ear and raised his voice. "You staying here, yeah?"

Taz shrugged.

"Want another can?"

"Yeah, if you want."

"Okay. I'll be back in a minute." And he stood up from the arm of the chair.

To Ryan it didn't seem that Rizza was very keen to move from where he was sitting next to Taz. His arm was almost

– but not quite – round her shoulders and Skank was lounging nearby.

Rizza didn't shift until Drew beckoned him a second time. Then he leaned in and said something to Taz before he got up. She shrugged, then nodded, but stayed put as Rizza and Skank left her and edged their way through the other party-goers towards Drew.

"What's up?" Rizza asked Drew, shouting to be heard over the music and noise.

"Where's Madder?" Drew demanded. "You seen him?"

"He was here," Skank said, glancing round. "Must've gone outside." He nodded to the open back door.

"Right," Drew said, and started to wend his way to the door.

Rizza signalled to the guy with tattoos and piercings behind the bar, indicating what he wanted by pointing: a can of cider and one of lager. He handed over a fiver and didn't look for change when he collected the cans.

"So what d'you reckon?" he asked Ryan, meaning the party in general. "All right, innit?"

Ryan made a so-so face, as if he'd seen better. "It's okay. How long've you been here?"

Rizza shrugged. "'Bout an hour." He cracked the ring pull on the cider.

"He thinks he's in," Skank said with a smirk and nodded towards Taz.

"Don't think – I *am*," Rizza said. "Specially with this."

He turned so he had his back towards Taz, then opened his hand and showed Ryan the tab in his palm before dropping it into the cider.

"What – you spiking it?" Ryan said.

"He's not gonna get a shag if he don't, is he?" Skank said. "No chance."

"More chance than you anyway," Rizza retorted. "Watch me." And he moved off, back towards Taz.

Skank watched him go for a moment, clearly envious, then looked back to Ryan. "You staying?" he said, leaning in to make himself heard. "Want a drink?"

Ryan knew Skank was only offering because he was on his own now and wanted someone to hang out with. Ryan also knew that if he accepted a drink he'd be stuck with Skank for ages and he didn't want that. He just wanted to get this over with and get out, so he shook his head. "I'm gone when Drew's finished – got something else on."

"Yeah? What?"

"Someone else to see." He left it deliberately vague.

"Oh. Right."

Disappointed, Skank moved to buy a can and Ryan took the opportunity to make his way to the back door and breathe in fresh, chilly air.

There were another two doormen just outside and from the step Ryan saw that someone had lit a bonfire in the centre of the run-down garden. It was burning high and a dozen or more people were standing around in its light, watching the flames and occasionally poking the embers with sticks, sending up sparks. It looked as if they were burning furniture, but it was hard to tell.

Off to one side by a fence, Ryan could just make out Drew's angular shape, standing close to Madder and away from the others, some kind of transaction going on. He watched it for a moment, then sensed someone beside him. When he looked round he saw Taz.

"All right?" she said as she too cast a glance towards Drew and Madder. "You and Drew tight now then? I seen you come in – and round the estate."

Ryan wasn't sure how to respond to that, so he shrugged. "We hang out a bit."

Taz nodded, as if that made it clear, then raised her can to take a sip before offering it across. "Want some?"

"Is that the one Rizza bought?" Ryan asked.

"Yeah. Why?"

He hesitated. "Come outside a minute," he said, then went ahead, down the steps to a paved patio area.

Suspicious, Taz followed. "What's up?" she said when he turned to face her again. It was just about possible to talk normally out here.

Ryan motioned to the can. "He spiked it – Rizza."

"What? No way."

"Okay," Ryan said flatly. "But he did."

She studied his face for a second, then relented a little. "You seen him do it?"

Ryan nodded.

"Wanker!" she exclaimed. "I'll fucking do him!"

She made to go back inside, but Ryan grabbed her arm. "Hold on," he said. "If you do that he's gonna know it was me who told you, yeah?"

"So?" she said. "You scared of him?"

"No."

"So?" Taz repeated.

"I don't need it now – trouble. I mean, not here, right?"

He nodded towards Drew and she followed the look, then seemed to understand the connection.

"Rizza's still an arsehole," she said, but slightly less vehemently. Then she tipped the can so its contents splattered on the ground and Ryan stepped back to avoid the splashes.

"That's a waste," Drew said. Neither Ryan or Taz had noticed him approaching.

"You can have it if you want," Taz told him. "It's got a fag end in it."

She stopped pouring and held it out but Drew ignored it.

"I'm staying for a bit," he told Ryan. "You don't have to if you don't want. Up to you."

"What about…?" Ryan looked towards Madder to finish the sentence.

"Sorted." Drew glanced towards Taz for a second. "I'll tell you tomorrow."

"Okay," Ryan said. "I'm gonna go then. This music's shit."

"Okay," Drew shrugged. "Whatever." And for Ryan it confirmed what he'd already suspected – that Drew had only wanted him to come along to prove he could make him. Now that he had he'd lost interest.

"Don't forget about the morning though," Drew told him. "I'll call you. Be ready. They won't want to piss about."

"Right," Ryan said, not keen to make it a fixed arrangement but knowing it would be anyway.

Drew nodded and without acknowledging Taz again he moved off towards the back door and went inside.

When he'd gone Ryan looked round to see if there was a way out that didn't involve going back through the house. There was a broken gate at the far end of the garden which seemed to give out onto some kind of side road, maybe a track. He took a couple of steps sideways to see it better.

"You going back to the Caddy now then?" Taz asked, moving with him.

"Yeah. Why?"

"Nah, no reason," she said. "Just I'll come with you, that's all. I ain't going back in there with Rizza and that lot. Waste of time. I'd rather go home."

It was pretty much how Ryan felt too – like he'd just found a way to duck out before his premonition came true.

"Come on then," Taz said, tugging his arm, and together they moved off down the garden, skirting the bonfire and heading away from the noise.

11.

Finally out of the van, Sam and the others stretched their legs and pulled on high-vis jackets. The whole idea was that everyone – but especially the local residents – should be able to see what was happening: that action was being taken.

When the next radio call came through Sam stayed beside Oz as they made their way towards the main road in a group. He could feel the anticipation mixed up with nerves and excitement as the phalanx of cops dropped their banter, holding themselves back until everyone was set.

"All Sierra units, move in. Move in."

Together they briskly rounded the corner onto Mill Hill Lane and Sam got a snapshot impression of the road, lined by residential houses and regularly spaced street lights. And at first nothing seemed out of place or unusual, until he saw that between the pools of orange light there were figures – maybe a dozen women – moving between one point and another, then back, all on high heels, all in tight skirts and low-cut tops.

One woman, wearing a leopard-skin jacket, was leaning into the passenger window of a car which had pulled up at the kerb. But as Sam and the other cops fanned out across the road in a walking cordon the woman must have seen them, because she backed off quickly and the car started away, only to be waved down by Mulvey and Kelly before it had gone twenty metres.

Then, through his earpiece, Sam heard their operation call sign on the radio: "*Sierra Three: IC1 male punter, about forty – jeans, light-brown coat. Heading in your direction on foot. He's approached most of them.*"

"There," Oz gestured and Sam saw the man the OP had described. He was crossing the road ahead of them towards a row of parked cars.

Oz and Sam changed course, speeding up a little to reach the man before he could get to his car.

"Excuse me, sir, could we talk to you for a moment?" Oz said. He was tall and bulky enough that most took notice when he approached them like that.

The man came to a halt. "Sure," he said. "Is there a problem?"

"Let's just move out of the road, shall we?"

Oz directed the man to the pavement and then gave Sam a nod.

Sam took the cue and stepped forward, hoping he could remember what he needed to say. "Sir, I'm TPO Marsden, this is PC Sitwell from Morningstar Road Station. At the moment we're conducting an operation to discourage prostitution in this area and the reason we've stopped you is that you've been seen approaching a number of women back there."

The man gave a bit of a laugh, but to Sam it sounded

nervous. "No, you've got it wrong. I wasn't doing it for that. – I mean, I can explain."

Believe nothing and keep control.

"You'll be able to do that in a moment," Sam said. "Could you tell me your full name and date of birth please?"

"Tony Steven Deakin, second of April 1971, but listen—"

Sam held up a hand. "Do you know it's an offence to solicit to obtain the sexual services of a prostitute?"

The man called Deakin shifted a little. "Yes. I mean, I suppose so, but I'm trying to tell you, that wasn't what I was doing. Look, can I show you?"

He went to reach into his coat pocket and Oz immediately took a step forward, alert. But when Deakin's hand came back into sight it was holding a printed sheet of A5 paper.

"I'm looking for my daughter," he said, handing the paper to Oz. "Her name's Andrea. She's a missing person – missing from home since January."

Oz tilted the paper so that Sam could see it as well. A photograph showed a smiling girl of about sixteen with shoulder-length brown hair. Above it was the word *"Missing"* and below *"Reward for information"*. There were more details at the bottom of the paper but the print was too small to read in the poor light.

"I'm looking for her," Deakin repeated. "That's why I'm here."

Oz shifted. "Where do you live, Mr Deakin?" he asked.

"Cardiff. Well, I used to. I'm not— It's complicated."

"Can you tell me your current address?"

"No. I mean, it's a bed and breakfast on Shapley Road – the Astoria. I can't remember the number."

"So you've got no fixed address."

"No, not at the moment. But look, I'm telling you the truth. I wasn't here for— I wasn't looking for sex. I just want information."

"Okay, could you wait there for me a moment?"

Oz gestured to Sam and they moved aside, although Oz stood so that he could keep an eye on the man.

"So?" Oz asked, keeping his voice down. "If this is you on your own, what do you do now?"

Sam knew that Oz was taking this as an opportunity to drop in an assessment. It happened a lot: put the trainees on the spot and see how they reacted.

"We could run a check and see if the girl really is a Misper," he said.

"Is that what you want to do?"

Sam thought it through quickly, glancing down the road to the dozen other officers dealing with the working girls and their clients. He knew that running a Misper check would take time so he shook his head. "No. I think we should take him in and sort it out later."

"Why?"

"Because he hasn't given us a permanent address, and even if his daughter *is* missing, it doesn't prove he wasn't soliciting."

"Right," Oz nodded, satisfied. "Rule One."

He moved back to Deakin and handed the leaflet back. "I'm not satisfied with your explanation of what you were doing here, Mr Deakin, so I'm arresting you on suspicion of soliciting for prostitution contrary to Section 51A of the Sexual Offences Act."

"What?" Deakin protested. "But if—"

Oz ignored him. "You do not have to say anything but it may harm your defence if you do not mention when questioned something which you later rely on in court. Anything you do say may be given in evidence."

"You're making a mistake," Deakin said.

"You'll be able to tell us about that later. For now, my colleague's going to search you, then we'll take you back to the station. Have you got any sharp objects in your possession or anything else we should know about?"

For a moment Deakin didn't move, then he let out a long sigh and shook his head. "No, nothing," he said.

"Okay. Sam?"

And Sam moved in to pat Deakin down.

12

Gemma came into the kitchen as Frank Chapman held the door and made a welcoming smile. "Hello, sweetheart. How're you doing?" he asked.

Because Dean was just behind her Gemma made herself sound cheery. "Me? Oh, I'm fine."

From the porch Fuller cut in. "I'll go and have a look," he said to Frank. "All right?"

"Help yourself," Frank nodded. "I'll leave the door on the latch for when you've finished."

When Frank closed the door Gemma finally relaxed. She knew Dean would be busy in the garage for at least an hour – maybe a bit more if he had a smoke while he was there.

"The kettle's just boiled," Frank said as he crossed to the kitchen units. "Want a cuppa?"

Gemma pulled a face. "Rather have a rum-and-Coke."

"Tea's better for you," Frank told her. "Don't want anyone saying I'm leading you into bad ways, do I?"

"Too late for that, innit?" Gemma said, but when she saw that he was about to say something else she added: "Go on. It's cold out there."

Frank hesitated, then nodded. "Yeah well, as it happens I bought some Coke yesterday, so I suppose... Just one though. – Go through to the other room, I'll bring it in.

The fire's lit. Put the telly on if you want."

"Ta."

Gemma went through into the sitting room and looked round. It was warm and the curtains were closed. There was an open newspaper on the footstool with Frank's reading glasses on top of it and on the sideboard there were two framed photographs of Frank and his wife – one from their wedding day, the other much later. Her name was Connie, he'd told Gemma. She'd died ten years ago.

There was a rug in front of the gas fire and Gemma stood on it, warming her legs and adjusting her skirt so it wasn't quite so high up her thighs. She knew it made Frank a bit awkward when she looked too tarty so she tried to tone it down a bit when she was here. Course, he knew *why* she dressed like that, but even so she didn't want to make him uncomfortable. Frank was okay – not a dirty old man, anyway; more like a grandad or something.

The first time Dean had brought her to the house two months ago he'd told her to wait in the car while he took care of the garage. But Frank had seen her sitting there and said it wasn't fair to make her stay out in the cold. He told Dean to let her come inside in the warm and after a bit Dean had agreed.

Frank had made her tea, that first time, and once they'd drunk it Gemma had just assumed that he'd want to do business next. But when she'd asked him he'd suddenly coughed a lot and then looked really embarrassed – not disgusted or anything; just, well, surprised. Then he'd said he didn't think so, not at his age. Thanks for asking though. After that he'd been quiet for a bit, and then he'd asked if she liked to watch *EastEnders*.

And that's how it had been every time since then. Dean came to look at the stuff in the garage every couple of days and whenever he brought Gemma with him – which wasn't always – she went in to see Frank. The hour or so they'd spend chatting or watching telly always made her feel normal again. It was tiring, always being on your guard, but with Frank she felt like she could be herself, just for a while as they drank tea, or something stronger if she could persuade him. She always tried harder for the rum and Coke if she thought Dean would make her go back on the street again afterwards. Sometimes it helped.

"Here we are then," Frank said, coming in from the kitchen. "Service with a smile."

He had a glass of beer for himself and a tumbler of rum and Coke for her.

"Oh, ta."

"You warmed up a bit?"

"Yeah. I love this fire. We don't have one, just radiators and half of them don't work."

"Better make the most of it now then," he said. "Take your coat off or you won't feel the benefit."

He held out her drink and when she took it she saw that he had a couple of plasters on the side of his hand.

"What did you do to your hand?"

"That? Oh, it's not much: just a graze. I had a bit of a tumble this afternoon."

"You all right? How'd you do it?"

Frank waved it away. "Just tripped, outside the newsagent's."

"You want to be careful," Gemma told him. "Don't want to break a leg or something, do you?"

"Me?" Frank chuckled. "Tough as old boots, I am. Shall I put the telly on? The lottery's on later. I'm gonna win tonight, I can feel it."

13.

There wasn't much to the centre of Collington, and what there was had pretty much closed by the time Holly got off the bus – everything except the pubs and a few fast-food places. The town had been swallowed up years ago as the city of Weston had expanded and now it lost out when people went shopping or on a night out. There was nothing much to keep them in Collington, unless they had no choice.

Swinging her bag onto her shoulder, Holly set off from the bus stop across the pedestrian precinct. It was only a ten-minute walk to the flat and because she'd grown up here the place was still familiar, even though she'd been dying to get away for as long as she could remember. Funny though: now that she had escaped, Collington didn't seem quite as bad as it used to.

She was crossing the small marketplace, glancing in the shop windows as she went, when she heard her name called from a distance. There was the sound of feet running to catch up and when Holly stopped beside the lighted window of an electrical shop she saw Jody Castle coming towards her across the damp paving stones.

"Holly! Hiya!"

Jody waved and jogged out ahead of two other girls and a

boy. They were all about the same age as Holly but she didn't know them.

"Oh, hiya," Holly said, slightly taken off guard by the other girl's rush to catch her.

She hadn't seen Jody since their last day at school, but the other girl hadn't changed much: still dressing a bit grungey, still bouncy and excitable.

And for some reason that struck Holly as strange; unexpected. In the past nine months everyone else she knew – all the other TPOs, at least – *had* changed. It wasn't just that they'd dropped their previous fashions and taken to practical, understated clothes when they were off duty; it was something more than that. But for the moment Holly couldn't work out what it was – why Jody being exactly the same seemed strange.

"So, how's it going?" Jody asked, slowing to a halt in front of Holly. Then she remembered the others and turned to introduce them in turn. "This is Em, Ali and Gino. We're at college together."

"Oh. Right. Hi," Holly said to the three of them.

"Holly was at Drayton with me," Jody explained to her mates. "She's in the police now."

"Oh shit!" the boy called Gino exclaimed. He took a step back and held up his hands. "I didn't do it, officer! Honest I didn't. Don't take me in!"

He grinned, pleased with his acting, and looked to the others for a reaction. The girls called Em and Ali both giggled.

Holly forced a smile. "You're okay, I'm off duty," she told him.

As if sensing that Gino had gone a bit too far Jody stepped in again. "So what're you doing back here? Have you seen anyone else – you know, from school? What about Sophie and Jaz?"

Holly shook her head. "I haven't seen anyone," she told her. "I don't get back much."

"Don't blame you," the girl called Ali said. "Nothing here, is there? It's rubbish."

"So how come you went in the police?" Gino asked. Now he'd found out about it he clearly wasn't going to let it go. "Don't you have to be eighteen or something for that?"

"I'm training," Holly said. "A TPO."

"Oh, right. So you're not a *real* copper then? I mean you can't arrest me or nothing?"

"Why, do I need to?"

"Dunno. You might want to try though. That's what coppers do, right? Stop and search, shit like that."

Holly looked him over coolly and made sure he knew she wasn't impressed. "Don't think I'd bother," she said. "Anyway, like I said, I'm off duty till tomorrow."

"So what you want to go on their side for anyway?" Gino said.

"Whose side?"

"The cops. – I mean, it's us and them, right? So why'd you want to go with them – 'less it's just so you can hassle people and stuff."

"Gino, shut up," Jody said, giving him a warning tap on the arm. She was looking a little uncertain now, as if she wasn't sure how Holly would react.

"Yeah, shut up, Gino," Holly said. "Otherwise I might smell that last spliff on your breath."

In fact she'd smelled it on his clothes almost as soon as he came within a couple of paces, but she just wanted to make a point.

"What? No way!" Gino protested, but he took a step back as he said it.

There was a moment of awkward silence from the others then, and although Holly knew she was entirely responsible for it she wasn't particularly sorry.

"Listen, we're going to McDonald's – just to hang out," Jody said with a bit too much forced cheerfulness. "Why don't you come too?"

"Actually, I'm going to see my mum," Holly said, gesturing away. "I've only just got here, so…"

"Oh. Oh, okay," Jody said, and Holly could tell she was a bit relieved to have been given a way out. "You can give me a ring though, yeah? We could meet up. Have you still got my number?"

"Yeah, sure," Holly said, not at all certain that she had. "I will. It'd be good to catch up. I'd better be going though."

"Yeah. Okay," Jody said. "See you later though, yeah?"

"Sure," Holly said. "Bye."

She started away but hadn't gone more than a couple of

steps when she caught part of something Jody was saying to the others: "…just from school. I don't know her that well…"

And that was really the truth of it, Holly realised: they didn't know each other very well, not any more.

And then she understood why it had seemed odd that Jody could be just the same as nine months ago. It was because Jody hadn't had any *reason* to change. She hadn't been dealing with muggers, domestic disputes and abusive drunks, or the victims of accidents and violence. That was an alien world that Jody and her mates wouldn't have understood, even if Holly had wanted to tell them about it.

For a moment, as she crossed the street towards home, Holly wondered what it would have been like if she hadn't left her old world behind. Would she be just the same as Jody now? But then she squared her shoulders and dismissed the thought. It was too late to wonder. The boy called Gino had been right about that: she *was* on the other side now. She was a copper, and that put her in a different place.

"Holly!" Archie shouted.

He jumped up from the sofa, the DVD of *Toy Story* forgotten. "Holly, Holly, Holly!"

Closing the door of the flat, Holly hardly had time to put her bag down before the nearly-five-year-old bundle of energy in Spiderman pyjamas and dressing gown was piling into her for a hug. She grabbed him round the waist and lifted him off his feet.

"Hello, little brother," she said, grinning. "I thought you'd be in bed."

"Mum said I could stay up till you got here. It's a treat cos tomorrow's my birthday."

"What? Not tomorrow. I thought that was next week."

"*No-ooo!* Tomorrow!"

Holly gave him a kiss, then put him back on the floor. "Good job I came then."

"Have you brought me a present, too?"

"You'll have to wait till tomorrow to find out," Holly said, but when she saw his slightly crestfallen expression she added: "I think there'll be something, don't worry."

"Yay!" He did a star jump and Holly laughed.

"Hey, no jumping around," Holly's mum, Lisa, said from the doorway. "It's bedtime and you'll never get to sleep. – Hiya, sweetie."

Lisa was still in her thirties, with good cheekbones and an easy smile. She was still a bit thinner than she should have been, but not much, Holly decided. She was looking better than she had in a long time.

She came over and gave Holly a hug and a kiss on the cheek. "You made it in good time."

"Thought I'd better not be too late," Holly said.

"Have you eaten?"

"Not since lunch."

"Okay, I'll make you something as soon as Archie's in bed."

"Can Holly put me to bed?" Archie said. "*And* do the story. *Please!*"

"Holly's had a long day," Lisa told him. "Let her have a rest."

"No, it's okay," Holly said, shrugging off her coat and draping it over the back of the sofa. "I don't mind. – You'll go straight to sleep if I do though," she said, looking at Archie. "Right?"

Archie nodded vigorously.

"Okay then."

"Did you catch any bad guys today?" he asked.

"No, not today. We didn't see any," Holly told him. Maybe not strictly true. "Come on, let's go. Have you brushed your teeth?"

"Yeah."

"Okay, you're all set then. Which story do you want?"

14.

"Come on, Shermain, either there was or there wasn't."

In the hard light of the cell the woman called Shermain gave Oz Sitwell a weary look, in no hurry to answer. She was in her early twenties, wearing red and purple make-up and an ultra-short skirt.

"Shouldn't he be tucked up with his teddy?" she said, looking at Sam. "How old is he anyway?"

"Older than you when you went on the game," Oz said.

"Yeah? Least I knew what I was doing. More than he does, I bet." She turned to Sam: "Tell you what, love – come and find me after, I'll give you a few lessons if you like. Free."

"No thanks," Sam said, but immediately knew he should have kept quiet.

"Ooh," Shermain said, mock-offended. "Listen, darling, you don't want to turn something down till you're sure you know what it is."

"Knock it off, Shermain," Oz told her.

Sam knew he needed to say something, if only to prove that he didn't need Oz to stick up for him. "We just need to know if there was a man looking for his daughter," he said. "That's all."

87

For a moment he thought Shermain was just going to give him another sarky answer, but instead she pursed her bright cherry lips and considered.

"Yeah," she said in the end. "There was a bloke. He went round most of the girls. I thought he was just a picky punter but he had some leaflets with a photo of this girl: had I seen her? He's her dad and he's trying to find her."

"*Have* you seen her?" Oz asked.

"Nah, not on the hill. I'd know if there was anyone new."

"Okay, thanks. That helps."

"So am I gonna get off with a caution this time then, for helping you out?"

"Caution?" Oz said. "How many times did you get done last year?"

Shermain shrugged. "Six or seven. – It ain't my fault. It's just the crack."

"So stop smoking it, or at least don't be so bloody slow to run when you see us coming."

"Don't want to stop, do I? What else am I gonna do?"

Oz shook his head hopelessly and stepped out of the cell.

"Thanks for your help," Sam said.

"See how long it's gonna be will you?" Shermain said. "I need to get out, yeah?"

"I'll ask," Sam said.

Outside in the corridor the Gaoler PC closed the cell door and Oz and Sam headed back to the custody area. The place wasn't as busy as it would be later when the pubs and clubs turned out, but there was still a background hubbub as the girls and punters from the tom sweep waited to be processed one by one.

Sergeant Brooks was dealing with a suspected drunk driver at the desk so Sam and Oz stood back till he'd finished. Oz scanned the printout from the PNC again and Sam could tell he still had some doubts, despite what he read.

The report showed that Andrea Jane Deakin had been reported missing from home in Cardiff two months ago. She had no history of going missing and her parents thought she'd run away because she'd packed a bag, clothes and money. Andrea Deakin would be sixteen in June.

"What?" Sam asked when Oz finished reading and handed him the paper.

"Nothing," Oz said. Then the drunk driver was removed from the desk and Oz went across.

"We'll have to release Mr Deakin," he told Sergeant Brooks. "Looks like he wasn't a punter after all."

"The daughter thing's genuine?"

"Looks like it."

"Okay, I'll get him pulled out," the sergeant nodded.

"Any chance you could process Shermain Taylor before too long as well?"

"Feeling helpful, was she?"

"More than usual," Oz said. "I think she fancies Sam."

Brooks looked at Sam and grinned. "You'll be in trouble if

she does," he said, then turned back to Oz. "Remember when she took a fancy to Dave Roper?"

"Oh yeah."

"Why, what happened?" Sam said.

Brooks shook his head. "You don't want to know," he said, mock-seriously. "Just make sure you're never alone with her though, that's my advice."

Five minutes later Tony Deakin was standing at the custody desk while his property was returned to him and he signed the release form. He hadn't been as pissed off as Sam had expected when he and Oz apologised for the arrest. Instead he had thanked them and said it was understandable: he could see how it had looked from their point of view.

If anything, Deakin's lack of resentment seemed to make Oz even more suspicious, but Sam couldn't see it. Besides, it made a change not to be on the receiving end of bad temper and threats of a complaint for false arrest when someone was released without charge. To Sam, Tony Deakin's reasonable attitude just made life easier.

Once he'd finished the paperwork, Sam and Oz led Deakin through the corridors towards the exit.

"So is there a reason why you're looking for Andrea in Weston?" Oz asked. It sounded as if he was just making conversation, though Sam suspected the question wasn't so innocent.

"Her grandmother used to live here," Deakin said. "And

one of her friends told me she used to say she liked coming here."

"But you haven't heard from her since you reported her missing?"

"No." He shook his head. "My phone's on all the time, but..." He shrugged, as if he accepted that it was a long shot, and for the first time Sam thought he saw a weariness in Tony Deakin's expression.

"How long have you been out looking for her?" he asked.

"Since she went – two months," Deakin said. "But only round here for a few days."

"Do you have any reason to think she might be working the streets?" Oz asked. "Was that why you were on Mill Hill Lane?"

"No, no, not at all," Deakin said quickly, not even trying to keep the fear of that idea out of his voice. "I've been going to homeless shelters, hospitals, churches, drop-in centres. I'm just trying to get people to look at her picture so if they do see her they might remember, or tell her I'm looking for her."

"What about your wife?" Oz said. "Is she here too?"

"No, she's— She's at home," Deakin said. "It's been difficult for her."

"Must be," Oz nodded.

They reached the door to the yard and Oz opened it, looked round and gave a wave to two regs by a patrol car. They were about to go out on patrol and had volunteered to give Tony Deakin a lift back to his car.

Deakin stepped out into the yard, then turned back. "Listen, can I give you these?" he said, holding out a couple of flyers and cards to Sam. "Just in case you see her. She's about your age."

Sam nodded. "Sure. I'll ask if I can put them up on the noticeboards."

"Thanks, I'd appreciate it."

Oz looked at the leaflets, then at Deakin. "A word of advice? If you give out leaflets saying there's a reward for information you're going to get a lot of nutters and con artists trying to cash in."

"I know," Deakin said. "I've had a few already."

"So if I was you I wouldn't carry any large amounts of cash or anything valuable," Oz said. "'Specially some of the places you've been going."

"I'll remember," Deakin said. "Thanks."

They watched him until he'd crossed to the patrol car, then Oz came back inside and let the door close. "All right," he said. "Let's get Shermain processed. Least you know where you are with her."

15

Ryan didn't say much but Taz was okay with that. In the ten minutes it had taken to walk back to the Cadogan Estate from the party they'd only exchanged a few words. It wasn't like they deliberately weren't talking or anything, just that there didn't seem any need to. And at least he wasn't like the others, always bragging about how they'd done this, that or the other; talking themselves up, trying to sound cool or connected.

He wasn't bad-looking either. Nice skin and teeth. A bit serious, maybe, but not nerdy. What she couldn't work out though was why he'd be tight with Drew Alford. They weren't anything alike. Drew treated everyone like they'd just challenged him and he had to keep them in their place, but Ryan seemed more easy-going – like he'd think before he did something. He must be able to stand up for himself though: if he couldn't, he wouldn't have gone in with Drew in the first place.

There was something else though – a bigger difference between the two lads. If Drew had seen Rizza was spiking her drink Taz knew he'd have thought it was a laugh, maybe put in some more. But Ryan hadn't – and he hadn't just kept quiet either. So why not? It wasn't like he knew her – only in passing, on the estate and at school – so why had he stopped her drinking the stuff?

They crossed the curve of the approach road under the orange street lights and entered the estate proper. It wasn't far now to Penrice House.

"So why'd you do it?" Taz asked then, like it was an ordinary question.

"Do what?"

"Tell me Rizza had spiked the can."

Ryan shrugged. "Cos it wasn't fair."

"Drew wouldn't have cared." She said it flatly – a definite statement – and looked to see what his reaction would be.

"I dunno."

"He wouldn't," Taz said again. "He'd do anything if he felt like it. – You heard about him and that girl from school – Ashleigh, right? Few weeks ago? Everyone knows what he did – tried to force her to have sex with him – 'cept no one's gonna say it in case he finds out and goes looking for them."

"I heard something about it," Ryan said non-committally, as if he didn't want to get into it. "I don't know if it's true."

"Yeah? Well it is," Taz told him. She left a silence, then said: "Anyway, I owe you."

"S'okay," Ryan said and he seemed a bit embarrassed. "Forget it."

They were close to Penrice House now, where Taz lived on the ninth floor. She gestured and came to a halt. "This is mine," she said of the block.

"What, all of it?" He exaggerated his look of surprise

so she knew he was messing about.

"Yeah. Didn't you know? I'm minted. I only use the top floor though – the penthouse. I let other people stay in the rest."

"That's nice of you."

"I'm a nice person," she told him. "Not to mention good-looking and funny and smart – right?"

"Can't say, can I? You said not to mention it."

Taz laughed. "Listen, you want to do something tomorrow? We could hang out for a bit – if you want. In the morning?"

Ryan hesitated, as if he hadn't been expecting her to say something like that. "I dunno," he said.

"Oh, okay," Taz said, making it sound just a bit disappointed. "If you don't want to, it's fine."

"No, it's not that. I just— I might have to do something – with Drew. That's all."

"Here?"

He shook his head. "My block."

"When?"

"I don't know yet."

"Okay, I'll give you my number and you can text me when you've finished. Got your phone?"

Ryan took out his phone and entered the number she told him. His face was illuminated by the screen and she liked the way he frowned a bit as he concentrated on what he was doing.

"So text me, all right?" she said when he'd finished. Then she touched his arm for a second before starting away towards the flats. "Don't forget!"

16.

In the kitchen Lisa watched approvingly as Holly ate her way through a plateful of fish fingers, chips and peas. Between mouthfuls Holly had been telling her about the street robbery call to Frank Chapman. Holly didn't tell Lisa about all the cases she dealt with because she knew her mum still had mixed feelings about her being a TPO. It wasn't that she disapproved, just that she worried about how safe it was, so Holly was always careful to edit out anything which might give her cause for concern.

"I'm glad he didn't catch them," Lisa said, meaning Frank Chapman. "You don't know what they'd have done if he had. I mean, they might have beaten him up or stabbed him or anything."

Holly nodded. "I reckon he gave them a surprise anyway," she said. "For a guy in his seventies he seemed pretty tough."

"Will you catch them – the lads who snatched his wallet?"

Holly shook her head. "Not now. We had a look, but they'd gone." She put her knife and fork down. "Thanks, that was great."

"Looks like you needed it," Lisa said of the empty plate. "Are you eating properly at the Section House?"

"Better than the lads do," Holly said. "Sam can just about manage scrambled eggs on toast but Tommo and Shiny Chris can't even cook that."

"Someone should teach them."

"Not me. If they're old enough to train as coppers, they're old enough to learn for themselves."

She stood up and went over to the kettle, switched it on. "So what's the plan for tomorrow?" she asked.

"Swimming at twelve, then McDonald's for lunch and back here for cake," her mum said.

"How many?"

"Six including Archie. I didn't think I could deal with any more."

"I'm sorry I can't be here. I couldn't change shifts."

"That's okay. It's nice that you'll be here in the morning. Anyway, Diane – Toby's mum – said she'll come to help."

"Anyone else?"

"No, that's it."

Holly knew it was now or never. "What about Liam?" she asked. "He could be on parole by now. Has he tried to contact you?"

For a moment her mum didn't seem to have heard, but from the way her back stiffened Holly knew that she had.

"He got out four weeks ago," Lisa said then, turning to face Holly.

"You've talked to him?"

Lisa nodded, as if she didn't trust herself to speak.

"When?"

"Just after he got out."

"Have you seen him?" Holly asked tightly. "Has Archie?

Lisa hesitated again and it was enough.

"Mum!" Holly said. "*Why?* For God's sake!"

"Don't be mad with me, Hol, please. I just— He wanted to see Archie. He *is* his dad."

"Yeah, and every boy needs a drug dealer and a thief in his life."

"Ssh!" Lisa said urgently, glancing round as if she expected to see Archie in the doorway.

"So how many times? How many times has he seen him?"

"Two or three."

"Here? He's been here?"

Lisa nodded.

"Christ!"

"Hol—"

"So what did you tell Archie? I mean, what did you tell him about Liam? He can't remember him from before, can he?"

"No, he— I told him Liam had a job where he had to go away a lot."

"Well at least that was true."

Immediately she said it Holly regretted the acid tone in her voice, especially when she saw her mum's face start to crumple.

"I didn't know what else to do," Lisa said hopelessly. "I couldn't just— He was really desperate – Liam. He said he wants to start again."

"Start again? Not with you?"

"No! No, he knows that's not going to happen. But with Archie. He wants to be able to see him, to get to know him so he can be a proper dad. That's what he said."

"He'll never be a proper anything," Holly said flatly. "He's an ex-con and he used to hit you. He'll never be anything else and the best thing for Archie would be to never see him again. He doesn't have to."

Lisa shook her head. "Liam said he'd talked to a solicitor. He said it was his right."

"What, so he's already trying to force you to do something you don't want to? What's that tell you, Mum? What's that say about him?"

"I don't think he meant it like that. – You weren't there. You— He wasn't being nasty about it. He just wants to see him."

"If I had been there I'd have decked him," Holly said. "I mean it." And then a thought came to her. "Is he going to turn up tomorrow?"

"I don't know. He asked what we were doing, but he didn't say he would."

"I can't believe this," Holly said, turning and pacing in the small kitchen. "How *dare* he?"

"Hol, listen, for Archie… He doesn't— It's weird enough for him already, seeing Liam again when he doesn't remember him from before. And if he does come round… It— I don't want you to do anything. Will you promise? I know I need to work this out. But I have to do what's best for Archie, too."

Holly could see how much her mum meant this and although she hated the idea, in the end she nodded. "Okay – for Archie. But I'm not going to be in the same room as Liam. I don't want anything to do with him."

"It's all right. You don't have to. And anyway, he might not come."

"He will," Holly said flatly, not sure how she knew, but certain she was right. "He never knew when he wasn't wanted. That was the problem."

17

"You ready?" Dean called from the back door. "Get your coat on."

Gemma looked towards the half-open door of the sitting room, expecting him to appear, but he didn't. Instead she heard him go out again. It hadn't taken very long this time.

She knocked back the last bit of rum and Coke in her glass and Frank used the remote to switch off the telly.

"I reckon he'll be finished out there soon," he said. "Then you won't be coming round any more."

"You gonna miss me?" Gemma said, sort of teasing.

Frank made a "*Huh*" noise but it wasn't a negative thing. He pushed himself out of his armchair.

"Maybe he'll want to do some more," Gemma said.

"Yeah, well, I dunno about that," Frank said. "I reckon it might get a bit risky. And anyway—"

He broke off, frowned a bit.

"What?" Gemma asked.

"Nothing," Frank shook his head. "*You* can come back though, you know that, right? I mean, you know where I am – in case you need something."

"Like what?" She didn't get what he meant.

"Like— If you need somewhere. Somewhere to go."

Gemma studied his face, the serious expression. He

seemed to mean it but she knew it couldn't be as simple as that. It never was.

And Frank seemed to understand what she was thinking. "Look," he said. "I'm not— I don't mean any funny business. I'm just saying. You don't have to stay with him."

Finally she realised he meant it. He wasn't trying something on.

"I can't," she said. "He'd just— He wouldn't let me."

"It's not up to him," Frank said, and his voice was determined. "It's you. It's what *you* want and if…"

He let the sentence trail off, as if he was embarrassed or thought he'd said too much. "Not everyone's like him," he told her. "That's all I'm saying."

Gemma knew there should be a way to show she'd finally understood what he meant, what he was offering, but she didn't know how to do it. She wondered if it was possible to forget how to show someone you liked them, that you were grateful, if there was never anyone to like or thank.

"I reckon you're just a dirty old man," she told him, and then made sure he knew she didn't mean it with a grin.

"Yeah, right," he said.

He picked up her jacket and held it so she could put it on, but she did it without thinking and turned her arm. The wrist, where Dean had twisted it, was still painful and Gemma let out a small "Ow!"

"You all right?" Frank asked, coming round in front of her, seeing the way she held her arm and the pain on her face.

"It's okay," Gemma said. "It's nothing."

"Did he do that?"

"I told you, it's all right."

Gemma pulled her jacket closed.

"No," Frank said, his expression setting. "It's not."

In the other room they heard the back door open and close again.

"Don't— Don't say nothing," Gemma said, urgently, lowering her voice. "Just—"

"You ready?" Dean said, opening the door of the sitting room but not coming in. When he saw the way they were standing he frowned suspiciously.

Gemma moved quickly away from Frank. "Yeah, I'm coming," she said.

"Wait in the van. I need to talk about something."

Without saying goodbye to Frank, Gemma ducked out through the door. If she wasn't there she hoped Frank wouldn't do or say anything. She hoped he'd realise what Dean might do, later, if he did.

Dean Fuller watched her go and once the back door had closed he turned back to Frank again.

"It'll be ready in a couple of days," he said. "He wants to know if he can do another grow straight after. Same as before: two grand and the electric, ten weeks. – You listening?"

Frank Chapman had moved away, turned his back, but now he faced the younger man again.

"What did you do to Gemma?" he said.

"What? What you talking about?"

"You know what. Her arm."

"Fuck off," Fuller said. "You don't know what you're talking about. She's nothing to do with this. You want another two grand or don't you?"

"Listen, you touch her again and—"

"What?" Fuller demanded. "You stupid old sod, you don't know nothing about it."

"I know enough to get you locked up," Frank said flatly.

For a moment after the words were spoken Fuller stood stock-still, then he took a step forward. "You think you're gonna do that, do you? – Eh? Is that what you think?" He pushed Frank in the chest. "Is it?"

Outside Gemma could hear Dean's raised voice as she stood by the corner of the house – not what was said, but the tone was enough. And then she heard nothing.

She knew she'd be in trouble – worse trouble – if Dean came out and found her standing there, so she moved quickly to the van and got in. Through the rain-speckled windscreen she watched the house, expecting him to emerge at any moment, but he didn't – not for several long minutes.

Then, finally, he rounded the corner and strode quickly round the van to the driver's side. He said nothing as he got in, banged the door closed, twisted the keys in the ignition.

Gemma sensed his fury. She knew it and knew not to say

anything, not to do anything. But it didn't make any difference. She only just glimpsed what was coming as he swung his left elbow round and struck her in the face. She felt her nose crunch, a pulse of pain in her cheek and saw a starburst of orange lights in her eye. She was too stunned to feel the blood well from her nose.

"You stupid bitch," Dean Fuller spat. "Stupid bloody bitch."

SUNDAY

1.

She felt his warm breath close to her ear and an arm over hers, under the duvet.

"*Holly?*" A whisper.

"Mm?"

"Holly?" Not so softly this time. "It's tomorrow now."

With a grunt, Holly rolled over and opened her eyes, tried to focus. She saw Archie's face right next to hers.

"What time is it?"

From the doorway her mum said: "Sorry, love, I kept him out as long as I could. It's nearly half eight."

"S'all right," Holly mumbled. And to Archie: "It's a good job I love you, you know."

"Can we do presents now?"

"What presents?"

"*Birthday* presents!"

"Mm, okay."

She rolled over a bit more. "Here's your first one," she said, and grabbed him round the waist and started to tickle him so he squirmed and screamed and laughed all at the same time.

2

In the semi-darkness from the closed curtains she felt Dean get out of bed and heard him rummage around for his clothes. She didn't open her eyes or move though, and after a couple of minutes he left the room, closing the door quietly behind him. She didn't know what time it was but outside the bed the room was still cold and she wasn't going to get up. The longer he left her the better. She'd stay there all day if he let her, even though she was starting to need a pee.

When she heard him in the bathroom Gemma finally pulled the duvet closer round her. If there'd been any choice she wouldn't have shared the bed with him, but there wasn't another one and he wouldn't let her sleep on the sofa. She knew he thought she'd try to get out of the flat if she was on her own all night.

At least he didn't want to touch her any more, which was good, so Gemma always slept at the edge of the mattress as far away from him as possible and pretended she had the bed to herself. It was only when morning came and she was woken by him getting up that the pretence was shattered. And this morning, now, she felt the dull blow of reality even more strongly than usual. She hated him. She never wanted to wake up near him again.

Still with her eyes closed, Gemma put a tentative finger to her cheekbone and felt the deep ache of the bruise. Her nose didn't feel so bad now, but she could tell her eye was swollen and she could imagine the purple-yellow colour it had probably become. Just like before.

He was a bastard. There'd been no reason for it. What had she done? Nothing. She hadn't even *said* anything. So how come he could just do that – for nothing?

Out of nowhere Gemma felt a warm, pricking feeling behind her closed eyelids and as soon as she realised it was tears she started to sob.

She made no noise, but she hugged her arms round her body and let the tears come. And as they did so, in a separate place in her head she made up her mind. That was it. No matter what he said or did now, that was it. No more.

After a bit she'd gone back to sleep and the next thing she knew was his voice.

"Gem? Gem, you awake?"

She knew he was standing over her and because he wasn't raising his voice or sounding bad-tempered, Gemma pretended that she was waking up for the first time. She rolled on her back, then opened her eyes.

He was holding a mug of tea but he had his jacket on and she could smell his aftershave so she knew he was going out.

"How you feeling?" he asked, like she'd just got a cold or

the flu or something. Like it was nothing to do with him.

"I dunno. Okay," Gemma said, still feigning sleepiness.

"I brought you a cuppa," he said, putting it down on the bedside cabinet. He sat down next to her and put a hand to her cheek, near the bruise but not on it. He stroked her skin.

"Does it hurt?"

"A bit."

He reached into his pocket and took out something small, put it next to her tea. It was half an E.

"Take that," he told her. "It'll make you feel better."

"Okay." She nodded, not wanting to question it or sound ungrateful. When he was in this kind of mood it was best to go along with it and make it last.

"Why've you got your coat on?" she said, propping herself up on an elbow.

"Got to see someone. You don't need to come though. Stay here and have a lie-in or watch telly or something."

"How long'll you be?"

"Dunno. Not too long."

He stroked her cheek again and she could tell he was assessing the damage.

"Does it look horrible?" she asked, sounding worried.

"Nah. You'll be able to cover it up, no problem. Be as good as new when you do."

"Okay," Gemma said, meekly. "I'll try."

"That's my girl."

He patted her arm and stood up from the bed then. "Maybe I'll get you something nice while I'm out, too," he said.

"What?"

"Don't know yet, do I? It'll be a surprise. – But only if you're good, all right?"

"I will be," Gemma said and managed to give him a promising smile before he moved to the door.

She stayed where she was, sipping tea and waiting for the sound of the front door being closed and locked. Even if he was in a better mood than last night he still wasn't taking any chances, and from the third-floor flat there was no other way out – not unless you went out on the balcony and jumped.

It wasn't until there had been silence for a couple of minutes that she was finally sure that he'd gone, and when she was she swung her legs out of bed and headed quickly to the bathroom to pee.

Afterwards, in the mirror over the sink, she examined her face and was surprised that the bruising wasn't quite as bad as she'd thought. Last night, when he'd finally calmed down, Dean had cleaned her up with a cloth and made her hold a cold flannel on the swelling, so maybe it had done some good.

The worst bit was under her right eye, and although the bruise was a sickly green and yellow, edged with purple, it probably would cover up if she used enough make-up.

Her nose was still a bit red too, but at least it wasn't broken. That had been her worst fear, especially when she'd seen how much it had bled.

The blood had coated her top so heavily that it had made her look like she'd been stabbed or something, but at least looking like that had meant he couldn't make her go out working again. No way she was going to get any punters with blood all down her front, not even at a tenner a time.

Gemma studied her reflection for a moment or two longer, then left it for the time being and went back to the bedroom to dress. The most important thing now was to remember what she'd decided as she lay in bed crying. She needed to get things sorted before he came back: sorted, so that when the time came she was ready.

3.

They managed to persuade Archie to have breakfast and get dressed before he opened his presents, but by ten o'clock the sitting room floor was covered in Lego – one of Holly's presents – and Scalextric – one of Lisa's.

Holly was kneeling on the floor, trying to connect the last parts of the racetrack together and Archie was building Lego obstacles to put in the way of the cars. The latest one was a solid-looking wall.

"I don't know if that's a good idea," Holly told him as he placed the barrier of bricks across the track.

"No, it'll be great," he told her. "We did it at Nathan's. If you hit them really hard you get a big smash and the cars fly off!"

He made the noise of an imaginary smash and showed how the cars would fly through the air.

"I thought the idea was to keep them *on* the track," Lisa said, but she was smiling as she stood over them, watching their progress.

Then there was a knock on the door, taking them all by surprise. Holly looked up, and when she saw her mum's face she knew they were thinking the same thing.

"I'll get it," Holly said, making to stand, but her mum held out a hand.

"It's okay, I'll go."

"Can we start the cars now?" Archie asked, but Holly wasn't looking. She was watching as Lisa crossed to the front door and turned the latch.

"Hol? The cars?" Archie tugged at her sleeve.

"Just a sec," Holly said.

As soon the door opened, Holly knew. His voice just confirmed it.

"Hiya," he said.

Lisa said nothing. Her hand stayed on the door.

"I've got something for Archie. Can I see him?"

Hearing his name, Archie's ears pricked up. "Who is it?" he called out.

Lisa didn't move for a moment, then finally she stepped back. "It's your dad."

Liam Mason came into the room with a wrapped present under his arm and Holly immediately stood up.

He was pretty much as she remembered him: stocky without being fat, hair a bit shorter but still curly, and he had the usual two days' worth of stubble on his face. Was it the *same* face she'd seen in the CCTV footage yesterday morning though? She still couldn't tell.

"Dad!" Archie yelled, scattering Lego as he raced round the sofa to greet him.

"Hello, big man," Liam said, gathering him into a hug. "Happy birthday!"

Over Archie's head he looked at Holly. "Hello, Hol," he said with a smile.

Holly said nothing. She didn't acknowledge the greeting, just stepped over the Scalextric track and headed out of the room.

A few minutes later, when her mum came into the kitchen, Holly was still standing beside the sink, sipping the cup of coffee she'd made, listening to the sounds of Liam and Archie in the other room.

"Hol—" her mum started.

"How long's he staying?" Holly said, cutting her off.

Her mother looked pained. "I don't know." She lowered her voice. "I can't just chuck him out."

Holly thought about saying that was exactly what she should do, but instead she looked at her watch, then back at Lisa. "I'll call the station," she said. "I'll tell them I'm ill or something: I can't come in."

"You can't do that, not if you're supposed to be there."

"People do it all the time," Holly said. "Anyway, I'm not going till he does. I want to make sure— I'm going to make sure he goes."

"He will," Lisa said, then took a couple of steps forward. She put a hand on Holly's arm. "Listen, you don't have to worry about it. I *can* deal with it, and you need to go to work. It's important."

"So's this."

"Please, Hol," her mum said. "I don't want you to."

"Why not?" Holly asked.

Lisa squeezed Holly's arm. "Because I can see what you're thinking right across your face. And so will Liam."

"I don't give a toss," Holly said, and meant it.

"No, but Archie will. Don't spoil the day for him. – Besides, we'll be going swimming in a bit and there'll be all the other kids there. I can't see Liam hanging around for that, can you?"

Even though she still didn't want to admit it, Holly could see that her mum was probably right. The idea that Liam would want to be surrounded by half a dozen five-year-olds at a swimming party wasn't very likely.

"Are you *sure*?" she asked, looking Lisa straight in the eyes, watching for any trace of nerves or a lie.

"Yes!"

Holly held her gaze for a moment longer, then nodded. "All right," she said. "If you are."

4

Whatever Drew wanted Ryan's help with, Taz couldn't see it happening very early on a Sunday morning. Even so, she set the alarm on her phone for half eight, just to be sure she wouldn't miss it. The trouble was, when the alarm went off she silenced it and went back to sleep, so it was ten o'clock before she left the flat, hurrying and hoping she hadn't missed her chance. Her mum was still in bed, dead to the world.

Taz hadn't asked Ryan too many questions last night in case he got suspicious, but even so she was pretty sure it would be worth finding out what Drew was doing. Every time they met at the safe house Holly asked what Drew was up to, so if Taz could find out she reckoned it would prove she was taking the informant thing seriously. And if the info was really good it would have to be worth a new pair of boots, surely.

It was still a dangerous game though – sticking your nose into Drew Alford's business – Taz knew that. Ever since the cops had decided not to bring charges against him for trying to rape Ashleigh Jarvis, he'd become even more cocky and dangerous than before, like he thought he was untouchable.

Now that he wasn't going out with her best friend, Bex, any more, Taz didn't see him as much as she used to, but on the Cadogan Estate it was hard to avoid Drew completely. He had the run of the place, went wherever he liked, and if she did bump into him – like last night – Taz still got that cold-shiver feeling when he gave her that look, like he knew what she was thinking. She knew it wasn't true, but even so the feel of it was enough to put you on edge and want to move away.

Even by ten o'clock there weren't many people about on the estate, so it was harder not to stand out. Taz did her best though, keeping away from open spaces as she headed for Cloudsley House, hoping to catch sight of Ryan or Drew without being spotted herself.

The guy who caught her attention wasn't Drew or Ryan though. And it wasn't so much who he was as what he was doing that took her interest – standing beside the rear doors of a blue van as if he was keeping guard.

The van was parked near the stairs at the south end of Cloudsley House, close to the side entrance to the block. But it was the way the guy next to it – thirties, leather jacket – kept glancing round that told Taz he was up to something. It might not have anything to do with Drew, but Taz reckoned it might still be worth knowing about if it was dodgy.

Because the guy had seen her, Taz pretended she was just passing by and slightly quickened her step. She didn't look at him after the first glance and when she reached a corner she went round it and disappeared from his sight.

Under cover she waited a few seconds, then edged back and sneaked a look round the corner, just in time to see Drew and then Ryan emerge from the stairwell. They were each carrying a large cardboard box in their arms, which they took round to the back of the van where the older guy opened the rear doors.

After a couple of seconds Taz ducked back from the corner and pulled out her phone. In her head she repeated the van's registration number over and over while she tapped it into the mobile. It was something Danny Simmons had specifically told her not to do in case someone else saw it, but Taz knew she'd never remember it any other way.

Then she heard the van start up and a moment later it passed her, heading away. Quickly she pushed her phone back into her pocket and took a glance towards the block of flats. She was just in time to see Ryan and Drew going towards the stairs and as soon as they disappeared Taz made her decision and trotted quickly after them.

Drew was counting the notes in his hand as he climbed the stairs to the third-floor landing. He'd already done that once, when the man called Dean Fuller had handed them over, but double-checking seemed to make him feel better and Ryan didn't interrupt. All he really wanted was for Drew to signal that he was no longer required.

"Three hundred," Drew said then, folding the notes and

shoving them into his jeans.

"For thirty? Seems cheap."

"Nah, don't you get it?" Drew said, like Ryan was being dense. "That's just deposit. He can't afford to pay it all up front so Tommy lets him have them on credit. Then, when Dean flogs them, he hands over another twenty or thirty quid each. If he's knocking them out at sixty or seventy he's still making a profit."

"So how much do we get?" Ryan asked.

Drew shook his head. "Included, innit? In what Tommy's paying for us looking after the place. Mind you, if we could find a few punters who want them – the Wiis – I reckon I could get Tommy to do us a deal. Better rates than Dean, too."

Ryan had mixed feelings about that. Moving boxes of bent gear from the flat to a van was one thing – you could always claim you didn't know what was in them, just helping out a mate, right? – but going out to sell stolen gear was different, and more risky. He said nothing and hoped Drew wouldn't pursue the idea.

They'd reached the flat by then – the first in the row – and Drew pulled out the key. "Stay here, I'll only be a minute."

He went into the flat but left the door slightly ajar behind him. Ryan stepped back and leaned on the railing to check the walkway. That was when he saw Taz in the stairwell.

For a moment she seemed surprised to see him, but then

she smiled and waved and came along the landing.

"Hiya!" she said brightly. "I was looking for you. Didn't know which flat was yours though. Stupid, aren't I? So is this yours then?"

"No, we're on the fourth," Ryan said. He was still wondering about her just appearing like that. It seemed a bit odd.

"Oh, right," Taz said, apparently losing interest in the flat. "Anyway, I found you. So we gonna do something, like we said yesterday?"

Before Ryan could answer Drew opened the door of the flat and came out. The moment he saw Taz his expression became a suspicious scowl.

"What you doing here?" he demanded, then cast a look at Ryan. "What you told her?"

"Nothing," Ryan said, defensive.

"I was looking for his flat," Taz said. "We're gonna go somewhere. We fixed it last night. Why? Whose place is that?"

"Never mind. Keep your nose out," Alford said, pulling the door closed behind him so it locked on the Yale. He looked back to Ryan. "That straight? You and her?"

"Yeah," Ryan said, knowing he'd been put on the spot. "I said I'd meet her."

Drew made a tutting sound. "Rizza's not going to like that." He looked to Taz. "He was telling everyone last night how you fancied him."

"He can sod off," Taz said. "I wouldn't fancy him if he

was covered in chocolate and giving out fifty-quid notes."

She turned to Ryan without giving Drew a chance to reply. "So, do you still want to do something?"

Ryan started to glance towards Drew, as if he was going to ask permission, but then he abandoned it. "Yeah, sure," he said with a nod. Then he did look at Drew, but it wasn't to ask. "We've finished, right."

"Yeah – for now. I'll call you later."

He gave Taz a last, dismissive look, then headed for the stairs.

Taz and Ryan both watched him go, each for different reasons, and then Taz stepped closer to Ryan and put her arm through his, moving them away. "So where we gonna go then? I fancy somewhere different from here – the park or the cinema or something... Be nice to get away, wouldn't it?"

5

In the bedroom Holly gathered her overnight stuff into her bag and remembered to add a couple of T-shirts and a bottle of perfume she'd been meaning to take back to the Section House. When she'd finished she collected her coat from the hall and put it on before going into the sitting room.

Lisa was sitting on the sofa, but Liam and Archie were on the floor in front of the TV, both holding controllers for the Wii that was Liam's present to Archie. They were playing Mario Kart and the Scalextric and Lego had been forgotten.

Holly leaned in and gave her mum a kiss on the cheek. "I'll call you later," she said. "Or call me if you need to. I'll have my mobile."

Lisa nodded and smiled. "I will. Have a good shift."

"Bye then, Archie," Holly said, straightening up. "See you in a few days."

After a moment's hesitation Archie tore himself away from the Wii and jumped up. He came round and took Holly's hand. "Aren't you coming swimming?"

"No, sweetie, I told you I couldn't. I've got to go to work. Sorry."

"Will you catch bad guys today?"

"I dunno. Maybe. Give us a kiss, eh?"

Archie planted a kiss on her cheek.

"See you soon," Holly said and ruffled his hair as she moved to the door.

Outside it was drizzling and she paused long enough to turn up her collar and settle the bag on her shoulder before heading towards the stairs. She'd reached the top of them before she heard her name called.

She knew who it was without looking round, so she didn't. Instead she just stopped and waited, hearing the jogging footsteps approach and only turning when they were almost upon her.

Liam came to a halt, puffing a little. He pushed the hair back from his forehead.

"Hol, listen, I wanted to talk to you," he said.

Behind him she saw the net curtains twitch in the neighbouring flat: Mrs Brodie, noseying as usual.

"About what?" Holly said, making no effort to make it sound friendly or interested.

"About— Just about Archie and your mum. – Look, I wouldn't blame you if you don't trust me – why would you? But all I want is to be a proper dad to Archie – like, be there so he knows who I am, and all the rest of it. – That's what I'm saying. I've changed. I mean it. It's different now – *I'm* different now."

"Yeah?" Holly looked at him coolly and held his eye.

"Yes!"

"Well, so am I."

Unflinching, Liam nodded seriously. "Yeah, yeah, I know. –

But that's all the more reason, right? I mean, more reason why I've got to stay straight – you being a cop and everything."

"You mean if I wasn't you *wouldn't* have to?"

"No! No, that's not—" He broke off, shook his head, then started again. "Look, I just hoped we could be friends again, that's all. I mean, if I'm seeing Archie... I just want it to be right for him, you know?"

Holly tried to gauge what she saw in his face but she couldn't. All she knew, from the past, was that Liam could persuade you of anything when he wanted to. Butter wouldn't melt.

"I'm not your friend," Holly said then, deliberately. "And I'll tell you something else: you *ever* hit my mum again – or you ever touch Archie – and you'll wish you'd stayed in prison. I mean that. Don't think I don't."

Turning away she took the stairs downwards, not knowing or caring whether he was still there, watching her go.

6

Gemma was on the sofa when Dean got back. He was carrying a bulky cardboard box, half-open at the top and almost too large to handle on his own. As it was, he had to kick the door closed behind him and he carried the box straight through to the bedroom without stopping or speaking.

Gemma knew better than to poke her nose in so she stayed on the worn leather sofa. She'd been watching the telly but she used the remote to switch it off in case he didn't like the noise. Instinctively she glanced at her bag where it lay casually on the floor – less chance of him suspecting something than if she hid it away.

She reached for a magazine and flicked through it while she waited for him to come back. When he did, a couple of minutes later, she could tell he was in a good mood. He kept one hand out of sight when he came and sat on the edge of the sofa.

"Do you love me?" he asked.

"Course I do," she said, with no hint of the lie.

"Really?"

"You *know* I do."

"Okay, just checking. You'd better have this then."

He brought out a small white box from behind his back and held it out to her.

"What is it?"

"Have to open it, won't you?"

She put the magazine aside and took the box, working the lid off. Inside, on a bed of cotton wool, there was a gold necklace: a St Christopher and a crucifix linked together on a thin chain.

It was cheap, she could tell, and she knew he was only giving it to her because of last night. He must think she was stupid if he thought she'd fall for that, but all the same she cooed when she saw it.

"Its gorgeous," she said. And then, as if she couldn't believe how lucky she was: "You sure it's for me?"

"Course it is. See, I'm always thinking about you. Put it on."

She took it out of the box, holding it up by the chain to admire it, then held it out to him. "You do it," she said.

She lifted her hair at the back so he could loop the chain round her neck and work the clasp, and when he'd done that she arranged the pendants on her chest, opening the collar of her shirt so he could see.

"It's lovely," she said. "Thank you."

She leaned over and kissed him to show she meant it, then snuggled in beside him. Taking advantage of his good mood, she said: "Why don't we stay in today? We could get a takeaway later, watch a DVD… Like we used to.

"Can't," he said, shaking his head. "We've got to see someone later: business."

Her heart sank. That would explain why he was being lovey-dovey; not just to make up for hitting her.

"What sort of business?" she asked, afraid of the answer.

"The stuff I went out for. There's more in the van. I've got a buyer."

"Oh, right," she said, relieved it was only that.

"We might go for a drink after though," he said, considering the possibility. "Could get a curry too, if you want."

"Oh, yeah, that sounds nice," she said.

"Maybe we will then," he said, settling back on the sofa and putting his feet up. "Make us a coffee, eh?"

7.

MORNINGSTAR RD STATION

The Sunday buses were slow and the one Holly was on was half empty. She sat midway to the back, watching the damp roads and listening to her iPod. Half the time she didn't register what she was listening to or really see what she was passing though. Her thoughts were centred on Liam Mason and whether his face really did match that of the man from the warehouse robbery, or whether she was simply reading it that way because she wanted it to be him.

She still hadn't decided by the time the bus reached the depot, but by then she had only ten minutes to make it to the nick, so she jogged all the way and changed quickly for the pre-shift briefing.

Having to hurry was enough to take her mind off things and the distraction would probably have continued if she could have gone out on a beat after that. She was partnered with Yvonne again, but immediately after the pre-shift briefing Yvonne was called away to complete a backlog of paperwork on an aggravated burglary case and because there was no part Holly could take, Sergeant Stafford put her in the front office until Yvonne was free.

Sunday afternoons on the front desk were usually a mixture of the boring, the trivial and the ridiculous: all the stuff that members of the public had been saving up through the week when they had more important things to do. "I've lost my glasses"; "The neighbours won't cut their hedge"; "They told me to bring in my documents but the dog ate the insurance certificate".

But this afternoon it was like no one in Weston wanted to report anything: no lost glasses, no annoying neighbours, no insurance-eating dogs. It was even too soon for the homeless drunks to come in for a warm, so for two hours Holly had nothing to do except tidy up the noticeboards and read the stuff she was supposed to have learned before her next assessment.

The trouble was, she couldn't concentrate. Her mind kept going over the same thing, over and over, trying and failing to make a decision. In the end she gave up and closed the training manual with a thud.

Steve Sollis, the reg PC in charge of the office, looked up from his book of sudoku.

"Make the most of it," he advised her. "One shift in fifty you get a quiet one like this – must be the moon or something. Then next time you're on they'll be five deep: pissed, annoyed, throwing up – and that's just the old ladies."

It was a pretty lame joke but Holly laughed anyway. Sollis was one of the regs who treated the TPOs more or less as equals and didn't come on all superior just because he had a lot more experience. She thought about it for a moment longer, then made up her mind.

"Is it okay if I go and check something with CID?" she

asked. "I should've sorted it out yesterday."

"Sure," Sollis nodded. "I'll shout if we get a coach party in."

"Thanks."

There were a few people around as she left the front office and walked along the corridors from the old part of the building to the more modern addition at the back, but even back here the nick seemed unnaturally quiet and empty. From the work rosta she knew Danny Simmons was down for duty cover until five, but almost as soon as she set off towards CID her decision to find him began to fade.

The truth was, she still couldn't make up her mind. Every time she thought she'd finally made a decision she began to doubt that it was the right one. It all came down to one question: whether to identify Liam or not.

If the pictures from the warehouse robbery had been clearer – if she could have been sure it *was* Liam – she wouldn't have had any doubts. Whether she wanted to or not, she'd have to speak up, and she'd have to face the inevitable questions too: *how did she know him? What relation was he to her? Did she know he had a criminal record?*

It would all come out then, it was bound to – all the stuff she hadn't mentioned during the selection process to become a TPO. She didn't know what would happen after that, but she could guess.

But what if Liam *wasn't* the guy in the CCTV? What if she opened up the whole can of worms and it turned out he was nothing to do with the warehouse raid? She'd have done it for no reason and Liam would still be on parole, still coming round to see Archie.

At the double doors leading into CID Holly hesitated, feeling the tightly wound ball of her decision start to unravel. On the basis of one grainy image was she ready to tell Danny Simmons the truth? Was she ready to let Liam Mason screw up that part of her life too?

"Holly?"

She looked round, startled for a moment, and saw Yvonne coming along the corridor from the direction of the Victim Support Unit. "I was just coming to find you," Yvonne said. "We've got a shout: a no answer at home."

"Oh. Right. Okay." Holly turned away from CID and fell into step with the older woman. In some ways it was a relief to have had the decision made for her – at least for the time being.

"What were you going to CID for?" Yvonne asked.

"Oh, nothing special," Holly said. "I was just going to catch up with Danny Simmons. It wasn't important."

She felt Yvonne look her over for a second, as if that didn't quite sit right.

"So what's this call about?" she asked, hoping to refocus Yvonne.

"Someone called Evans, can't see any sign of his neighbour so he's worried. – That street robbery outside the hairdresser's yesterday – Mr Chapman? It's his house."

"Frank," Holly said, remembering.

"Yeah, have-a-go-Frank," Yvonne said.

8

It had been Ryan's idea to go to the canal. Taz had never been there before and even though it was a half-hour walk from the estate she didn't complain – didn't even think about it really, just because it was nice to be going somewhere, not just hanging round the Caddy with all the same places, same faces, same shit.

And when they got there she'd been amazed by how different it was. Not like it was pretty or anything – they were still in the city, there were still houses and buildings and brick – but it was greener and natural, with bushes and proper trees overhanging the path beside the water, not the spindly useless things the council planted round the estate just to die or be snapped off when someone got bored.

Even the litter and rubbish along the canal side didn't spoil it. Or the fact that there was a cold wind that made her cheeks feel tingly. It was almost like being in the country or something, where the air was fresh and new and better.

They stopped every now and then, watching anglers trying to catch something in the dark waters; looking at a pair of swans gliding along the smooth surface; eating pasties they bought from a garage near a road bridge over the canal. And after that they crossed over the bridge and walked back on the other side of the waterway, the breeze at their backs, helping them along.

Ryan didn't talk much – just enough. Sometimes he went for ages without saying anything, and when he did Taz walked quietly too, because she didn't want him to think she was stupid and couldn't shut up. After a while, she got used to his quietness though, and she started to like it because it meant she could think about what to say next before she said it, instead of just running on as she usually did.

She did want to know things about him though, and when she asked him about his family he told her about his dad and his brother, Charlie, and how their mum had died of cancer.

"That's tough," she said, seeming to mean it. Then after a pause she added, "I wish mine would've. Least then she wouldn't be on my back all the time, you know?"

Ryan shook his head. "You shouldn't say that," he said seriously. "You don't know."

Taz shrugged. "I don't care, cos it's true." But the way she said it was a little less belligerent now.

"What's she say?" Ryan asked. "I mean, what's she go on about?"

"Everything. All the stuff she don't want me doing. Except it's all stuff *she* does do – and did. If she hadn't I wouldn't be here, you know what I mean?"

Ryan nodded then. "What about your dad?"

"Who knows?" Taz told him. "I never seen him. He

136

could be Prince Charles, I wouldn't know. – What's yours like?"

"He's always going on about school – how we've got to do better than he did so we can get decent jobs."

"So what *will* you do – you know, when you leave?"

Ryan gave it a moment, taking the question seriously rather than just shrugging a "Dunno" like most people would.

"Maybe law or something," he said then, glancing at her. "I'd need the exams first though... It probably won't happen."

"You mean going in court?" Taz said, unable to keep the surprise out of her voice. "In a wig and all that?"

This time he did shrug, as if he thought he'd said too much. "I dunno, maybe. It's what my dad'd like, but..."

"No, shit, that'd be really good," Taz told him, hoping she could smooth it over again. "That way, if I ever get nicked, you can be my lawyer and get me off."

He looked at her for a second, then chuckled. "Yeah, I suppose, maybe," he said.

"What d'you mean, '*maybe*'?" Taz said, mock-offended. "You wouldn't let them send me to prison, would you? I thought we were, you know, *mates*."

Ryan laughed again. "Nah," he said. "I'll get you off, seeing as it's you."

"You'd better," she warned. "Otherwise I'll tell them you were in on it too."

"In on what?"

"I don't know, do I? The jewel robbery I've done – or the murder. Yeah, that'll be it. I'll've murdered my mum with a carving knife and you'll have to prove how I couldn't have done it because I was with you all the time, here by the canal."

"Jesus, you're mad," he said, but he was smiling. "But that's good."

"Why?"

"Cos it's a better defence – you're just insane."

By the time they left the canal and started back towards the estate it was late afternoon. And as the estate got closer the other stuff – real stuff – seemed to loom in again and Taz realised she still hadn't got Ryan to talk about Drew and the flat. And in some ways it was harder to bring it up now, just because she wanted the information.

They were crossing the open space of the rec area when Ryan's phone rang and as he looked at the screen Taz saw him hesitate before dismissing the call.

"Was that your dad wanting you to come in for tea?" she said, deliberately making it sound teasing and innocently playful.

Ryan shook his head and for the first time in hours his expression was serious and closed down rather than open and relaxed. "Drew," he said.

"Oh. Right. – You don't want to talk to him?"

Ryan shook his head. "Later."

Being careful not to overplay it, Taz said: "So what is it with you and him? I mean, I don't get it."

"What?" He sounded a bit uncomfortable with the subject but not quite enough to refuse to talk about it.

"I dunno," she said. "I mean, I don't get why you bother hanging out with him. I mean it's not like you're the same, is it?"

He frowned. "What d'you mean?"

"What I said. Like, before, I thought you was just – I dunno – just gonna be all arsey an' stuff. Like you'd be full of it. Like Drew. But you're not – you don't think you can boss it over everyone else, like they don't matter. So that's what I don't get – why you bother with him, cos you ain't nasty like that."

Ryan shrugged, as if he didn't have a better answer – or not one he could put into words.

"No, come on," she said. "I mean, you and your lot used to keep seeing him off. But now…"

She let it trail off but looked at him sideways so he'd know she still wanted to know.

"It's – complicated," he said. "There's reasons."

"Like what?"

But Ryan shook his head, refusing to be drawn, and after a moment Taz let it go.

"Okay," she said. Just that. Not sulky, just accepting, because she realised that she didn't want to know if there was a chance that pushing him to talk would screw things up now. It wasn't worth it. So she hooked her arm through his again and walked close beside him, both of them quiet.

9.

"It's not like Frank," Mr Evans said. "I mean, he never leaves the curtains closed all day. And the newspaper's still in the door."

They were standing on the pavement, looking at a red-brick bungalow which stood about thirty metres back from the road. The space in between was covered by a lawn, a few well-tended flower borders and a paved driveway leading to a garage. On the drive Holly recognised Frank Chapman's Rover saloon from yesterday.

"You've tried knocking?" Yvonne asked.

"Yeah, course. And phoning," Evans said. He was in his mid-fifties, unremarkable, but he seemed to be genuinely concerned as far as Holly could tell.

"So when was the last time you saw Mr Chapman?"

"Yesterday afternoon. Not to speak to. I was in the garden." Evans gestured to the next-door garden, mostly hidden by fence panels. "He came back from somewhere and I waved when he got out of the car."

Yvonne looked, then said: "You don't think he could just have gone out somewhere today?"

"No. His car's there. He always drives, even if he's just going to the shops. And why would the curtains be closed all day?"

Yvonne considered for a moment, then nodded. "Okay, Mr Evans, if you'd like to wait there we'll have a look round, okay?"

She gestured to Holly and together they walked up the drive, leaving Evans on the pavement.

"Okay," Yvonne said. "You're assessing this. What's the first thing you want to do – bearing in mind he could be asleep in front of the telly, or down the bingo."

"See if there's any answer at the doors?"

"Right, go on then."

This was the way it usually went when Yvonne decided to use a call as a training opportunity. "Wind up and point", she called it – letting the trainee negotiate the situation for themself and only stepping in if they were about to make a mess of something.

The wooden front door was solid – no window – and as Mr Evans had said there was a thick Sunday newspaper wedged in the letterbox. The protruding section was damp enough to have been there all day.

Aware that Yvonne was assessing her reactions, Holly pressed the doorbell and heard it ring inside. There was no reply.

"Can I move this?" Holly asked, gesturing to the newspaper.

"If you want."

Holly pulled the newspaper out and bent down to peer through the letterbox. Inside it was dim but she could make out a hallway. Nothing moved.

"Mr Chapman?" she called. "It's the police."

Nothing. She straightened up. "Shall we try the back?"

"You forgot something."

Yvonne leaned in and tried the door handle. It turned but the door didn't open. "Never assume a door's locked till you've tried it."

"Oh. Yeah. Sorry."

"Come on then, round the back."

They left the front door and Yvonne let Holly lead as they made their way round the bungalow. All the windows they passed had their curtains closed except the kitchen. There Holly cupped her hands against the glass to look inside, but again nothing moved or seemed out of place.

The kitchen door was half glazed and after she'd tried the handle Holly knocked hard on the glass.

"Frank? It's the police. Can you hear me?"

Silence.

"Okay," Yvonne said. "Tell me your assessment."

Holly drew a breath, then counted it off. "There's no reply, the curtains have been closed all day and the car's outside. The neighbour says Mr Chapman should be here and he's worried."

"So what d'you want to do?"

"Break in and see if he's all right?"

"Break in how?"

"Kick the door?"

"Look at the locks first," Yvonne said. "If it's a mortise lock, yeah, you'd have to kick it in, but that's a Yale." She pointed it out. "So, if you break the glass you can reach in and open it. Plus, glass is cheaper to replace than a whole door. Okay?"

"Okay," Holly nodded. "Do you want me to do that – break the glass, I mean?"

"Next time. Pass me your hat."

Holly took off her beret and handed it to Yvonne.

"Why mine?"

"Cos I don't want mine covered in glass," Yvonne said simply.

She took the asp from her belt, flicked it out to full length, then held the beret against the glass next to the Yale lock.

"One good hard tap," she said. "The hat stops the glass flying back but you want to look away when you do it anyway. Stand back a bit."

Holly did as she was told and then Yvonne aimed the baton, brought it back and whacked it against the beret.

The glass broke with a crack and then tinkled as part of it fell on the kitchen floor. Yvonne removed the beret, shook it out and handed it back to Holly before using the asp to tap some loose shards away from the window. It left a ragged hole the size of a football, which she reached through to turn the Yale lock inside. She opened the door just as Mr Evans appeared round the corner of the bungalow.

"Is he there?" he asked, looking worried.

"We don't know yet," Yvonne said. "Could you wait back on the drive for me please? I'll let you know if we find anything, but you need to stay out here, okay?"

Under Yvonne's firm gaze Evans nodded and reluctantly went back round the corner.

"Smell anything?" Yvonne asked, turning back to Holly.

"No. Why?" But as soon as she said it Holly knew the answer.

"Sometimes you'll get a good whiff if there's a body inside – 'specially if it's been there for a while and the central heating's been on. – Okay, let's have a look. You lead."

Holly couldn't tell if Yvonne really thought they were going to find a body inside, but now it had been mentioned she realised that it hadn't even crossed her mind before. Sure, she'd thought that Frank Chapman might have collapsed or had a fall, but the possibility that they might find him dead suddenly changed things. Abruptly, what had been a simple training assessment seemed a lot more serious.

There was a stillness inside the house and with no lights on the grey afternoon created a semi-dark gloom which only got darker as Holly moved from the kitchen into the hallway beyond.

"Hello?" Holly called out. "Anyone here? It's the police."

Silence.

There were several doors leading off the hall, all closed except the nearest one which was partially open. Aware that Yvonne was waiting, Holly stepped forward and pushed the door wider.

That was when she noticed the smell, not like anything she'd smelled before but something she instinctively knew wasn't good. It reminded her a little of dustbins in summer and nappies. When she hesitated she felt Yvonne's hand on her shoulder.

"Okay," she said, reassuringly. "Want me to go first?"

Then Holly knew. She steeled herself, shook her head.

"Okay. In your own time."

Holly took one step, then another until she was clear of the door. She let her eyes get used to the dimness, making out shapes of furniture, the TV and then Frank Chapman's body.

He was sitting on the floor, his back propped against the sofa, head forward with his chin on his chest. He had tartan slippers on his feet and a cardigan over his shirt.

Then Yvonne put the light on and moved to stand beside Holly. "Just stay there for a minute," she said. "Are you going to chuck up?"

Holly shook her head, still looking at what she now knew was a dead body. "No, I'm okay."

Yvonne handed her an evidence bag. "Just in case. Or go outside."

She moved forwards towards Frank's body, squatted down and pressed a couple of fingers against the man's neck. After a few seconds she stood up again.

"He's dead," she said, simply but not callously. "Fairly cold, so it's not recent."

"Do you— Are you sure?"

"Yeah, but the FME'll have to confirm it."

Holly hesitated. She knew what she ought to do, even though it was against all her instincts.

"Can you— Will you show me how you checked?"

For a second Yvonne didn't move, then she nodded. "Okay. Put some gloves on."

Holly did that, then moved closer. Yvonne took her right hand. "Two fingers, press here under the jaw." She held Holly's hand against her own neck to show her, then let go.

"Okay," Holly said.

She knelt down on one knee next to the body, easier to recognise now. Odd that he looked as if he was asleep; the smell of faeces and urine; the small detail that he needed a shave; the moment before touching him when it seemed inappropriate…

His skin didn't really feel different but it wasn't warm. Under the bone of his jaw she felt his whiskers through the rubber glove but no pulse. She kept her fingers there and made herself count to five, then she stood up.

"Well done," Yvonne said.

"I think I need some air," Holly managed.

"Go on," Yvonne told her, nodding to the door, and she followed when Holly turned and walked – didn't run – out of the room.

10

Gemma's bare legs felt raw and icy cold, but she kept walking – up to the corner, stand for a bit, then back to the building with the red doors. Moving wasn't just to keep warm but because she knew Dean would be watching. The van was parked in the entrance to one of the industrial units, inconspicuous but positioned so he could keep an eye on her and check out the punters – if there had been any.

Gemma had been out for nearly an hour now and in that time there'd been no business at all. A couple of times cars had slowed down and crawled alongside her for a moment, but each time she'd stopped and turned to give the drivers a better view the men had straightened up in their seats and moved off again. The last one had been twenty minutes ago and she was getting really cold now. It would almost be worth pulling, just to get into the warmth of a car for a few minutes.

Of course, if the guy called Jon-Jo had turned up to buy the stuff in the back of the van she might not have been here now. But he hadn't, and after they'd waited for half an hour Dean had been really pissed off. That was when he'd said they'd go round to the industrial estate and Gemma had known better than to argue or complain.

The best hope when it was like this – no other girls out and no punters – was that Dean would get fed up of sitting around and decide to jack it in. Gemma wasn't hopeful though, not unless she could turn a couple of tricks. She knew Dean had been counting on the money from Jon-Jo and now he didn't have it he'd expect her to make up for it.

A car turned into the road and headed towards her. It didn't show any sign of slowing even as it passed her so Gemma didn't break her pace. But then she heard its engine note change and saw the brake lights shine as it pulled in to the kerb.

It was several metres past her, so she kept walking, waiting to see if he'd reverse back for a better look. Instead though, the engine went off and she saw the driver's door open as a middle-aged guy in a brown leather jacket got out.

Gemma was immediately suspicious. By now she knew that punters almost always waited for you to go to them, but sometimes the cops would try something like this, coming up to you out in the open, acting like a punter to try and get you to make the first move so they could nick you. This guy didn't act like a copper though – he seemed too eager for that and he had some kind of paper in his hand.

Casting a quick glance back at Dean's van, Gemma stopped by the kerb and waited as the man came towards her.

"Hi," he called, still some distance away. "Can I talk to you for a minute?"

"What's up?" Gemma asked, instead of the usual *Looking for business, love?*

"My name's Tony," the man said. He stopped a short distance away, as if he didn't want to scare her. "I need some help. I'm looking for a missing person – my daughter."

"So?" Gemma said, still suspicious.

"I just wondered if you might have seen her. This is her."

He held out the paper in his hand and took a step closer so she could take it.

Gemma glanced down at the flyer. In the fading light it was almost impossible to make out what she was supposed to be looking at – a photograph, yes, but it could have been anyone.

"I dunno," she said with a shrug.

"Hold on, let me— I've got a torch."

From his pocket he produced a small penlight torch and snapped it on. He shone the light down on the paper so she could see it more clearly.

"Her name's Andrea," he said. "Andrea Deakin."

Now Gemma could see the face of a smiling, good-looking girl. She also read the wording above it.

"This for real?" she asked, looking at him directly.

"Yes, absolutely. She's fifteen, nearly sixteen. She left home two months ago and I think she might be here – in Weston."

Gemma looked back at the flyer. "I dunno," she said, squinting a little. "She ever change her hair – you know, the colour?"

"Not at home," Deakin said. "But she could have – I mean, since she left. Why? Do you think you've seen her?"

"I dunno," Gemma repeated. She gazed hard at the photo, as if trying to visualise the girl with different hair. "There was a girl a bit like her – blonde though – kind of streaky. Could've been her."

"Where? I mean, where did you see her?" The man's voice was immediately urgent and pressing, but Gemma didn't answer directly. Instead she took a half-step back.

"How do I know you're really her dad?" she said. "You could be anyone."

"No, listen, I am," Deakin said. "I've got more pictures in the car. Me and Andrea, when she was born."

"Oi!"

She hadn't heard him coming, but as soon as she heard his voice she knew there was going to be trouble. She knew from the tone and she stepped back from Deakin, distancing herself as Dean came in.

"You looking for business or just pissing about?" he demanded of Deakin.

"Business? No, I—"

"So get lost."

Gemma saw Dean plant himself squarely in front of the other man, short-tempered, aggressive and not to be messed with.

"No, listen, I'm— I just want to talk to her for a minute," Deakin said.

"She's not out here to talk and I said piss off."

To make the point he gave Deakin a shove in the chest – hard enough to make him step back. Instinctively Gemma also moved further back.

"Hold on," Deakin said with a note of desperation. "Just let—"

It was too late though. Without warning Gemma saw Dean lash out. It was a punch – a short jab straight to the man's mouth. Deakin let out an exclamation of pain.

"You gonna piss off now or what?"

Dazed by the suddenness of the blow, Gemma could see that Deakin didn't know what was happening. And because he continued to stand there Dean seemed to take it as a challenge. He struck out again, twice more to Deakin's face, landing both blows even when Deakin belatedly tried to dodge. When she saw the blood Gemma looked away.

She only looked back when she heard the sound of footsteps. Deakin was lurching away now, stumbling back towards his car as quickly as he could. For a moment she thought Dean would go after him, but instead the short act of violence seemed to have been enough to satisfy him and now he gestured to Gemma. "Sod this. Let's go."

Grateful to be packing it in but wary in case his temper was still up, Gemma ran to keep pace as he strode towards the van. By the time they got there he seemed to have calmed down though.

"So what did he want anyway?" he asked as he opened the van door.

"Dunno," Gemma said. "Just some crap about a girl he knew."

"Huh. Tosser."

Pushed deep in her pocket, Gemma still had the flyer, crumpled up small and unobtrusive.

11.

"He's in the front interview room," Steve Sollis told them. "Said he'd talked to you yesterday."

"Yeah, he did," Oz nodded. "Thanks, mate."

He moved away from the counter and Sam followed him across to the interview room.

"This'll be interesting," Oz said.

The front interview room was the first port of call for anyone who came in off the street and needed to talk privately, or just wait out of the way. Inside, the room was fairly shabby, grubbied by a procession of unfortunates over the years since it had last been painted. The furniture was standard issue: a table and four mismatched plastic chairs.

On one of these Tony Deakin was sitting with his back to the wall, a tissue pressed to his lip. He looked up when Sam and Oz came in, then got to his feet.

"Hello again, Mr Deakin," Oz said. "My colleague on the desk says you want to report an assault."

"Yeah. Well, sort of," Deakin said.

"Are you okay? Do you need to go to A&E?"

From what Sam could see it looked as if Deakin had been punched on the left side of his jaw where a red mark was swelling. In addition there was also whatever damage was hidden by the bloodstained tissue he held to his mouth.

"No, I'm okay. I mean, I can go later if I have to. I need to talk to you about Andrea first."

"Your daughter, right?"

"Yes. I found someone who said she'd seen her – might have seen her – but this guy she was with wouldn't let her tell me."

From the way he rushed it out Sam knew he was excited, eager to tell it, but Oz wasn't going to be hurried.

"Okay, have a seat and start from the beginning."

As Tony Deakin told them his story Sam made a note of the details – not a full statement, just the bare bones – time, location, incident, description of attacker: IC1, medium height, brown hair, black leather jacket, jeans…

"Would you recognise him again?" Oz asked when Deakin had finished his description.

"Yeah, definitely," Deakin said. "But it's not about that, is it? I mean, I don't care about the assault, I'm not bothered about that – it's the girl. If she's seen Andrea, *she's* the one I need to find again. But if this guy won't let me talk to her – if he's her pimp or something…"

Oz took a beat and Sam knew it wasn't a good sign.

"So what are you asking for, Mr Deakin?"

"To go back there with me, so I can talk to her without him stopping me."

Sam glanced at Oz to gauge his reaction. He didn't look very convinced.

"If what you've told me is right, I can't see this bloke – or the girl – still being there," Oz said. "Chances are they moved on soon after you did – 'specially if he thinks you might report the assault."

"But it's got to be worth a try," Deakin said, leaning forward to emphasise the point. "Can't you just come with me to look?"

Oz shook his head. "Like I said, I doubt they'll still be there, and if you don't want to make a complaint about the assault there's not much more we can do."

"What if I did? I mean, what if I did make a complaint?" Deakin said, and Sam could hear the need in his voice.

Oz pursed his lips. "You said you'd recognise the man again?"

"Yes. Yeah, I'm pretty sure."

"Well, if we knew who he was – if you could identify him from mugshots – we might have a chance of picking him up."

"Well, can I do that then? Can I report it and look at the pictures?"

Oz tapped a couple of fingers on the table, then pushed his chair back. "Okay, Mr Deakin, if that's what you want to do. Just give us a minute, okay?"

He gestured to Sam and stood up.

Outside the interview room Oz closed the door for privacy and said: "Get a full statement. I'll find a laptop for the mugshots."

"Wouldn't it be quicker just to go back there and look?"

"We might do later," Oz said, still uncompromising. "But not till he's made a statement. Otherwise all we're doing is providing a private bodyguarding and taxi service. Not in the job description."

Sam knew Oz well enough to recognise that this hard line was unusual, but it didn't seem like the time to question it so he just nodded. "Okay."

12.

On the drive beside the bungalow Yvonne Dunlop and Sergeant Eddie Stafford were talking together as the last of the daylight drained out of the sky. Stafford's car was parked across the entrance to the drive and beyond it several neighbours had gathered to stand and watch, although there was nothing to see.

Holly waited by Frank Chapman's car, still glad of the fresh air, until Yvonne and Stafford separated and the sergeant came across to her.

Stafford was in his late forties, well built and sometimes hard to read. He had overall responsibility for the TPOs at Morningstar nick as well as his normal duties. On the whole, Holly knew he was a pretty good guy, although he could be tough if you did something when you should have known better.

"Feeling okay?" he asked.

Holly nodded. "Yes, Sarge, I'm fine." She said it with more conviction than she felt.

"Think you can do an assessment with me? Say if you don't want to, but Yvonne says you've done all right so far."

Holly couldn't help feeling pleased when she heard that, despite the circumstances. Yvonne rarely gave anyone much praise. And although going back into the house wasn't what

Holly really wanted to do, she also didn't want Stafford or Yvonne to think she couldn't take it.

"No, I'd like to," Holly said. "I mean— I'm okay."

"Good, come on then."

He led the way to the back of the house, pulling on a pair of latex gloves.

"Okay, let's start here," he said, brisk and businesslike when he got to the door. "Closed and locked when you arrived?"

"Yes, Sarge. Yvonne broke the glass."

"Okay."

He pushed the door open and stepped inside, but only far enough to let Holly join him, then he stopped and looked round. "Any signs of disturbance?" he asked. "Anything look odd or out of place? Take your time."

Holly looked round carefully, more than she'd done when she first entered. As far as she could see everything looked normal though.

"It looks fine to me," Holly said.

"Right. Show me the sitting room then."

They retraced the steps she and Yvonne had taken earlier. The sitting room door was still open and Holly couldn't help her gaze being drawn back to Frank Chapman's body on the floor when they walked in.

"Same again," Stafford told her. He, too, had glanced at the body, but for the moment it didn't seem to interest him. "Stand still and look. Is there anything that could tell you what might have happened here?"

Again Holly looked round, assessing. Having to focus on the practicalities helped.

Under a box of matches on top of the gas fire she noticed a lottery ticket and realised she knew what the numbers would be. They'd match Yvonne's collar number and her own.

"Any sign of violence or a struggle?" Stafford asked. "Anything you wouldn't expect to see?"

"I don't think so," Holly said, moving her gaze round the room. "It all looks normal."

"Okay, so what about the body?"

Holly looked. It wasn't as hard as the first time. She knew it was there, knew he was dead, so she tried to think of it as a thing, not a person.

"What's the most obvious thing?" Stafford said.

"He's on the floor?"

"Right."

Stafford moved forward. "He's on the floor, which isn't usual, but he's resting against the sofa. So maybe he had a fall or collapsed and couldn't get up, but managed to get this far, into a more comfortable position."

He knelt down to look at Frank Chapman's face and then at his hands.

"What am I looking for?"

"Injuries?"

"Right. And there's nothing showing, except he's got plasters on his hands."

"He fell over yesterday," Holly said. "Some youths stole his wallet."

"Yeah, Yvonne told me."

He looked for a moment longer, then stood up.

"Okay. As far as I can see there's no reason to think this is suspicious, so we'll check the other rooms to make sure, then we'll wait for the FME and CSE to get here, okay?"

Holly nodded. "Yes, Sarge."

"Just one other thing," he said, and motioned to a side table between the sofa and armchair. "One beer bottle and two glasses, see?"

Holly looked, then realised. "You think someone else was here?"

"Possibly. Also possible he used them both. Still, it's worth noting for the CSE, okay?"

"Yes, Sarge."

"Right then." He nodded. "The other rooms, then out."

13.

"That's him," Tony Deakin said, pointing to the laptop.

On the screen there were six faces arranged in two rows and for the past ten minutes Deakin had been examining similar pages of photographs: all white males of similar age and physical characteristics to the description he'd given of his attacker. Under each photograph there was an ID number – the only way to differentiate the pictures.

"Are you sure?" Oz asked.

"Yes. Definite. That's him." Deakin tapped the second photograph on the top row.

"Okay, you're identifying this man as the one who attacked you."

He read out the ID number to Sam, who wrote it down.

"So what happens now?" Deakin said. "I mean, will you go out and arrest him?"

"We'll have to see what information there is on file, but with what you've said we'll definitely talk to him."

"What about the girl – the one he was with? I need to talk to her. I need to ask her about Andrea."

Sam could hear the note of determination in Deakin's voice

and knew that finding the girl was the only thing that was important to him. Oz clearly didn't see it like that though.

"I think we need to concentrate on finding your attacker first, but if the girl was a witness we'll obviously try and talk to her as well. Let's see how we get on, okay?"

He reached to the laptop and closed the lid, a sign that the interview was over. Deakin wasn't quite ready to let it go though, even when Oz stood up.

"You'll go and look for him now?"

"Like I said, we'll see what information we've got first. The best thing you can do is go to A&E and get them to look at your injuries. We'll call you when we have anything."

"Later today?"

"That's hard to say. We'll do what we can."

"So if I waited here…"

"I think it'd be better to let us call you," Oz said, clearly unwilling to be pushed. "We've got your number. – Thanks for coming in, Mr Deakin. Sam will show you out."

Reluctantly Deakin stood up and allowed himself to be shown out of the interview room. Sam took him to the main entrance door and Deakin half opened it before stopping and turning back.

"If you find her – the girl I talked to – will you bring her in too?"

"That depends," Sam said, knowing the cagey reply sounded like something Oz would have said. "If she volunteers to give a witness statement she might come to the station, but we can't make her."

Deakin nodded. "Would you make sure she's got this then?"

He held out one of the postcard-sized photos of his daughter with his contact number on the back.

"Tell her – ask her – to call me. Tell her there's still a reward."

"I'll try," Sam said, taking the card.

"Thanks. Thank you."

He hesitated for a second, as if he was about to suggest waiting again, but then he changed his mind and went out of the door.

Sam watched him go down the front steps, shoulders hunched and downcast, as if he'd done all he could but knew it wasn't enough.

Oz was logging on to a computer terminal when Sam joined him behind the counter in the front office.

"Has he gone?" he asked as Sam came to stand beside him.

"Yeah."

"Ask you to talk to the girl if we find her?"

"Yeah."

"And you said?"

"I couldn't promise."

"Good."

He looked back to the computer screen where a PNC record was being displayed alongside the arrest photo Deakin had identified.

Surname: Fuller

FORENAMES: DEAN PATRICK
BIRTH DATE: 29/5/1981

Beneath that the entry detailed height, eye colour, ethnicity, marks and scars and other features before going on to Intelligence Information: address, occupation, driver number and so on.

Oz scanned it as he scrolled down the page, then hit return to move on to arrests and convictions. There were half a dozen for Dean Patrick Fuller, including assault, handling stolen property, possession of a Class C drug and possession of a Class B drug with intent to supply.

"What do you think?" Sam asked.

"Pond life," Oz said flatly.

"I mean, do you think he did it – the assault? There's nothing on there about pimping."

"So what?"

"Mr Deakin said—"

But Oz cut him off, sounding unusually short-tempered. "Listen, whatever Mr Deakin thinks, whatever he's trying to get out of this, he reported an *assault*. That's it, and that's what we're investigating, nothing else. And he's identified Fuller as his attacker, so that's all we need, okay?"

"Okay," Sam said, knowing better than to say any more.

"Right," Oz said, ending it. "Looks like Fuller's about due for a tug anyway. Last nicked eighteen months ago."

He closed the screen window and logged out. "Let's see if we can find him and ruin his evening."

14

In the growing darkness below, Taz caught a glimpse of Ryan as he crossed the courtyard towards Cloudsley House, then disappeared from view amongst the shadows and grey concrete.

She hadn't heard everything Drew had said when he'd called Ryan again five minutes ago, but she'd heard enough. He was up to something and he wanted Ryan there.

"I've gotta go," Ryan had told her when he came off the phone. They were standing near the entrance to Penrice House where Taz lived.

"Oh. Okay," Taz said, like it was no big thing.

"What're you gonna do?"

Taz shrugged. "Go home, I suppose." Then, making a joke of it: "Up to the penthouse."

"Right."

"It was nice – today, I mean. I liked, you know, hanging out."

He nodded. "Yeah. Me too."

Then there was that awkward moment, neither of them knowing exactly what they should do or say, until Ryan gestured with his phone and said again: "I gotta go."

He made to move but Taz reached out and held him back for a moment. "Call me later, yeah?"

"Yeah, sure," he said, then gave her a strangely shy smile before he started away.

Taz turned and headed inside Penrice House to the stairwell. She didn't go far though – only up to the first-floor balcony, where she watched as Ryan crossed the courtyard, then disappeared. As soon as she lost him from sight she left the railing and headed quickly back down the stairs, the way she'd just come.

There was part of her that felt guilty about doing this, like she was tricking Ryan or something. But it wasn't really like that. She wasn't doing it because she wanted to get him into trouble – if anything she thought she might even be able to get him out of it.

Taz knew now that Drew had some kind of hold over Ryan, and although she didn't know what it was, it didn't matter. What *did* matter was finding out what Drew was doing. That way, when she next called Holly and Danny Simmons, she'd have something to tell them – something they couldn't ignore. As long as she was clever, as long as she was careful not to mention Ryan, she could tell them what Drew was mixed up in and they'd nick him. Then Ryan would be in the clear *and* she'd have shown that she was taking the informant thing seriously. All ways round it would work out – *if* she could get the info on Drew.

She was too late though. By the time she'd taken the longer route round the tower blocks to Cloudsley House, Ryan and Drew were already at the roadside next to a metallic silver car. There was no way Taz could get close enough to see what was going on without being spotted, so all she could do was watch from a distance as Drew leaned in at the open passenger door to talk with the lone man inside.

A couple of metres away from the car Ryan was keeping watch and Taz stayed back in the shadow of a wall to make sure he wouldn't see her. She strained to make out what was happening, but even as she did so Drew was withdrawing from the car, closing the door. Then the car's headlights came on and it pulled away.

Taz didn't see much more than that. She caught a fleeting impression of the man inside the car but not really clearly, not to be certain of anything except he was white, dark haired, thirties maybe. But while she was looking at him she missed seeing the car's number plate and swore to herself because she knew it wasn't enough.

By the road Drew signalled to Ryan before heading into the entrance to Cloudsley House. Behind him Ryan followed, but Taz could see from the slouch of his shoulders and the unenthusiastic trudge of his feet that she hadn't been wrong about him. No way he wanted to be in this with Drew.

15.

Oz Sitwell pounded on the door of the flat with the side of his fist but there was no sign of life from inside – no lights on and no sound. After a few seconds of waiting he pushed the letterbox open and peered in for a moment before straightening up.

"Out," he said flatly.

"So what do we do?"

"Nothing *to* do. Maybe come back later. See how it goes. Come on."

He started off back towards the stairs and Sam fell in beside him.

"So how come you don't like him?" he asked after a couple of paces.

"Who?"

"Tony Deakin."

Oz shrugged but didn't bother to deny it. "Just cos someone reports a crime doesn't mean we have to like them."

"But his daughter *is* missing."

"*Runaway* is what the report says. There's a difference."

"You think she was running away from him?"

"Can't tell, can we? – And then there's the obvious question."

"What's that?"

"Why's he keep looking for her in the local tomming areas? Mill Hill Lane yesterday, the industrial estate today… "

Sam frowned. He hadn't thought about that. "You mean he could think she is one – a tom?"

"Some runaways do go on the game. He might know that – or there might be something he's not telling us."

"So we could ask him some more questions about it – about his daughter."

Oz shook his head. "How'd we know what he told us was true? We wouldn't – that's the point. So it's Rule One, and we just deal with what's in front of us."

They were on the first floor now. As they passed the iron railings they had a view over the car park and a set of headlights swung round from the entrance, illuminating a line of parked cars as they did so. Oz glanced down, then paused and looked harder.

"What was the vehicle Dean Fuller was listed as driving – a blue van?"

"Yeah." Sam moved to share the view Oz was looking at. Below in the car park a dark blue, lightweight van had pulled into a space and a second later its lights went out.

"Might be lucky after all," Oz said, and Sam heard a note of satisfaction in his voice.

"Stay there," Dean told her as he switched off the engine and opened the driver's door. "I'll be two minutes, all right?"

"Can't I go in and wait?" Gemma asked. "You don't need me there, do you?"

"Depends, don't it?" Fuller said. "If he doesn't show up again…"

He left the sentence unfinished as he got out of the van, but Gemma knew what he meant.

The man called Jon-Jo had phoned ten minutes ago and Dean had sworn at him for not meeting like they'd agreed. But when Dean had finally calmed down and let the other man speak, Gemma had heard enough of what was said to know that the meeting was being rearranged. And that whatever Dean was selling, Jon-Jo now wanted to take the whole lot rather than just some of it. That was why they'd come back to the flats, so Dean could get the rest of the stuff from inside.

"Can I have the heater on then?" Gemma asked as Dean made to close the door.

He leaned back in, annoyed. "No. Just fucking wait. I told you: I'll be two minutes."

Gemma huddled back in her seat. "Okay," she said, anxious not to make him any more irritable.

The blue van was about twenty metres away and a figure was just getting out of the driver's side. In the light of the single street lamp illuminating the car park it was impossible to see clearly whether the man matched the arrest photograph of Dean Fuller, but Sam reckoned he was about right, even though he had his back turned.

Sam matched Oz's jog, trying to cover the distance before the van driver looked round and caught sight of them. He seemed preoccupied with something still inside the van though, and the two cops got to within five or six metres before he heard the sound of their feet.

"Dean Fuller?" Oz called, not breaking stride. "Police. Stand still."

For a second Sam saw Fuller's expression shift in realisation and then he pushed himself off the van into a run.

"Sod it!" Oz said, annoyed. "Head him off!"

Sam broke away, adrenalin kicking in, trying to beat Fuller's sprint towards the far side of the car park as Oz piled on a turn of speed from behind. Over his pants of exertion the only other noise he could hear was that of his feet on the wet tarmac and the jangle of the equipment on his utility belt.

And although Sam was lighter it was Oz who caught up the distance fastest, and as Fuller made to break away to the side Oz launched himself in a flying rugby tackle. He caught Fuller round the waist and brought him crashing down on the ground with an audible grunt.

Even then, Fuller still struggled, kicking against Oz's weight on top of him, fighting to get free.

"Get his arm!" Oz shouted as Sam ran in, panting, and added his weight to help pin the man down. "Get a cuff on!"

Sam fumbled to get the handcuffs off his belt for a moment, one-handed as he fought to hold Fuller's wrist with the other.

He managed to snap the steel jaws in place though, and forced Fuller's arm back till it caused a shout of pain.

"Agh! Fuck! You're breaking it!"

"Hold him," Oz said, shifting position. He got to one knee, dropped the other into the centre of Fuller's back and pulled the man's free hand round to take the other loop of the handcuffs.

With both hands now secured Fuller couldn't go anywhere and for a moment Oz sat back on his haunches, panting.

"So why'd you run, Dean?" he asked. When there was no response he tapped Fuller on the shoulder. "I'm talking to you."

"Piss off. No comment," Fuller said.

"Right," Oz said dryly and stood up. "You're being arrested on suspicion of assault. You do not have to say anything but it may harm your defence if you do not mention when questioned something you later rely on in court. Anything you do say may be given in evidence. Understand?"

Fuller spat on the tarmac.

"I'll take that as a yes then."

Gemma's heart was beating fast, not just from running but from the fear of what she'd just done. She hadn't even stopped to think about it for more than a second: she'd just grabbed her bag and bundled out of the van as fast as she could.

She'd almost tripped as she pulled off her high heels so she could run better and quieter. All the time she expected to hear a shout as one of the coppers saw her, but none came and she made it to the end of the flats, where she ducked round a corner and hid in the darkness.

It was only then that she dared to breathe for a moment, then peer out round the corner and look back, just in time to see the two coppers struggling with Dean on the tarmac. Even at this distance she could see that his wrists were being handcuffed together behind his back and she continued to watch as the coppers hauled him upright, onto his feet.

Gradually her thudding pulse slowed a bit. She caught her breath and her thoughts became clearer as the coppers led Dean back towards the van. She knew this was it: this was the moment. If she wanted to go – if she really did want to get away – now was the time.

Just go! she told herself. *You decided this morning. You promised. Touch the bruises! You hate him, remember?!*

But still she couldn't quite bring herself to leave her hiding place and start moving again.

What if, for some reason, the coppers didn't do anything? What if, in a couple of minutes, they just let him go? He'd know she wasn't there then and the first thing he'd do was come looking for her. And if he found her running away…

No, she had to be sure first. She had to know that she would have time.

There were no windows in the back of the van, but when Sam used his torch it illuminated a grubby mattress wedged tightly into the space. On top of it there were two large cardboard boxes.

"Passion wagon, is it?" Oz said, of the mattress. And to Sam: "Check the boxes."

Sam reached for the nearest one and pulled it to the back of the van where there was more light. It was quite heavy and he opened the flaps by their edges, then shone his torch on the contents. Inside, neatly packed, were at least a dozen boxed Wiis. Sam pulled one out and turned it so Oz could see.

"So what's your favourite – tennis or golf?" Oz said to Fuller. Then, without waiting for a response, he turned to Sam. "Let's get some back-up down here, then we'll go up and have a look in the flat."

At the dark corner of the flats Gemma shifted, trying to see better what was happening at the van. All she wanted was a sign, but it was so hard to tell, so hard to decide.

The adrenalin rush she'd got from running this far was starting to wear off now and she shivered, pulling her jacket closer round her. As she did so she realised her bare feet were freezing on the cold ground, and for a moment she risked looking away while she bent to pull her shoes on, tight and awkward.

When she straightened and looked back towards the van she saw that something was happening. One of the coppers was holding a box or something up to the light to see it better and behind him the other copper was tugging Dean towards a patrol car.

He didn't want to go, but the copper wasn't giving him a choice and when she saw that Gemma finally felt his hold on her melting.

This was what she'd waited for. *Just go!* she told herself again. *It's safe now. Just go!*

It was like a physical wrench to make herself go, but then Gemma found herself moving and each step got faster until she was walking as fast as she could – away from Dean Fuller and the cops and all the rest of it; not daring to hope, but still hoping more than anything that she had really, finally, torn herself free.

16.

Through the closed curtains the flash of the Crime Scene Examiner's camera had punctuated the evening darkness at irregular intervals for a while. It had been the only visible indication of what was going on inside the house, but the flashes had stopped a few minutes ago when the Forensic Medical Examiner went inside. So far he hadn't come out again, and neither had Sergeant Stafford.

By the gate at the end of his drive Holly was standing with Frank Chapman's neighbour, Mr Evans. Most of the other spectators had gone away – bored by the lack of anything to see and tired of the cold – but Evans had lingered, as if he felt it was his duty to see this through.

"Had Frank got any family, do you know?" Holly asked.

Evans shook his head. "There was Connie, his wife, but she died. Must be ten years ago – before we moved here anyway. He's been here on his own since I've known him. I think they had a daughter – he mentioned her once, but I think it was one of those things – you know, they didn't get on. She never came to see him as far as I know – least not while I've been here."

"Can you remember her name?"

"No, sorry." He shuffled his feet and cast a glance towards

the house. "Terrible thing, isn't it? – I mean, I saw him yesterday and then he's just gone. – He was all right, too; a nice bloke. Not one of them pushy types, always wanting to know your business, but if you asked him for something it was never too much trouble, you know?"

Holly nodded. "I think so."

"So what'll happen now?" Evans asked. "I mean about a funeral and stuff."

"I'm not sure. I think that'll depend on the relatives – if we can find them."

Evans nodded solemnly, then shivered a bit, distracted. "Do you need me any more?" he asked.

"No, thank you, you've been a great help," Holly said.

"If there is anything else you'll let me know?"

"Of course. Thanks again, Mr Evans."

As Evans headed back towards his own house Holly jotted down a couple more notes then closed her pocketbook and debated what to do next. If Frank had a daughter she knew they'd need to try and trace her, but until the FME and CSE had finished there wasn't anything she could do.

She glanced at her watch and then, on an impulse, she took out her mobile and checked the screen. No missed calls. After a moment's hesitation she keyed through the menu and hit *call*.

"Hiya, it's me," she said when it was answered at the other end.

"Oh, hiya, sweetie. I didn't expect you to be calling," her mum said. "Everything all right? You got to work okay?"

"Yeah, fine," Holly told her. "I just wondered how the party went. Did Archie have a good time?"

"Oh, yeah, it was great," Lisa said. "He wore himself out with swimming, then ate two burgers and loads of cake. He had a really good time."

Holly could tell from her voice that her mum was moving. There had been music in the background, but now it was fading, then she heard a door close.

"What about Liam?" Holly asked.

There was a brief hesitation, then: "Oh, he was all right."

"How long did he stay?"

"Oh, not long."

Holly had a fine-tuned sense for when her mother was covering something up, and she felt it now. "He didn't try to hang about or anything when you went out?" Holly asked. "He didn't cause any problems?"

"No, he was okay. You don't need to worry. It was fine."

Holly didn't say anything for a second or two because she couldn't think of anything that wasn't *I don't believe you*. But she didn't. She knew there was something not right.

"Sweetie? You there?"

"Yeah. Yeah. Sorry. I'm still at work." She cast a look towards the bungalow and saw the FME come out of the house and head down the drive, black bag in his hand.

"Listen, I've got to go," she told her mum. "I'll call you tomorrow, okay?"

"Oh, okay then, sweetie. Love you."

"Me too."

"Bye."

But as Holly rang off she couldn't decide. Had there been a note of relief in her mother's voice when she'd said goodbye, or was it just her imagination?

She didn't have long to think about it though. By the time she got back to the bungalow, Sergeant Stafford was outside, waiting.

"Dr Carson's certified the death," he said as Yvonne came up beside them. "Possible heart attack or stroke between twelve and twenty-four hours ago."

"So he's leaving it at unexplained, not suspicious?" Yvonne asked.

"Yeah. Saves us some trouble, anyway. I've called the undertakers so when they get here he can be moved." He looked to Holly. "Did you get anything on relatives?"

"Not really, Sarge," Holly said. "His wife died a few years ago but there could be a daughter, only Mr Evans doesn't know her name. He thinks they might have fallen out though – her and Mr Chapman."

"That's families for you," Stafford said, not sounding particularly surprised. "Come on then, let's see if there's anything to tell us how to contact the daughter or any other relatives. I'll take the sitting room, you two do the bedrooms and kitchen. Be nice to get it wrapped up before end of shift if we can."

17

She wished she'd thought to bring a different pair of shoes – and clothes, even just a pair of jeans: anything warmer that wouldn't make her look so much like a prozzie.

It was too late now though. Even if she went back to the flat she couldn't get in, and if Dean was there – if the cops had already let him go – she'd be right back where she started. No, she had no choice. If she was really going to get away she had to stick to her plan, such as it was.

Her first thought had been to go to Frank's house. She knew he'd let her stay: that was what he'd said. But almost as soon as she thought about it she knew it wouldn't work. Frank's house would be one of the first places Dean would look for her. Perhaps in a day or two, when the stuff in the garage was gone, she might be able to risk going there, but not yet.

Instead she walked along the main road, heading west and trying to avoid drawing attention to herself. It was a long walk, especially in high heels, and at first she wasn't even sure she was going the right way. She wasn't used to going anywhere on foot because whenever they went out Dean always drove. Things looked different from the van and distances seemed shorter.

It wasn't until she saw the high-rise flats of the estate

after twenty minutes of walking that she finally felt confident that she knew where she was. Then, on a side road, she spotted the chippy she was looking for and from there she knew the pub was at the end of a road to the right.

The Bunch Of Grapes stood on its own on a plot of land with a tarmac car park at the back. It had been built at the same time as the Cadogan Estate, which rose up above it. It was an ugly, rectangular building with a concrete slab over the entrance where the smokers went for a fag. There were two of them out there now, and as Gemma passed them to go inside she knew they were looking at her and knew what they were thinking.

Inside she entered the lounge bar, immediately feeling the warmth as a welcome relief from the damp cold outside. There was a thick, patterned carpet and about half a dozen tables were occupied with Sunday night drinkers, most of them middle-aged or older. Gemma looked round quickly as she approached the bar, but it was immediately obvious that Evvie wasn't here – she would have stood out, like Gemma.

Hesitating for a moment, she wondered if she should check the other bar, but then the landlord moved up to the beer taps.

"All right, love?" he asked.

Gemma had seen him before when she'd been in with Dean. His name was Bryan and he was in his early fifties, wearing a floral pattern shirt – open to show a gold cross on his chest.

"Hiya," Gemma said, trying to make it sound natural and light.

Bryan cast a glance back at the door. "On your own tonight?"

Gemma nodded. "Just for a bit. Have you seen Evvie?"

"No, she's not been in yet."

"Do you think she'll be in later?"

"Maybe. She usually is." The man studied her more closely and Gemma knew he was looking at her swollen eye. "You all right?" he asked.

Gemma nodded. "Yeah. Just cold. Can I use the ladies?"

Bryan hesitated for a second, then nodded. "When you gotta go, you gotta go," he said with a grin.

In the toilets Gemma examined her face in the mirror, then applied some more make-up carefully over the puffy bruise. It still hurt, but not quite as much as before. Even so, it was a reminder of why she was here, why she was doing this.

When she went back to the lounge Bryan was still at the bar, as if he'd been waiting.

"Can I have a rum-and-Coke?" Gemma asked.

Again Bryan looked her over. "No business in here, you know that, right?" he said.

"Yeah, course," Gemma said. "I'm just waiting for Evvie."

"All right then," he said and went off to get the drink.

Gemma dug deep in her bag to find money to pay. Near

the bottom there was a roll of notes – mostly fivers – that she'd managed to keep to herself instead of handing over to Dean. In six months she'd managed to save eighty-five quid like that, keeping it concealed in places where he wouldn't look, like tampon applicators and panty liner packs. She knew it wasn't much – 'specially compared to what she'd handed over to Dean in the same time – but it would have to be enough.

"Three twenty, love," Bryan said, putting the rum-and-Coke in front of her.

Gemma handed a single note across and when he returned with change he nodded to a small table in the corner. "Sit by the radiator," he told her. "It's warmer there. Out of the way."

Gemma took the hint and nodded gratefully. "Thanks," she said, and meant it.

18.

There was something really sad about standing in someone's bedroom when you knew they'd never be there again, Holly thought. It was like everything had just stopped, and for Frank Chapman there didn't even seem to be anyone who would care that he'd gone.

She closed the final drawer of the dressing table and stepped back. For a moment she looked at the silver-framed wedding photograph sitting on a piece of lace above the drawer. The picture was black-and-white and it showed a much younger Frank Chapman in a grey suit standing next to his new wife. She was smiling, in an ankle-length gown with a bouquet in her hand, and Frank looked as if he thought he'd just done the best thing ever.

Strangely, looking at the photograph made Holly smile – just a little – then she looked away and moved briskly out of the room, switching the light off behind her.

In the kitchen Sergeant Stafford had just emerged from the sitting room. He had a small collection of documents in an evidence bag. The Crime Scene Examiner had gone a few minutes ago and a guy from a property maintenance company was supposed to be on his way to repair the back door.

"Anything?" Stafford asked.

Holly shook her head. "No, Sarge."

"Okay. There's an address book and some house documents from the sitting room. They might give us something to go on when we get back to the nick."

Yvonne opened the back door and looked in. "Undertakers are here," she said.

"Okay, send them in."

"Right." With a nod, Yvonne disappeared again.

Stafford looked at Holly. "Can you do me a favour? Go round the outside of the house and check everything's secure, okay? Doors and windows."

"Sure," Holly said, relieved to have the excuse to get out of the way. She didn't want to watch while the undertakers put Frank's body into a bag and carried it away.

Outside she saw that a black van with the words *Private Ambulance* on its doors had been backed onto the drive. Two undertakers in dark suits were leaving it and Holly kept herself from looking too closely at the black body bag one of them was carrying. Instead she occupied herself with taking the torch off her belt and when the men had gone inside she started a slow circuit of the bungalow, shining the beam over the window frames as she went.

Even though she didn't hurry it only took a few minutes to go round the whole house. She knew the undertakers would still be inside, so as a way of occupying a little more time, she crossed a short path to check out the garage as well.

186

The single window was blacked out and there was a new-looking padlock on the side door, so it all looked secure. She switched off the torch, about to turn away, but just before she did so she noticed a thin sliver of light escaping from inside the garage under the door.

It was probably nothing – a light left on by mistake – but just to be on the safe side Holly went down the drive to the IRV where Yvonne was standing watch.

"There's a light on in the garage," Holly told her. "Do you think it matters?"

Yvonne cast a quizzical look towards the building. "You sure? I didn't see anything."

"The window's covered, but you can see it under the door. It's locked though."

"Any keys around?"

"I think there were some by the back door of the house."

"Okay, see if any of them fits. If not, leave it – it won't hurt."

"Right." Holly nodded and went back to the house.

In the kitchen she could hear voices from the sitting room – Stafford and the undertakers – but she didn't listen to what they were saying. Instead she quickly took a set of keys from the hook by the door and went out again.

In the light of her torch she selected the only key that could belong to a padlock and when she tried it the padlock snapped open. She lifted it off the hasp, then twisted the door handle, opening it inwards.

The first thing to hit her was the dazzling brightness from six overhead strip lights, the glare bouncing back from foil-lined walls. The surprise of the brightness was followed almost immediately by a wave of heat carrying an overpowering, pungent smell from a small forest of plants.

The bushes were all as tall as Holly, growing from black plastic pots spaced out at regular intervals. Their foliage was so dense that it was almost impossible to see to the far end of the garage and every so often the leaves were stirred by the breeze from two oscillating fans fastened to the walls.

Holly didn't move for several seconds, still not quite believing what she was seeing, then she backed out and closed the door behind her, blinking her way back to the house.

"Sarge?" she called from the door. "I think you should come and look at something out here."

19.

"For the benefit of the tape, TPO Marsden has just entered the room."

Oz nodded Sam to the seat next to him and Sam took it, putting a folded piece of paper in front of the PC, although for the moment Oz didn't look at it. He turned back to Dean Fuller instead.

"So how come you've been identified by Mr Deakin as the person who attacked him on Norwood Avenue then, Dean? How do you explain that?"

Dean Fuller had his arms folded, a stony look on his face. Beside him the duty brief, a solicitor called Norton, looked bored.

"He's lying," Fuller said flatly. "I wasn't there. Prove I was."

"So where *were* you at five o'clock this evening?" Oz asked him.

"I told you, at home."

"Can anyone verify that?"

"No."

"Does anyone else live there with you?"

"No."

"So the female clothes and belongings we found in the flat – they're yours, are they, for when you want to dress up?"

Norton shifted. "Constable…" he said, letting it trail off.

Fuller didn't rise to the bait though. "They're my ex's," he said. "Ex-girlfriend. She left loads of shit when she went."

"When was that?"

Fuller shrugged. "Few months ago. Can't remember."

Sam could tell this wasn't going to go anywhere, especially when Oz didn't ask anything else. Instead he picked up the sheet of paper Sam had brought in and looked at the information on it. He took his time, but Fuller didn't seem worried – just sullen.

"All right," Oz said in the end. "Let's talk about the Wii game consoles we found in your van and your flat. What can you tell me about those?"

"No comment."

"Are they yours?"

"No comment."

"What were they doing in your van and your bedroom?"

"No comment."

"Did you know they were stolen?"

"No comment."

"According to the serial numbers they were stolen in a raid on a warehouse in Shenford on the twenty-third of January this year. Anything to say about that?"

"No comment."

"Did you steal them?"

"No."

"So where did you get them?"

"No comment."

"What were you going to do with them?"

"No comment."

"Right."

Oz sat back and drew a breath. "So is there anything else you'd like to add or explain at this time?"

"No comment."

"Okay, in that case I'm going to terminate this interview. The time is now 20:08 hours." And he reached across the table and stopped the tape.

Outside the interview room Sam and Oz stood a short distance from the open door so they couldn't be overheard by Fuller and his brief.

"Who's the case officer on the warehouse raid?" Oz asked.

"DC Simmons."

"Is he in?"

"No, I checked."

"Okay, we'll charge Fuller with handling and kick him out. There's no point trying to hold him, not on handling. Danny can always pick him up again tomorrow if he wants."

"What about the assault though?" Sam said. "We *could* hold him on that."

Oz shook his head. "It's not going to fly."

"But Deakin ID'd him. And if we get him back in to look at

a video ID parade..." But even as he said it he could see Oz's expression stiffening up.

"It's still Deakin's word against Fuller's," Oz told him. "There's no CCTV and no witnesses."

"There was the girl."

"Was. She could be anywhere."

"What if she's gone back to Fuller's place? I bet that was her stuff we saw in the flat."

"Probably."

"So if we find her..."

"You're not thinking it through," Oz told him. "If Fuller's her pimp, what's she going to say when we ask her if she saw the assault?"

Sam knew the answer immediately and kicked himself for walking into something so obvious. "She'll say no, or that Deakin started it," he said, downbeat.

"Right. So then it's two against one *and* you've wasted the time it took to find her. And even if you stick it in front of the CPS, they're going to say it's not winnable. You need to know when to draw a line."

Sam nodded morosely. "Yeah, I see. – I just thought if she *had* seen Deakin's daughter..."

"I reckon Mr Deakin's already had his money's worth out of us tonight, don't you?" Oz said flatly.

He moved across to the interview room door. "All right, Mr Norton. If you and your client want to come through to Custody..."

And Sam moved aside, waiting for them to come out.

20

"I can't," Evvie said.

She was a tall girl, mixed-race, with high cheekbones and really long legs – the sort punters went for. At a guess Gemma thought she was about twenty-two or -three, but she didn't know.

The truth was she didn't really know anything much about Evvie, apart from the fact that she was another tom and that they occasionally worked the same roads. They chatted sometimes, when it was slow, or if Dean decided to come in for a pint at the Grapes. For some reason he'd never seemed to mind when Gemma talked to Evvie – not like he minded if he thought she might be getting friendly with anyone else – and sometimes Gemma had wondered whether it was because he fancied the other girl, or hoped he could get her to work for him as well.

"It's just for tonight," Gemma said, her voice more pleading than she'd expected. "I'll go in the morning, I promise."

"I can't," Evvie said again. "I've already had a warning from the housing. If someone tells them I'll be out."

"No one'll know," Gemma said. "I'm not going to do business or nothing. I just need a crash. Just till tomorrow."

For a moment she thought Evvie might change her mind

when the other girl turned her gin and tonic glass in her long fingers, but then she shook her head.

"It's too risky," she said. "Not just the housing. If Dean knew… You know what he's like."

"I know, but that's why—" Gemma broke off, shook her head. She knew it was useless now.

"I'm sorry, babe," Evvie said. "I've got to think about Ethan, too."

"Who's Ethan?"

"My little boy." She looked at Gemma sadly for a moment, as if she really did regret it. "Listen, maybe you should just go back to him, eh? Least for a bit. Just till you get yourself sorted."

Gemma made a half-nod, but didn't say anything. She sipped her drink and then Evvie stood up.

"I've got to go," she said. "I told my mum I'd only be out for a bit. She's looking after Ethan."

Gemma looked up. "You won't tell him – Dean – if you see him?"

Evvie shook her head. "I won't tell him nothing."

"Thanks."

"I'm really sorry," Evvie said.

"It's okay." Gemma forced a smile. "I'll think of something."

She didn't watch as Evvie crossed the room to the door. She felt too much like crying. Evvie had been her best hope – her only hope – of a safe place for the night, and with that gone Gemma suddenly felt lost. There was no one else she could ask, and without different clothes she knew she'd freeze if she tried sleeping rough like she had when she'd first arrived in the city. It had been cold enough then, and that was in summer. Now, in March...

"Dean, was it?"

Gemma looked up quickly. She hadn't noticed him come over, but now Bryan sat down on a stool and placed another rum and Coke in front of her.

"What?" Gemma said, not sure what he meant.

"Hit you," Bryan said. "I always thought he was a bit too handy with his fists. No call for that though. No call." He pushed the drink towards her. "On the house."

"Thanks," she said, picking up the glass and taking a sip.

He nodded. "So what happened?"

She hesitated, unsure how much she wanted to tell him, but wanting to be sure he wouldn't give her away.

"He was nicked," she said in the end. "Dean. They took him away."

"When?"

"Before I came in."

"Do you know why?"

Gemma shook her head, then looked at him over the glass for a second before she spoke. "I need a crash," she said. "Just for tonight. You know anywhere I could go? I can't go back."

She held his eye for a moment, just enough, and when

she glanced away she knew he was looking at her in a different way – the way she was used to being assessed.

"I might," he said.

"Where?"

"There's a room here, at the back. Not up to much. Better than roughing it though, all the same."

Gemma looked back at him. "I haven't got much money," she said. "I can't pay – I mean…"

She let it trail off, but looked at him so he'd know. This would be when he decided, so she said nothing else, waiting to see.

He took a moment longer. "I don't want your money," he said then. "Can't have you wandering around with nowhere to go, can I?"

"Yeah? You mean it?" Gemma said, making it bright and grateful.

"Course I do," he said. "You'd better wait till closing though. – Don't want everyone knowing I'm a soft touch, do we?"

"No, course not."

He pushed back his stool and stood up. "I'll give you the nod then – in a bit. You can go round the back way, okay?"

"Sure," Gemma said, giving him a bright smile. "That's great. It's really nice of you."

"Me? I'm a nice bloke," Bryan said. "Ask anyone."

And he turned to head back to the bar.

21.

Holly was waiting beside Sergeant Stafford when Inspector Williamson came out of the garage and drew a deep breath of fresh air.

"Christ, Eddie," he said. "I thought you were talking about twenty or thirty plants, not a whole bloody jungle. There could be a lost tribe of Amazon Indians living in there."

Stafford nodded, as if that wasn't beyond the bounds of possibility. "It's about ready to cut, too," he said.

"Did you count them?"

"Didn't fancy staying in there that long. I want to drive home."

Williamson chuckled. He was a lanky man in his early thirties with a Home Counties accent which didn't always make him popular with the PCs on the relief. A lot of them thought he was snooty and on a fast track to higher rank. Like everyone else who'd looked in at the garage door though, Inspector Williamson clearly thought the discovery of that many cannabis plants was a cause for celebration.

He turned to Holly. "It's a good find," he told her. "By the time we work out the value it might even put us ahead of the Drugs Squad on goods seized this year. Pleased with yourself?"

"Yes, sir," Holly said, trying to make it convincing. In truth though, she felt oddly half-hearted about the find, even though she was getting the credit for it. For some reason she just wished it had fallen into her lap at another time or place.

"So how's it relate to the deceased male?" Williamson asked, turning back to Stafford. "Do we still think that's natural causes?"

"The FME was happy," Stafford said. "I can't see how this makes any difference unless the PM shows something else. The body's bagged up now anyway."

Williamson nodded thoughtfully. "So was he the grower, or was he renting the place out for a bit extra on top of his pension?"

"It looks like a professional set-up to me," Stafford said. "There's some money gone into it – air filters, insulation, lights... Holly met him though." He turned to her. "What do you think – was your Mr Chapman a grower?"

"I don't think he was the sort, sir," Holly told the Inspector. "I mean, he was in his seventies and he seemed like a nice guy when Yvonne and I talked to him – not like he had anything to hide."

"No – just the hundred cannabis plants in the garage," Williamson said dryly. "Any drugs paraphernalia in the house?"

"No, sir. I didn't even see any cigarettes."

"Right. Well, if Mr Chapman wasn't the grower then someone else is going to be pretty pissed off. – What do you reckon, Eddie – thirty or forty grand's worth on the street?"

Stafford shrugged. "Could be getting on that way, yeah."

Williamson looked pleased by the confirmation. "Pretty good for one garage. Okay, let's work out what we're going to do about forensics and removal then. Thank you, Holly. Like I said, it was a good find."

"Thank you, sir."

She moved away, leaving Stafford and the Inspector to talk. On the drive she found Yvonne with a couple of newly arrived regs. One of them, known as Pogo, was pretty short for a bloke – something his partner, Andy, was fond of mentioning.

"You get a pat on the head?" Yvonne asked Holly shrewdly, nodding towards Williamson.

"Yeah, I think so," Holly said.

"Make the most of it," the PC called Andy told her. "You wait, tomorrow it'll all be down to *'teamwork'*." – He made rabbit ears in the air. "And *'dedicated response policing'*. Led by you-know-who, of course."

"I don't mind," Holly said, because it was true. "It was an accident anyway – finding it, I mean."

"Christ, don't say that!" Pogo said in mock horror. "If you don't count accidents that's half Andy's arrests out the window right there."

"Piss off, you laptop," Andy told him.

"Laptop?" Holly said.

"Cos he's a small PC – get it?" Andy said, enjoying it, even when Pogo thumped him on the arm.

And then Holly found herself giggling, not particularly at the joke, but just because she needed to let something out.

Yvonne eyed her, deadpan. "I reckon you've been standing too close to that garage," she said.

And for some reason that made Holly laugh again – until she heard a rattling behind her and looked round to see the undertakers wheeling a trolley bearing a black body-bag from the house to the ambulance. Then her laughter stopped short in a kind of hiccup and changed to something different – harder and deeper.

A second or two later she felt Yvonne's hand on her shoulder.

"Come on, we need some stuff from the car," the older woman said. And to the others: "See what Stafford wants to do, eh?"

Then Holly felt herself propelled away towards the road by Yvonne's grip, but by then she wasn't really paying any attention as the tears finally came and her chest heaved with deep sobs.

22

In the car park near to his van Dean Fuller paid off the taxi, then stood looking round. After a moment he raised a hand to his mouth and shouted: "Gemma!"

There was no answer and no sign of the girl and after calling out for a second time he strode off bad-temperedly towards the stairwell.

Less than two minutes later he was back, swearing under his breath as he unlocked the van and got in. *Stupid little tart.*

He jammed the keys in the ignition and as soon as the engine caught he revved it hard, backing out of the parking space in a tight turn before accelerating away, tyres squealing, towards the road.

It took him five minutes, no more, to drive the two miles and it was only when he made the last turn into the avenue of detached houses that he let the van slow down to the speed limit.

She could have got this far, even walking it, and if he knew Gemma this was where she'd head for. So he watched the pavements on both sides of the road as if he expected to see her, trotting on her high heels.

Instead though, Fuller's gaze found the white, orange

and blue of a police car parked by the kerb up ahead. Then another, caught by the lights of a black van as it eased out of the drive to the bungalow.

"Fuck!"

He said it aloud, angry, head still turned to see two uniformed figures by the side of the cop car, conferring. Then he looked away, accelerated and swore again as he thumped the steering wheel. "*Shit!*"

23.

"Here," Yvonne said, holding a tissue so Holly could take it.

Holly accepted it, grateful. She blew her nose, then dabbed her eyes.

"Sorry," she said, knowing it sounded pathetic. She couldn't meet Yvonne's eye yet, but she knew what Yvonne must be thinking and she hated herself for losing it like that.

"Don't be. – You okay now?"

Holly nodded and finally looked up, expecting to see the older woman looking stiff and unimpressed. Instead though, Yvonne shifted to put an arm round her shoulder.

"It's my fault," she said. "I should've thought about it when we got the shout. It's always harder if you know the deceased."

"It wasn't that," Holly said. "I don't know— I was okay, then…"

"Shock," Yvonne told her. "You don't get it right away, not always. – My first body, I was with her all day, then went to tell her parents what had happened. I was fine – went for a curry afterwards too, but as soon as I got home I cried for an hour, maybe more."

"Is that true?" Holly looked at her and wanted it to be.

Yvonne nodded. "I've seen guys do more than that, right

there, as soon as they go in the room. – It's not just you, and if anyone says they don't get affected by it, that's crap. Okay?"

Holly dipped her head. "It does get easier though – I mean, after the first?"

"A bit, yeah. But you don't have to be Superwoman. If you don't have feelings you're not human, are you?"

She patted Holly on the shoulder, then took her arm away and stepped back a pace. "At least you didn't chuck up," she said. "That's a real pain – and the CSEs hate it."

"Because it contaminates the scene?"

"Nah – just cos they have to keep stepping round it."

Holly managed a smile at that, then took a breath to straighten her shoulders. Finally she looked towards the house.

"So what do we do now?"

"Back to the nick, write it up, soon as I've cleared it with Sergeant Stafford."

"We don't have to," Holly said. "I mean, if it's because—"

But Yvonne shook her head. "We'll be due off by the time we get back anyway, and they won't want to dip into overtime." She gestured towards the two other PCs – Andy and Pogo – on the drive. "Wallace and Gromit can look after the rest – 'specially if it's just standing around looking gormless."

24.

"You jammy sod," Sam Marsden said.

"What?"

"Sudden death *and* a bloody cannabis factory. How jammy is that?"

He dropped into a nearby chair, then leaned forward to look at the collection of documents on the desk in front of Holly. He'd already changed out of uniform, so she knew he must have clocked off.

"What did you get?" Holly asked.

"Nothing as good as that," Sam said. "Just a guy called Fuller on handling stolen goods. He had forty Wiis in his van from a raid on a warehouse in Shenford."

"Wiis? Did he do it – the raid?"

Sam shrugged. "He went no comment. DC Simmons is going to talk to him tomorrow, it's his case. – So how long had it been there?"

"What?"

"The body?"

"Him," Holly said. "His name was Frank Chapman."

She knew she sounded stuffy but she didn't care. She

wanted to make the point.

"Okay, so how long had *he* been there?"

"Less than a day."

"So it wasn't too bad then? – Hurley told me about this guy who died in front of a gas fire while it was on and—"

Holly saw Yvonne glance up from the computer where she was typing her incident report. "Oi! If you want to chat, go to the canteen. We're still working."

"Oh. Yeah. Sorry," Sam said, chastened. He knew better than to cross Yvonne and stood up again. "How long you going to be?" he asked Holly, voice lowered.

"Ten minutes, probably."

"I'll wait in the canteen then," he said. "Come and find me, yeah?"

"Okay."

When he'd gone Holly went back to the address book Sergeant Stafford had removed from Frank's sitting room. It was old and worn at the corners and a lot of the pages were blank. Those that did have entries had often been updated several times, with old addresses crossed out and new ones written in. The trouble was, most of the people listed had no surname against them. Frank Chapman must have known who Lizzie, David, Fiona and all the others were, but that was no use when it came to identifying a possible next of kin.

Holly reached the end of the book and closed it. She'd really wanted to solve this – to find Frank's lost daughter – but there was nothing more to do. She felt better for trying though, and it had finally put her moment of grief behind her. At least *someone* had tried.

She bundled the documents back into their bag and went across to Yvonne.

"I can't find anyone," she said when the PC looked up. "I mean, there are names in the address book but you can't tell if any of them are relatives."

"Anything from the house documents?"

"I found the name of the solicitors Frank used when he bought the house: Parker, Hall and Bird."

"Well if he left a will he probably used the same firm – people usually do. I'll email Sergeant Stafford and he can follow it up tomorrow or pass it onto the Coroner's Office."

She took the documents and put them aside on the desk.

"We could call some of the numbers in the address book, see if anyone can give us any more information."

Yvonne shook her head. "Not tonight," she said, closing it for debate. "Go and get changed."

"Okay," Holly said, finally accepting it.

Then her phone chimed and when she took it out and looked at the screen there was a message with an attachment tagged *B.day boy! Mum xx.*

Holly tapped it and the image opened to show Archie leaning in over a birthday cake, cheeks ballooned to blow out the candles. Around him there were half a dozen kids the same age. It made Holly smile and wish she hadn't missed it.

"Joke?" Yvonne asked.

"Uh-uh. Picture of my brother from my mum," Holly said.

"Let's see."

Holly turned the phone to let her see the screen.

"Cute," Yvonne said, although Holly could tell it was mostly out of politeness.

Holly looked at the screen again, then put the phone away. It had reminded her of something else, but she waited till she was at the door before saying anything.

"I forgot to ask you," she said, as if she'd just remembered it. "If someone's on parole and they're caught doing a crime, they go straight back to prison, is that right?"

"Probably. Depends what they've done – the original crime and the one on parole." Yvonne gave her a quizzical look. "Why?"

"Oh, it was just something Sam was talking about earlier. I just wanted to check."

"Go on, go home," Yvonne told her. "Have a bath with a load of smelly stuff and get an early night. It'll help."

Holly nodded, grateful, and finally opened the door.

25

"I've got you something," Bryan said, standing by the open door. In his arms Gemma saw a jumble of clothes by the light from the corridor outside.

She'd been sitting and waiting, more than half expecting him to come, but still hoping she'd be lucky and he wouldn't. The bedroom light was off, only a lamp on beside the bed, which she'd been using to look at the flyer for the missing girl, thinking it through.

Now she put the paper aside quickly, folded, as he came a couple of steps into the room and dropped the clothes on the bed. They were a mixture of sweaters and jeans, a couple of shirts too, and Gemma stood up to look at them.

"Where are they from?"

"My ex's." He gestured away. "What she left when she went. – Probably couldn't get into them any more," he added sourly.

He looked at Gemma then, gauging her size. "Might be a bit big for you, some of them. I thought you'd want something though. Can't walk around like that all the time, right?"

"It's really nice of you," Gemma said. She was wary, not trusting this gift to come without strings. Nothing ever did.

"I keep telling you, I'm a nice bloke," Bryan said, but she

saw he was assessing her again, like he had in the bar. Then he gave her a smile. "Not many of us left. – Sleep tight, all right?"

And with that he turned and left the room, closing the door behind him.

For a moment Gemma stood still, listening, not quite trusting that there wouldn't be anything else. But under the door she saw his shadow move away and after a second or two longer she let herself believe it. For the first time in a long time she felt herself relax.

MONDAY

1

BRIEFING ROOM
MORNINGSTAR RD STATION
08:36 HRS

"Three-One-Seven and Six-One-Four, you're on Five Beat. Special attention to the burglary artifice attempts in Park Road last week, okay?"

"Yes, Sarge," Sam said, making a note.

"And before you go out I've got a request from DC Simmons for an update on an arrest re stolen goods yesterday. Make sense?" Sergeant Stafford asked Oz.

"Yeah, got it," Oz said.

"Right."

Stafford turned back to address the room generally. "Okay, anyone not already assigned to a beat, you're on house-to-house in Oakleigh Road. Probably take a couple of hours. Stay put for a briefing by DI Connors in five minutes. Everyone else, up and at 'em."

The briefing broke up with the noise of chairs being pushed back and conversations being restarted, leaving Holly, Yvonne and three other PCs in their seats.

"What's that for do you think?" Holly asked Yvonne. No one had talked about doing a house-to-house last night, but if it was in Oakleigh Road Holly knew it must be associated with Frank Chapman's death.

"Looks like CID's going to muscle in on the skunk farm," Yvonne said. "Bet that's not gone down well with Inspector Williamson." She looked at the TPO beside her. "Did you do what I told you last night?"

Holly nodded. "Not a bath, but a ten-minute shower. I did feel better after."

"Sleep okay?"

"Yeah, fine." Which was true, if unexpected – almost as if her body and brain had just decided to shut down as soon as she gave them the chance.

"Good," Yvonne nodded, then stood up: enough said. "I'm going to grab a coffee."

"What about the DI?"

"She'll be late. She always is."

2

As Taz hurried across the walkway overlooking the precinct the wind sliced through her tights and robbed her legs of any warmth. She had to keep a hand on the strap of her school bag to keep it on her shoulder and she wished she had gloves.

When she got to the steps she cast a glance out over the handrail and saw two hunched figures moving away from Penrice House, heading towards the road that circled the estate: Drew Alford with Ryan alongside him.

They were all heading in more or less the same direction and for a moment Taz wondered if she should try and catch up with them but make it look as if it was coincidental. It might give her chance to ask about the things she'd seen yesterday – if she was careful and didn't make it too obvious…

Then her attention was taken by the sound of a car horn and she saw a shiny-grey BMW slowing down on the approach road. The horn sounded again and this time Drew stopped and looked. Then, as two men got out of the car, Drew changed direction and jogged quickly towards them. Ryan went too, but he hung back a little, as if he wasn't sure he was invited.

The older of the two men was a square-set guy with short

cropped hair and Taz knew him immediately: Tommy Vickers. Everyone on the estate knew Tommy Vickers – if not in person, then by reputation. And by reputation was enough: most people didn't want to know him – or for him to know them – better than that.

Walking more slowly than before, Taz got a clearer view of the second man as he came round the car – stocky, with dark curly hair. He might have been the same man she'd seen with Drew last night, but she couldn't be sure. That didn't matter though because now she could see him better she recognised him. He was the guy Danny Simmons had shown her, the one on the CCTV of the warehouse robbery. Even from this distance she was certain: he was the one Danny Simmons had nicknamed "The Bandit".

"You seen Dean Fuller this morning?" Vickers asked and his tone made it abundantly clear that he wasn't asking for nothing. Beside him the BMW's engine ticked over, issuing a thin trail of exhaust in the cold air.

Drew Alford shook his head. "Not since yesterday when he picked up the Wiis. Why?"

Vickers ignored the question, looked at Ryan. "You?"

Ryan shook his head but didn't say anything. Tommy Vickers made him wary and he didn't want to have anything more to do with him than was absolutely necessary.

"You see him you call me, soon as," Vickers said, looking back to Alford now. "Where you going?"

"School."

"No," Vickers said, not a request. "I need you to watch the flat." He gestured at Penrice House. "From a distance though. If there's anyone snooping round I want to know."

"Like who?"

"Anyone," Vickers said, as if Alford was being dense. "Dean was nicked last night with the stuff he got from us. Now he's gone missing."

"You think he could've told them where he got it?"

"Not if he wants to keep his kneecaps, but he could have. So keep an eye on the place – and I mean properly. If there's no sign of anything by tonight we'll shift the gear, but not till it's dark. I'll come back later, or Liam will—" He nodded to indicate the other man. "Just watch the place, all right?"

"Yeah, okay," Alford said. "Sure."

"Right. Go up there now."

And with that he turned and got back in the car, followed by the other man who had said nothing.

As the BMW pulled away Drew Alford looked back towards the estate. "You'd better come with me," he told Ryan.

As soon as he said it, Ryan felt the same sort of dark premonition that he'd felt on Saturday night at the party – the same feeling that as soon he let himself be drawn into this he was opening the door for things to go wrong, badly and fast, with no way to stop them.

"No, man, I can't," he said. "I've got coursework and stuff to give in."

"Fuck that," Drew said dismissively. "This is *real*, man. We stay in with Tommy so we *earn*, right?"

Ryan knew that once Drew had made up his mind he was hard to shake. You had to give him a better alternative, so he thought fast.

"Yeah, but keeping a lookout doesn't need two of us," he said. "And anyone sees us hanging round it's gonna look *more* suspicious, right? – Two of us, like we're up to something. – Listen, you do it this morning and I'll come back later, give you a break."

Drew's expression was still reluctant, but finally the idea seemed to make sense to him and then he nodded. "All right," he said. "But you'd better."

"I said, didn't I?" Ryan told him and started away before he could change his mind. "I'll be back at lunch."

But even as he headed across the tarmac, Ryan knew he'd only postponed the black premonition, not avoided it. And he knew it would keep coming back, just as Drew's demands on him would keep growing until, inevitably, the premonition became a reality.

What he really needed was a way out, for good. The problem was that he couldn't think of one – at least not one that didn't involve Drew Alford being either dead or in prison.

3.

CID was noisy and busy, as it usually was on a Monday morning when the plain-clothed officers started to wade through the cases from the weekend. Everything that hadn't been dealt with by the Duty CID officer would be assessed, prioritised and followed up, and that was on top of the cases that were already being investigated from previous weeks.

As he followed Oz through the swing doors into the CID office Sam immediately felt the buzz of the place and wanted to be part of it. He knew it would take five or six years – three to finish training and probation and a couple as a PC before he could apply for transfer – but it would be worth the wait and the perseverance. This was the place to get to the heart of a case, rather than just reacting to whatever came along and then handing it over, losing any involvement.

In the glass-walled conference room DI Connors and two or three other plain-clothed officers were having a meeting, and at a desk near a window DC Danny Simmons was gathering case notes together. He was frowning in concentration and wearing a suit and tie rather than his usual jeans and sweater. He'd also had a shave.

"Whose funeral is it?" Oz asked as he wandered up to the desk.

Danny Simmons made a tight, humourless grin, then immediately dropped it. "What's up?"

"Dunno. Staff said you wanted to see *us*. Dean Fuller?"

"Oh, yeah. Right." Simmons dug out a printed report from the other papers on the desk. "How many Wii consoles did you catch him with yesterday?"

"Forty," Oz said.

"All down to the Shenford job?"

"Yeah, I checked the serial numbers," Sam told him. "They all matched."

"He didn't have anything else – no laptops, hard drives, anything like that?"

"Not that we found. Just the Wiis."

"Right." The DC looked back to Oz. "Anything from the interview? Could Fuller have been in on the raid or do you think he'd bought them to knock out locally?"

Oz made a face. "He no-commented all the way through, but if it was me I wouldn't take Dean Fuller on a job – too flaky. I reckon he's more likely to be a middleman. Most of the stuff was in the back of his van, so he could've been going out to flog it when we nicked him. Just his bad luck that we found him before he got rid."

"Why *were* you looking for him?"

"Alleged assault. Didn't fly though."

"Nothing to do with stolen goods?"

"Not till we found them."

"Right."

"Has anything else from that warehouse raid shown up yet?" Sam asked. He still had a slim hope that finding the Wiis might bring them in on the case.

"Not so far," Simmons said. "I'm still trying to pull in some intel."

While he was talking his mobile rang and after looking at the screen he said: "I need to take this. Thanks for the info."

"No probs," Oz told him and nodded Sam towards the corridor.

Behind them, as they headed out, Sam heard Simmons say: "Hi. Hold on a sec."

And when he glanced back the DC was going into an empty office, closing the door behind him for privacy.

4

"*Hi. Hold on a sec,*" Danny Simmons said.

In the shelter of a concrete overhang Taz glanced round to make sure there was still no one else nearby. Through the mobile she heard background noise, then a door close and silence for a moment.

"*Hello?*" Danny Simmons said.

"It's me," Taz said.

"*Yeah, how's it going?*"

She thought he sounded a bit hassled, as if he'd had to stop in the middle of something to take the call.

"Okay," she said, making sure it sounded positive. "Listen, I've got some information for you. I've seen that guy you want."

"*Which guy?*"

"The Bandit – on the video, you know, from the other day."

"*Okay, where and when did you see him?*"

"Just now. He was with Tommy Vickers. You know him?"

"*Doing what?*"

"Vickers was talking to Drew – Drew Alford – and the other guy was with him. – There's some other stuff been going on, too – with Drew. If you want to meet I'll tell you all of it."

For a second, nothing. Then Danny said: "*Go back a minute. How sure are you that the guy with Vickers was The Bandit?*"

"It's him, definite."

"*Okay, if he is that's fantastic. Have you got a name?*"

Taz knew then that he wasn't convinced. It was because he'd said "if" and then "fantastic", like it was what he thought she'd want to hear.

"*Taz?*"

"What?"

"*Do you know his name?*"

"No. I mean, I haven't talked to him or nothing. I told you."

"*Okay, but can you find out? I need a name, first or last, or a nickname – whatever you can get. Can you do that?*"

"I suppose. You don't want to meet? I've seen some other stuff too – like I said. It's good. You need to know."

There was a momentary pause on the other end of the line, then Danny said: "*It's a bit difficult at the moment – I've got something on. Listen, see what else you can find out about the guy you saw, yeah? Then let me know – or call Holly if I'm not available. Concentrate on getting that name.*"

"It's gonna be worth something though, right – if I find out?"

"*Yeah, yeah, it will be; I'll make sure. – Listen, I've got to go. Call me or Holly later, all right?*"

"Okay," she said and rang off.

For a moment she was annoyed that he hadn't been more enthusiastic or willing to take her word that she'd recognised the guy. But more than that she was frustrated that he hadn't wanted to meet. That was what she really wanted, so she could tell him about Drew Alford and the flat, so that Alford would be picked up and done.

But if she got the name of the guy with Vickers that would *make* Danny take notice, she was sure of it. It would prove she was doing the business and then he'd have to listen to her about Drew. All she needed was the name.

5.

"Can I have a word?"

Danny gestured her aside, away from the others. Holly stood up and went with him so they could speak privately.

"I've just had a call from Taz," Danny told her. "My pep talk must've gone in, or else she's seen another jacket she really likes. Anyway, it sounds like she's been busy over the weekend – she reckons she's seen our target from the Shenford warehouse job – The Bandit."

Holly felt her heart trip. Trying to keep her voice matter-of-fact, she said: "Did she identify him?"

Danny shook his head. "No name yet, but she saw him with a guy called Tommy Vickers and Vickers would easily fit the frame for a warehouse raid too. That's by the by for the moment though. The thing is, I'm in court – probably all day – so I told Taz to call you if she gets anything else before I'm free. You don't need to do anything if she does call – just make a note of any info and tell her what a fantastic job she's doing."

"You mean keep her sweet."

"Yeah. If she has got a decent lead I don't want her going off the boil, so say I'll call her to fix a meet as soon as I'm free, okay?"

"Okay."

"Good." He looked at his watch. "I've got to go. Text me if you need to but if I'm on the stand I won't be able to reply straight away."

"What's the case?"

"The Matteson attempt-murder. He's trying to wriggle by saying he was assaulted."

"By you?"

"Yeah. But if I'd assaulted him for that he wouldn't be standing in the dock – he'd be leaning on crutches. Scumbag."

"Might be best not to say that though, eh?"

He gave her a wide-eyed look, joking. "Oh, you think?"

Holly smiled. "Good luck."

"Thanks. See you later."

But as he headed away Holly's smile dropped. What was the likelihood that Taz would get an ID on The Bandit? And if she did, what were the chances that he would turn out to be Liam?

Even though Holly still wasn't certain that Liam and the man in the grainy CCTV images were one and the same, she knew that the possibility of Liam being identified had just taken a sickening jump forward. And maybe it was now so close that she *had* to say something, even if her suspicions turned out to be wrong.

She trusted Danny, and although she knew he'd probably be annoyed with her, she thought he'd understand why she hadn't said anything until now. She could explain that and she should.

But even as she turned to look for Danny again, the door of the Briefing Room was swinging closed behind him. Still resolute, Holly took half a step towards it, but then the step faltered as another thought struck her: what if he *didn't* understand? What if he looked at it differently and thought she'd kept quiet in order to *protect* Liam for as long as possible? What if it looked that way to everyone? It might.

"They tell me you're the one responsible for this, TPO Blades."

Holly jumped, then saw DI Connors approaching, her steps clipped and brisk.

"Sorry, ma'am, I don't—"

"Thirty grand's worth of skunk and an unexplained death," the DI said, tapping a sheaf of papers in her hand.

"Oh, er, yes, I suppose so."

"Well I'm glad you don't look very happy about it cos I've just come off the phone with the pathologist and he's not happy either."

"He isn't?"

"No, so now I've got to go and have a look at the scene and you can give me the VIP tour when we get there, all right?"

"Yes, ma'am."

"Right. So let's go through what we know first, shall we?"

And as the DI moved up to the whiteboards at the end of the room, Holly slid onto a seat beside Yvonne, trying to pull her thoughts away from Liam and back to the Frank Chapman case.

6

Gemma didn't know what time it was but she hoped it was still early. There was grey daylight around the edges of the curtains in the small bedroom, so it was possible. She took a moment just to lie there and listen. Nothing. If she was lucky she might be able to leave without seeing anyone or having to answer any questions.

Pushing the duvet aside she stood up and navigated her way to the door round the assorted boxes and junk that were stored in the room. She twisted the handle and after listening at the crack for a moment she closed it again and crossed quickly to the pile of clothes Bryan had brought last night.

She'd slept in her bra and knickers and when she held a pair of jeans against her bare legs she knew straight away that they were too big. Bryan's ex-wife must have been taller and broader by a couple of sizes at least. Even so, Gemma knew she needed something to wear instead of her short tomming skirt and she went through the clothes quickly. In the end she took a pair of grey jogging pants with a drawstring waist and a purple sweater that had probably been skintight on its previous owner.

Once she was dressed she checked her bag, then pulled on her jacket and went back to the door, listening again.

She knew she must look odd in the strange combination of clothes but she didn't care: it would only be for a bit, and at least she wouldn't stand out like a prozzie any more.

There was still no sound from the rest of the pub, so she slipped quietly out of the room and went barefoot along the corridor to the stairs, trying to remember the layout of the place and the quickest way out. She emerged from the stairs at the back of the lounge bar, saw part of the countertop lifted up and was heading through it when Bryan came round the corner.

"Morning," he said brightly. "I thought you were going to sleep till lunch."

"Yeah, sorry," Gemma said, suddenly feeling caught. "I didn't know what time it was."

"You're all right, no rush: the cleaners don't come in till ten."

He came to the other side of the bar and put down a mug of coffee.

"Oh. Right," Gemma said. "I'd better go anyway though. I've got to see someone. Thanks for letting me stay."

"Nah, come on, you don't have to go yet. Have some breakfast first."

"No. Thanks. I never eat breakfast."

"Have a cup of tea then. Go on. Sit down. I haven't unlocked at the front yet anyway."

His insistence seemed a bit odd, but after the clothes and the fact that he hadn't tried anything on last night, Gemma couldn't see that a cup of tea would hurt, not if she was quick drinking it. Maybe he was a Christian or something, wanting to save her soul before she left.

"Oh, okay, then," she said. "A cuppa'd be nice. Thanks."

"Milk and sugar?"

"Ta."

He waited until she'd sat down on one of the bar stools, then went off round the corner. When he was out of sight Gemma checked her bag, then pulled her shoes on.

Then she heard the door open behind her and looked round. Tommy Vickers came into the lounge, followed by a slightly taller guy with dark curly hair.

"Where's Dean?" Vickers demanded without any preamble as he crossed towards her.

Gemma slipped quickly off the stool, grabbed her bag and clutched it tight. "I don't know," she said. "I haven't seen him."

"Since when?"

Vickers was in front of her now, as impassable as a brick wall.

"Yesterday," Gemma said. "Last night. He— The cops nicked him."

"I know that. I want to know where he is now."

"I don't know," Gemma said again. "I haven't— I didn't go back to the flat. He could be there. "

"Yeah, well he's not."

It was obvious that Tommy Vickers was more than pissed

off and Gemma started to take a step back, but he reached out faster than she could move and grabbed hold of her arm, painfully tight.

"Did he ever take you to a place on Oakleigh Road – a bungalow? An old bloke lives there, called Frank."

Instinctively Gemma shook her head. "No, I don't know anything about it."

She tried to pull away but he squeezed her arm harder, making her wince in pain.

"You sure?" he demanded.

"Yes! I've never been there!"

Vickers studied her for a moment longer, then let go of her arm. Gemma stepped back immediately, eyes watering with the pain.

"You see Dean, you tell him to call me," Vickers told her. "He's in trouble already – worse if he don't. Got it?"

"Yeah. Yeah, I'll tell him." She nodded quickly to show that she meant it.

"Right."

With that Vickers turned away and headed out of the bar. The man with him followed, still not having said a word.

Gemma held her breath till she heard the front door of the pub swing closed after them, then she sensed a movement behind her and looked round to see Bryan by the corner of the bar. Now she knew why he hadn't wanted her to leave.

"You okay?" he asked.

Gemma ignored the question, massaged the place on her arm where she could already feel the bruise forming. "You told him I was here," she said, hard and bitter. "I thought—" But she cut it off, knowing she'd been stupid to even think it.

"He wants Dean," Bryan said. "If I hadn't told him… Listen—"

But Gemma turned away, started towards the door.

"You're just like everyone else," she told him over her shoulder. "You can fuck off."

7

57 OAKLEIGH ROAD
09:56 HRS

Forensics weren't ready to let them in when they arrived at Frank Chapman's bungalow so they had to wait. The forensic examination of the scene took precedence and even DI Connors couldn't hurry it up, although Holly knew she'd have liked to.

While they waited Connors used the time to examine the garage where two PCs were cutting down the cannabis bushes and bundling the plants into bin liners for disposal. The approximate count was a hundred plants and even with the garage door and windows open, the smell of the place was still pretty overpowering.

A Crime Scene Examiner was dusting various bits of electrical equipment – lamps and heaters – for prints and Connors talked to him for a bit, then went over to an electricity meter by the door. "Did they bypass the meter or run it off the mains?" she called across to the CSE.

"Off the mains."

"Right," Connors said.

"Does that make a difference?" Holly asked, coming to look.

Connors nodded. "It means Mr Chapman would've got bills

for the electricity being used. It wouldn't have been cheap, so he probably knew what was going on. – There was a garage key inside the house too?"

"Yes, ma'am."

Connors nodded. "So even if he wasn't actually growing this stuff himself, he must have known it was here. My guess is that he was renting the place out."

"Renting?"

"Sure. The grower gives him a grand or two to use the garage for a few weeks, pays for the power, then harvests the crop and flogs it. If he's got three or four set-ups like this he could be turning over a hundred grand every three months, easy. And if one gets busted he's still got the others, all in nice quiet neighbourhoods where we're not likely to find them."

"And the owners would all know what was going on?"

"Usually," Connors said. "It's safer for the grower that way. Means the owner's not going to call us because they've got suspicious."

"But it's still risky," Holly said. "I mean, if the homeowner *does* get caught."

"Sure – they can get up to fourteen years. But times are hard. A couple of grand tax-free, just for having a few plants in a back bedroom or shed? Even people who pay their TV licences and stick to the speed limit can't see the harm. It's easy money."

"Jackie?"

Holly turned and saw the lead CSE – a woman called Mel Greenberg – had put her head in at the garage door. "You want to look at the house before we start moving furniture?"

Five minutes later Holly and Connors were suited up in forensic overalls and followed Mel Greenberg into the house.

Nothing had changed, Holly saw as they went through the kitchen to the sitting room, but now she felt better able to cope with the place. It was no longer somewhere that an old man lay dead. Instead it was a crime scene – or at least a *potential* crime scene, depending on what the DI decided.

Connors had a bundle of photographs in her gloved hand, all taken last night before Frank's body had been moved, and when they entered the sitting room she paused to look at them, matching the scene as it had been to what it was now.

"This is the way you found him, sitting on the floor?" she asked Holly, tapping a photo.

Holly looked. The photograph made the scene less real somehow and wasn't as hard to look at as she'd thought it might be.

"Yes, ma'am," she said. "We didn't move him."

"Good. Just wanted to check. No sign of a struggle, nothing upset?"

"No."

"Right," Connors said.

She looked at the photos for a moment longer, then handed them to Holly and glanced at her notes.

"The pathologist says he'd had a blow to the back of the head, here." She turned to Mel Greenberg and indicated a spot at the back of her own skull. "Not much external bleeding and covered by his hair so it was hard to spot without a full exam. It could have been enough to render him unconscious if not kill him. – Something triangular, causing a right-angle wound about two centimetres long. Did you find anything to match that?"

The CSE nodded. "The only trace of blood we found is on here."

She stepped across the room and indicated the corner of the wooden gas fire on the chimney breast opposite the sofa. "It was only a smear and we'll have to test to see if it belongs to the deceased, but my guess is it will."

"So if it is his, what do you think – a fall, hits his head?"

"Could have been that, yeah, but he'd have to have gone backwards and most people fall forwards if they trip or collapse."

"Okay, so could he have been pushed – goes down, hitting his head?"

"Yeah, that's possible too."

"Well don't commit yourself," Connors said dryly.

"Wasn't going to," Mel Greenberg said, giving her a wry look. "I just present the evidence."

"Huh."

Connors drew a breath and pursed her lips. "Okay, so then there's the other question: if he went down here, how did he get to be in a sitting position over there? Did he crawl there himself and then die, or did someone else drag him?"

Greenberg shook her head. "Sorry, can't tell you that either – least not till we look at any fibres on his clothes. If there are carpet fibres on his hands and knees it might indicate that he crawled there by himself, but if not…" She shrugged.

"Great."

"Hardly worth coming in for, was it?"

"Nah, well, it's not like I've got anything better to do," Connors said, but she defused the sarcasm with a look. "Thanks, Mel."

And she gestured Holly back towards the door.

Outside DS Ray Woods was standing with Yvonne Dunlop and another PC who had just come back from doorstep enquiries with the neighbours. When he saw Connors and Holly emerge, Woods left the others and crossed towards them as they took off their forensic suits.

"Door-to-door's not given us anything new," he told the DI. "No one noticed any activity around the time of death or anything unusual over the past few weeks. One lady says she *thinks* she's seen a blue van parked on the drive once or twice, but she can't remember when."

"So much for Neighbourhood Watch then," Connors said, unimpressed.

"What's it look like inside?"

Connors shook her head as she disentangled herself from the legs of the forensic suit. "It's still either/or: a push or a fall.

I'll call the SIO Homicide. He can decide if he wants to take it, but I bet he won't."

She handed her suit to Woods and moved away to use her mobile.

When she'd gone, Woods cocked an eyebrow at Holly. "So how's it been then?" he asked conversationally. "Your first sudden death."

Holly took a moment, thinking it through.

"It was...okay," she said in the end. "I mean, it's not a great thing to do, but..."

"Someone's got to?"

"Yeah, I suppose."

Woods nodded, understanding. Holly hadn't seen much of the DS since the Ashleigh Jarvis case a month ago – just an occasional nod when they passed in a corridor – but she was pleased that Woods still felt able to be friendly like this.

"So, do you think it's suspicious?" he asked.

"Me? I don't know," Holly said, taken a bit off guard by the question. "I sort of hope it wasn't though."

"Oh? Why?" He gave her a inquisitive look.

"Cos he was a nice old bloke," she said. "Or he seemed like it. And you don't want to think of someone like that being killed, do you?"

"No, I suppose not," Woods said and seemed to approve of her answer. "It happens though – and more often to the nice people. Fact of life."

Holly took his point, then hesitated before asking the

question that had been on her mind since they arrived. "Sarge, if it does turn out to be suspicious will we be in trouble for not spotting it last night?"

"Was there anything *to* spot?" Woods asked.

"No, I don't think so, but..."

"And you did it by the book?"

"Yeah."

"So you're covered," he said, matter-of-factly. "Can't see what's not there, can you?"

As he said it DI Connors came off the phone and as she approached them Holly knew from her expression what the result of the call had been.

"Homicide don't want it unless we can say for sure it's suspicious and not just unexplained," she told Woods.

"No surprise there then."

"Nope. So we're stuck with it."

She cast a glance at the house and garage. "Anything we haven't covered here?"

"Don't think so."

"Well we're not going to figure out who was growing the stuff until we get the forensics back so we might as well put that to one side for now. – Let's take it back to the nick and assess what we've got on the death."

8

Gemma knew Dean would still be looking for her. She also knew the only thing that would stop him was if Tommy Vickers found him first and maybe – if she was lucky – put him in hospital, or at least beat him up badly enough that all he could do was stay in the flat and lie on the sofa. But that would only happen if she was lucky, and Gemma knew she couldn't rely on that.

Instead she knew she had to be careful and stay away from anywhere that Dean might think to look for her. That was why she'd walked as far and as fast as she could when she left the pub, away from streets she knew, until she finally found a high street cafe where she could rest and think.

Sitting at the back of the cafe, away from the windows, she finally felt safer. She hadn't eaten since yesterday and the smell of frying bacon was impossible to resist, so when the waitress came over she ordered a full breakfast with tea and it was only after she'd finished it all that she finally relaxed and started to think about her escape plan.

Originally she'd intended to go to Frank for help and ask him if she could crash there for a couple of nights. That would have been long enough to persuade him to give her some cash for the coach fare to London and a bit extra for when she arrived. She knew he'd want to help her get a fresh start, away from Dean. Hadn't he said so?

But that idea wasn't any good any more, not after she'd told Tommy Vickers that she didn't know Frank and hadn't been to the house. She'd have risked being found there by Dean, but not Tommy Vickers. If he knew she'd lied to him there was no telling what he might do and Gemma was scared of him much more than she ever had been of Dean.

So going to Frank's was out and there was only one other way she could think of that would get her the cash she needed and the chance to be on the bus out of Weston before tonight.

On the tabletop beside her empty plate she unfolded the crumpled piece of paper she'd kept in her jacket pocket, examining the face of the girl called Andrea, who looked back at her, smiling. She reread the print below the picture, then found some change in her bag and went to the payphone at the back of the cafe near the toilets.

After a glance round to see that no one was listening, Gemma punched out the numbers that were printed on the flyer and then listened as the line started to ring.

"Hello?"

"Is that Tony?"

"Yes, speaking. Who's this?"

"I talked to you yesterday. On Norwood Road. You said you were looking for Andrea."

"Yes, yes, I am," Tony Deakin said. "Do you know her?"

Gemma noticed the sudden upturn in his voice. "I might've seen her," she said.

"Can you tell me where – where you saw her?"

She didn't answer immediately. Instead she looked at the flyer.

"Hello? Are you still there?"

"It says there's a reward," Gemma said.

"Yes, if I find her there is."

"I don't know if she's still there."

"Where?" Deakin said, a note of desperation in the word. "Listen, if you've got *any* information… I'll make sure it's worth your time. If we can just meet…"

"How much?"

"A hundred pounds. More if I find her. I'm not going to cheat you, I promise. I just want to find her. That's all I care about."

"A thousand," Gemma said. She held her breath, waiting to see what he'd say.

"That's too much – I mean, without proof. I'd need to know more."

Gemma gave it a moment, then said: "If I tell you, how do I know you won't just rip me off?"

"I won't, I promise," he said. "Listen, if you want I can—"

Gemma cut him off. "Half then. Half when I tell you, the rest if she's there."

"I'd still need to know more first," he said and she could

tell he was suspicious now. "I don't even know who you are."

"Look, I don't care," Gemma said flatly. "Please yourself, right? But the guy she was with, he's nasty. I don't want him knowing it was me that told you. I mean, even if it's not her. Understand? I'm not getting him mad at me. Not for nothing. So if you don't want to know…"

There was silence for a moment then finally Tony Deakin said: "No, I do. I'd just need to get the money, that's all."

9

"You can't be here, Paddy. You know that. It's private property."

The man Oz was talking to clutched a bottle of cider in a grimy hand and Sam could smell the heady combination of old sweat, unwashed clothes and several other equally off-putting scents.

To be fair, not all of them came from the mumbling drunk sitting on a low wall at the back of the disused chapel though. The overgrown plot around the building was littered with bottles and cans, syringes and crap – crap as in rubbish, and crap as in crap.

"Paddy, come on," Oz said again, more firmly. He tapped the man's leg with the toe of his boot, but only enough to get his attention. "Time to go."

"Fuck ov! L' me 'lone."

The man started mumbling to himself and Oz sighed. "Gloves," he told Sam. "Let's see if he'll go if we get him on his feet."

He pulled on a pair of blue latex gloves and Sam did the same. "You don't want to take him in?" he asked.

"What for?"

"D&D?"

"He's not disorderly though, is he?" Oz said. "He's harmless – as long as you keep downwind of him, anyway. Five or six years ago, yeah, he'd have been fighting us by now, but since he had his stroke he's been gentle as a lamb."

"A stroke?" Sam said, surprised. "How old is he?"

"Take a guess."

Sam looked. It was hard to tell through the grime and the beard and the deeply etched lines on the man's face. "Fifty?" he asked.

"Thirty-eight."

"You're joking."

Oz shook his head. "If he *gets* to fifty he'll be lucky – that's if you think living like this for another twelve years is lucky." He shifted his attention to the drunk. "Paddy, come on, mate – we're going to get you on your feet, okay?"

They took hold of Paddy's arms from each side and hoisted him to his feet. He was unexpectedly light, Sam discovered, and after a moment's initial resistance the man started a stumbling walk towards the gap in the fence.

"Keep him moving," Oz said. "As long as he heads off under his own steam we're sorted."

"B'stards," Paddy protested. "Not my— You b'stards."

"Not us, mate," Oz told him mildly. "We're the good guys, remember? Come on, keep going."

Sam wasn't surprised by the way Oz treated the drunk – with a mix of gentleness and firm insistence. Oz's bark was often worse than his bite, but seeing it now made Sam realise that Oz hadn't been his usual self for the last couple of days and he didn't know why.

They kept Paddy moving as far as the chain-link fence and then Oz's radio came to life. *"Three-One-Seven from Delta Mike One, receiving?"*

Delta Mike One was the call sign of the Duty Inspector and Sam recognised Williamson's voice.

"It's okay, I'll deal with Paddy," he told Oz. "Come on, Paddy, through here."

While Oz took the radio call Sam went ahead through the hole in the fence and then reached back to guide Paddy out by the arm. The drunk had a hard time coordinating his feet and his arms, flailing against the fence as if it was trying to hold him back, but in the end he broke free of its grip and staggered out onto the pavement beyond, tripping a bit as he did so but managing to stay upright.

"You all right, Paddy?" Sam asked, ready to grab him if he looked like going down.

"Fuck off."

"You need to leave the area now, okay?" Sam told him. "D'you understand? You can't come back, okay?"

There was no way to tell if Paddy understood this or not. For a moment he looked round, as if only just realising that his surroundings had changed, but then something in the distance caught his attention and without another word he set off towards it with a shambling, half-limping gait.

Sam watched him go for a moment, then looked back for

Oz. He was still talking into his radio and when he signed off he didn't look happy.

"What's up?" he asked as Oz came up to the fence and pushed through the gap.

"Your Mr Deakin again," he said. "He's back in the station, only this time he's got the Inspector involved. We're wanted, asap."

"Did he say why?"

"No, just to get our arses in gear."

And with that Sam knew that Oz's mood of understanding had evaporated again.

10.

"So what was your impression of Frank Chapman when you met him?" Connors asked Holly. They were standing in front of whiteboards and the DI was tapping a marker pen against her thumbnail. Yvonne had been tasked with coordinating the door-to-door statements and DS Woods had gone off to take a phone call.

"I liked him," Holly said. "He seemed like a nice guy – cheerful. Bit of a rascal, my mum would say."

"Even though he'd just been robbed?"

Holly nodded. "It was like he wasn't going to let them beat him."

"Right."

Connors picked up the single-page robbery report and scanned it for a moment. "He'd had a fall though. Was that serious?"

"No, just grazes. He went after the youths who took his wallet and tripped. He wouldn't let us call an ambulance."

"Okay, we'll see if the pathologist thinks there's any link between that incident and his death when we get the full PM. For the time being let's assume there wasn't though."

She dropped the robbery report on a desk.

"So what do we know about Mr Chapman from the neighbours? Was he the sociable type – many visitors, family or friends?"

"Mr Evans – the man next door – said Frank kept himself to himself most of the time. It didn't sound as if he had much company and I looked through his address book last night – it was pretty empty."

"Next of kin?"

"Mr Evans said he thought there was a daughter, but I couldn't find out who she is."

"Okay. – So, he lives on his own, keeps himself to himself and has no criminal record. He's a model citizen – except for the fact that he's got thirty or forty grand's worth of skunk in his garage."

Connors pursed her lips, thinking it through, and Holly knew she wasn't required to say anything. She'd seen the DI work this way before: she just needed to use the nearest person as a sounding board to order her thoughts.

"So, we've got two alternatives," Connors said then. "One: the death was an accident. He fell, hit his head and died from the injury and it's just a coincidence that he also had a garage full of weed.

"Or, two: there *was* someone else in the house. There was an altercation, Mr Chapman was pushed, hit his head and died. The cannabis *could* be the reason for that, or again it could have nothing to do with it."

She pulled a face, clearly not happy, then looked away as Ray Woods approached. "When are we likely to get the full PM? We're whistling in the bloody dark without it."

"By lunch was all they'd say," Woods told her. "But that was the lab on the phone. They've got an ID on prints taken from a glass near the body. They match a girl called Gemma Hoskin. She's got form for tomming."

"Really?" Connors looked mildly surprised. "Anything else?"

Woods scanned the information sheet in his hand. "She's had two tugs for prostitution – last time in January. She claimed to be eighteen, but from her picture, I dunno, I reckon sixteen's more like it…"

He ran a finger further down the page. "Blah, blah, blah… – Yeah, okay, this is something. She's also flagged to a file on a Dean Fuller. Same address. Intel says he might be her pimp."

"Interesting," Connors said. "Maybe she was making outcalls and Mr Chapman was a client. – Don't look at me like that, TPO Blades. I said *maybe*."

"Sorry, ma'am," Holly said, trying to adjust her expression. She hadn't realised her thoughts were so easy to read.

Connors looked to Woods. "Let's see what we've got on Fuller as well, okay?"

Woods nodded and moved to a computer terminal while Connors wrote up Gemma Hoskin's name on the board.

"Ma'am?" Holly caught the DI's attention again. "It might not be the same guy, but PC Sitwell and TPO Marsden arrested a Dean Fuller yesterday for handling stolen goods."

Connors frowned. "Are you keeping tabs on the *whole* station?"

"No, ma'am. It's just that Danny was interested in Fuller because the stuff he was caught with came from the Shenford warehouse raid and that's one of the cases we're trying to get intel on."

Holly could see that Connors had understood what she meant: that this was something they had an informant working on.

"Okay, well maybe Fuller was at Frank Chapman's house last night too," Connors said. "But Gemma Hoskin definitely was, so it's her we need to concentrate on – why?"

"Because if she was there she might have been the last person to see Frank alive?"

"Correct. Always a good place to start."

11

INTERVIEW ROOM 1
MORNINGSTAR RD STATION
10:42 HRS

By the time Sam and Oz returned to the nick Tony Deakin had already told Inspector Williamson his story and now, sitting on an interview room chair, he was repeating it for their benefit.

"She said if I gave her £500 she'd tell me what she knew about Andrea," Tony Deakin said, looking at Oz. "I told her I'd need time to go to the bank but she wouldn't give me her phone number. She just said she'd call me back at twelve and tell me where to meet her."

Sam saw him glance anxiously at his phone where it lay on the table, then at his watch. By the door of the interview room Inspector Williamson was talking to a female PC who'd just brought him something.

"You're sure it's the same girl?" Oz asked Deakin dubiously. "The one who was with Fuller when he assaulted you?"

Deakin nodded emphatically. "She said so. I mean, she said she'd spoken to me yesterday on Norwood Road and I didn't talk to anyone else there, so it must be the same girl."

"Is this her?" Williamson asked, crossing to the table and putting a photograph in front of Deakin.

Tony Deakin looked for a moment, then nodded. "Yes. Yes, I think so. Her hair was a bit longer, but yes."

"Okay, good," Williamson said. "If you'll just give us a minute, we'll decide how best to tackle this."

The Inspector took the photograph back, but as he did so Deakin spoke up. "Inspector, I don't want you to— I don't want her arrested or anything – I mean, that's not why I'm here. If she *does* know something about Andrea I don't want to scare her off. I need to talk to her."

Williamson nodded reassuringly. "Don't worry, Mr Deakin. I understand your concern and I'm sure we can work something out."

"Thank you. It's just that this is the first real lead I've had."

"Don't worry," Williamson repeated. "We just need to discuss the best way forward."

In the corridor Sam was last out of the interview room and he closed the door behind him before joining Oz and the Inspector.

"Who is she?" Oz asked when Williamson handed him the photo.

"Her name's Gemma Hoskin. She's on record for prostitution, linked to Dean Fuller's file by address."

"Right." Oz handed the picture to Sam.

Williamson shifted. "So is it correct that Mr Deakin asked you to look for this girl yesterday?"

"He wanted us to look for *a* girl, yes, sir."

"So why didn't you?"

"Because she hadn't done anything. She was a possible witness to an assault, which was what Mr Deakin was reporting, but he identified Dean Fuller as his attacker so we went looking for him. The way Mr Deakin told it, the girl was tomming for Fuller, so if we found him I thought we'd probably find her as well."

"But you didn't."

"No, only Fuller."

"Pity."

Although it wasn't a direct criticism, Sam could tell from the stiffness in Oz's back that he felt he was being blamed for something.

"Like I said, the girl hadn't done anything."

"Well, clearly the situation's changed," Williamson said. "As it stands, she's now offering to sell him information about the possible whereabouts of his daughter."

"I still don't see what it's got to do with us though," Oz said. "Deakin's offering a reward, so it's not blackmail or extortion."

"No, but after what happened yesterday he's worried in case it's some kind of set-up to rob him," Williamson said. "He might be right too – especially if Dean Fuller's involved. He could see it as a way to settle the score for being arrested last night. In which case we're looking at conspiracy to rob."

Sam could tell that the further Inspector Williamson pushed this the less Oz liked it. He still didn't know why Oz was being this way, but he knew Williamson wasn't going to convince him.

"We can't go along every time someone offers to sell Mr Deakin information though, can we?" Oz said. "And if he gives out leaflets saying there's a reward for information he's bound to get people trying it on."

"Perhaps," Williamson conceded. "And I will talk to him about the way he's going about this, but for the moment I'm inclined to think Mr Deakin deserves some support. He's understandably anxious to find his daughter and the least we can do is make sure he isn't being drawn into a dangerous situation today. – So, if Gemma Hoskin calls back I want to be ready. Mr Deakin can arrange to meet her and we'll set up an obbo. Then, if there's any trouble, we'll be on hand to deal with it, okay?"

"Just us?" Oz asked.

"I think the three of us can cope with it, don't you?" He looked at his watch, then stepped back towards the interview room. "I'll tell Mr Deakin what we're planning to do and you two had better get changed into civvies."

"Yes, sir," Oz said neutrally, but when Williamson had gone Sam saw his expression change.

"This," Oz said flatly, "is going to be a right royal waste of bloody time."

12.

"Hello? It's the police. Show yourself now please."

There was no response and behind her Holly could hear Yvonne calling out much the same thing.

Raising her asp to shoulder height as she'd been trained, Holly took the last couple of steps along the hall and stood in front of two doors. One was closed, but the other stood wide open, giving a view of a bedroom with an unmade bed and untidy piles of clothes littered around.

Holly went in, but it only needed a cursory inspection and a look under the bed to see that there was no one there. The bathroom took even less time and when she'd finished she headed back down the hall to where Yvonne was waiting beside the splintered frame of the front door – the only way in or out of the flat.

"Nothing," Holly said.

"Or here."

They moved out onto the walkway and Yvonne considered the broken lock and the smudged boot-print on the door beside it for a moment, then closed the door as best she could. "Let's see if the neighbours know anything."

They separated, each taking a flat on either side of Dean

Fuller's broken door. At the one on the left Holly knocked a couple of times, then stood back so she'd be clearly visible through the spyhole. Like most of the other flats the woodwork round the windows and door was faded and in need of painting.

There was a short pause, then Holly heard the sound of a chain being unfastened inside and when the door opened a woman in her late twenties looked out through the narrow gap she'd made. Her hair was scraped back and it gave her face a slightly pinched look.

"Hello," Holly said, making it cheerful. "Sorry to disturb you. I'm TPO Blades from Morningstar Road station. Could you tell me if you've seen your neighbours today – this side?" She gestured to Dean Fuller's flat.

The woman shook her head. "I haven't seen him," she said.

"Actually, we're looking for a girl who might live there – Gemma? Have you seen her at all?"

Again the woman shook her head.

"Did you hear any kind of disturbance there recently?"

The woman hesitated and glanced away as Yvonne came to stand beside Holly. "It was earlier," she said in the end, reluctant.

"Can you remember what time?"

"I dunno. Early. About eight. All I heard was a crash and some shouting. It sounded like two men. I dunno. I didn't see." She started to close the door. "I've got to go."

"Thanks for your help," Holly said, but the door was closed before she'd finished the sentence.

"It wasn't our lot," Yvonne said as they moved away from

the flat. "The door. So someone else has got an interest in Dean Fuller by the look of it. – Anyway, there's nothing else we can do here. We'll get back and tell the DI."

They went down the stairs and into the parking area, heading for the patrol car. As they did so Holly glanced at the other cars, then looked again.

"Yvonne?"

"Yeah, I've seen him."

In the far corner of the car park a metallic blue Ford Mondeo was parked in a slot. The man in the driver's seat had a newspaper open on the steering wheel but he was watching them rather than reading. He was in his mid-fifties, heavyset, holding a cigarette near the partly-open window.

By now Holly had learned that most people avoided eye contact when they realised a copper was looking at them, but this man didn't. He just continued to look.

"I know him from somewhere," Yvonne said, opening the car. "Stay there a sec."

She sat on the driver's seat and pulled the in-car PNC terminal round to face her.

"Can you see the index?"

"Yeah. Romeo Foxtrot zero four – er—" Holly squinted. "Kilo Zulu Alpha."

Yvonne tapped it in, then waited for the check to be processed. Holly looked away from the man in the car to see the result but before it came through there was a call on Yvonne's radio.

"*Delta Mike Five-Nine-Two from DS Woods, free to speak?*"

"Yeah, go ahead, Sarge."

"*Any joy at your location?*"

"Negative. No one home. Looks like someone paid an early morning visit though – the door's been kicked in."

There was silence for a moment, then Woods said: "*Okay, you'd better get back here. We've got a change of situation.*"

"Will do. Out."

"What's that about, do you think?" Holly asked.

"Dunno," Yvonne shrugged.

Then the vehicle check came through. "Right," Yvonne said, with a note of satisfaction when she saw it. "Malcolm Kerrigan."

"Who is he?" She cast a glance towards the man in the car.

"Works for a guy called Tommy Vickers," Yvonne said. "Heavy mob. And if he's sitting there it's not because he likes the view."

"You think he's waiting for Fuller?"

"If he is Fuller's in serious trouble. Tommy Vickers doesn't send Malc Kerrigan out to ask you round for tea and cake. – Come on, get in." And she started the car.

13.

"What're you doing here?" Holly asked when Sam Marsden and Oz Sitwell came into the Incident Room just a couple of minutes after she and Yvonne had got back. Yvonne was talking to the DI by the whiteboards and off to one side DS Woods was talking to Inspector Williamson.

Sam shrugged. "Dunno," he said, but kept his voice down. "Williamson just told us to report for a briefing." He gestured to the whiteboards. "Is this the unexplained death?"

"Yeah. I don't know why Williamson would be involved though."

Holly shifted a little to get a better view of the boards as Connors added a couple of new names at the bottom: *Kerrigan* and *Vickers*.

"Okay, listen please," Connors called, tapping a marker pen on a desk to get attention. "Right, here's the situation. Despite the wonders of coordinated policing it turns out that while we've been looking for Gemma Hoskin in relation to Frank Chapman's death, Inspector Williamson is also looking at her for a possible conspiracy to rob. Whether or not the two things are connected we don't know, but we've all got an interest in her, so let's pull this together and see if we can't satisfy everyone, okay?"

She turned to the whiteboard and used her pen to illustrate as she spoke.

"Starting with the unexplained death of Frank Chapman. We know Gemma Hoskin was in Mr Chapman's house sometime close to his TOD because her prints were on a drinking glass. As of ten minutes ago we can also link a Dean Patrick Fuller to the cannabis found in Mr Chapman's garage because Forensics have identified Fuller's prints on the garage door frame."

The DI had drawn on the whiteboard as she spoke and now she stood back.

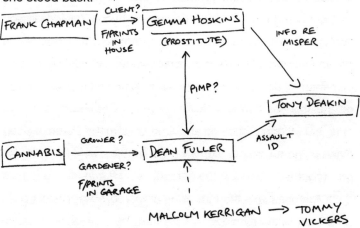

"So, we have Gemma Hoskin connected to the house, Dean Fuller linked to the cannabis and both of them probably there at or around the time Mr Chapman died, all of which means we need to speak to them."

She indicated a line linking Gemma Hoskin's name with

Fuller's. "We're pretty sure Fuller is pimping for Gemma Hoskin, so it looks to me as if we've got Fuller coming to the house to look after the plants and he's bringing Gemma with him, possibly to entertain Mr Chapman while Fuller plays at *Gardeners' World*. Everyone clear so far?"

There were nods and Connors looked to Williamson. "James?"

Williamson stepped up. "From our side, we've got Mr Tony Deakin who has been contacted by Gemma Hoskin with an offer to meet him and sell information on the whereabouts of his missing daughter, Andrea. This offer may be genuine, but there's also a chance that it's a set-up to rob Mr Deakin, and that Dean Fuller might be behind it."

Connors shifted, taking over again. "Inspector Williamson has generously agreed that our sudden death trumps his conspiracy to rob –" she made a mock bow towards the uniform Inspector – "so instead of the original plan just to put an obbo on the meeting, we now want to detain Gemma Hoskin and bring her in for questioning about Mr Chapman's death. If Dean Fuller is there with her, so much the better – we'll nick him for growing the cannabis in the garage. Just bear in mind that he's got form for assault though, so be prepared. – Any questions?"

No one said anything.

"Right," Connors said. "In that case we're three teams: me and Ray, Yvonne and Holly, Oz and Sam – Oscar One, Two and Three. Channel six for radio. Study the photographs on the board and as soon as we know where the RV's been fixed we'll plot up. Street clothes all round."

14

She hadn't wanted to text or call him because that would be too easy for him to ignore and too hard for her to find out what she wanted to know. Instead Taz waited till the lunch break and found a spot where she could look out for Ryan amongst the noisy, milling crowd of pupils all released for a while into the dampening air.

Even then she almost missed him though – only just catching sight of him as he dodged out through the school gates and headed quickly away in the direction of the estate.

Taz moved quickly to follow and didn't bother to check whether she'd been spotted by a member of staff as she went through the gates. By then he was almost at the end of the road and she ran to catch up, putting on a happy face when he heard her footsteps and turned to see who was coming.

"Hiya," she said brightly. "Where you going? Bunking off? I'll come with you if you are."

She put her arm through his, like it was the most natural thing to do.

"Nah, it's— I've got to do something," Ryan said and she could sense his reluctance to join in with her cheerfulness.

"I could still come with you," she said, persevering. "I've only got science this afternoon and that's a waste of time.

Like I'm ever gonna need that working in Tesco's. – Come on, where you going?"

"You can't," Ryan said then. "I've got to see Drew. He won't— You don't want to be there."

"Why? What's he doing?"

"Nothing, just— It's just something I said I'd help him with."

"Is it something for Tommy Vickers and that other guy?" she asked. "I saw you with Drew and them this morning."

"Where?" He sounded wary now – defensive.

"On the road," Taz said, as if it was no big deal. "I waved but you didn't see me. – Least, you didn't wave back."

"I didn't see you," Ryan said. "Listen—"

"So what was it?" Taz asked, cutting him off, but making it seem like an accident. "Has Drew got something on with Vickers, or is it the other guy? I've seen him before somewhere. What's his name – Steve or Simon or something?"

She hoped that by running on like that he'd just think she was being naturally curious, not really expecting an answer to any of it.

Ryan shook his head. "Liam."

"You sure? I thought it was Steve. – Liam what?"

"I don't know." And as he said it he turned so that she had to let her arm go from his. His expression was serious. "Listen, you can't come," he told her, sounding definite. "I mean, you don't want to."

"You don't sound like you want to either," Taz said.

"I don't, but I said I would, so…"

"Why though? I mean, if you don't want to do it tell Drew to piss off."

Ryan hesitated, then shook his head. "I can't," he said. And then, as if to make up for it: "We could meet later though – if you want."

Taz looked at him hard then, assessing his expression, trying to read what was behind it. Then she nodded and smiled. "Course I do," she said and leaned in to kiss him, just briefly. "Call me, okay? Don't forget, all right?"

"I won't," Ryan said, his expression lightening a little.

"You'd better not," she told him, jokingly stern. Then she gave him a wave and started back along the road the way she'd just come. It was starting to rain and in her head the name was going round so she wouldn't forget it: *Liam… Liam…*

15

In the changing room of the charity shop Gemma dressed quickly. It had taken longer than she'd thought to find something decent to fit her, but at least now she was rid of the horrible, oversized clothes from the pub, with their lingering scent of Bryan's ex-wife.

Instead she had a pair of clean jeans, white trainers and a warm jumper that zipped up to the neck. As she put her jacket on over the top she looked at herself in the mirror and felt like a regular person again; not like a prozzie; not like someone in stupid, too-big-for-her clothes. She could blend in and disappear dressed like this and no one would look twice. That was all she wanted.

She gave Bryan's wife's clothes to the grey-haired woman at the till and told her to recycle them or put them in the bin, then she paid for the stuff she had on and left.

Outside the shop, she paused under the awning to find some change for the phone and also to count the money she had left. It wasn't so much now, after buying breakfast and the clothes, and for a moment that made her feel vulnerable again. If this didn't work…

But it had to – she had to *make* it work because she knew what he'd do if he caught her now. She'd got away from him once before, in November, just for a few hours, but his anger and the beatings had gone on for days after he found her. She didn't want to think how long and savage his punishment would be if he caught her after being away all night and all morning.

No, there was no choice. She knew he'd still be looking for her so she *had* to go through with this; she had to get right away – from everything and everyone. If she could just manage to do that she could start again: a new life, better and different. Away.

Holding that determination, Gemma stepped out from the awning's shelter and crossed the short distance to the phone box down the street. It had started to rain while she was inside the shop and she moved briskly to dodge it, pulling the heavy door open and stepping in quickly. As the door closed behind her she unfolded the leaflet and put it on the metal shelf so she could see the phone number, then pushed in her coins and tapped out the number with care.

For a moment there was nothing, then in the earpiece she heard the *burr-burr* as the phone rang at the other end. She counted the tones, forcing herself to be calm despite the hollow, jittery feeling in her stomach.

Four rings, then five. Then: "Hello?"

She thought his voice sounded anxious, nervous perhaps.

"It's me," Gemma said. "Did you get it?"

"Yes, it's— Yes, I've got it," Tony Deakin told her. "Where can we meet?"

16.

"Sod this rain." DI Connors cast a black look at the sky, then across at the park entrance. "We'll stand out like idiots if we just hang around waiting in this."

Holly had been thinking the same thing as she and Yvonne joined the others beside the DI's car. The car park and the entrance to Ellsworth Park were almost deserted except for one or two people hurrying away towards shelter. The small refreshment kiosk by the gates was closed and locked up too: no chance of using it as cover for an obbo.

Connors glanced across to Oz's car where Tony Deakin was holding an umbrella, looking restless and nervous beneath it, waiting to be told what to do.

"Okay," Connors said, making a decision. "Oz, you and Sam plot up in your car: you can see the main entrance from there. Yvonne, you and Holly take the north and east gates. If you can find shelter, use it. Ray and I will do circuits near the bandstand, God help us. She's going to be heading for that anyway, so let her get there, then we'll move in, okay?"

The others nodded.

"Right, you two go now," she said to Holly and Yvonne and

when they headed off towards the park gates she crossed to Tony Deakin.

"Okay, if you're ready, Mr Deakin. It's going to be just like we discussed. Go to the bandstand and wait underneath it – at least you'll be dry. When Gemma Hoskin turns up just keep her talking until we move in, okay?"

Deakin nodded, but Sam saw the worried look on his face and knew he was investing a lot in all this going to plan.

"Don't worry, it'll be fine." The DI gave him a reassuring smile. "Go through the gates and follow the left-hand path. You'll see the bandstand. We'll follow a few metres behind but just ignore us and pretend you're on your own, okay?"

Deakin nodded, tight-lipped. "Should I go now?" he asked, uncertain.

"Yeah, now would be good – and like I said, we'll have you in sight all the time."

"Okay."

With a last nod, Tony Deakin started quickly away towards the park gates and Oz gestured Sam to get into the car. By the time he had and they were settled to watch the wet tarmac entrance, DI Connors and DS Woods were following Deakin at a slower, discreet pace.

"Think she'll come?" Sam asked, placing the radio by the gearstick, within easy reach.

"For five hundred quid?" Oz said. "Probably. It's worth getting wet for that kind of money."

He wiped the windscreen with a rag, clearing a patch of

condensation so they could see the gates. The heater was on but it wasn't making much difference.

"Do you think it could be genuine then?" Sam asked.

"What?"

"The girl – Gemma Hoskin. You think she could really know where Mr Deakin's daughter is?"

Oz shrugged. "Anyone's guess, isn't it? We'll find out one way or another if she turns up."

Sam knew he should leave it alone – over the last couple of days Oz had put out enough signals. But it was bugging Sam because in many ways Oz was the reg he liked best in the station.

A lot of the other coppers just looked on the cases they dealt with as problems to be sorted as quickly as possible. To them, *people* were the problem – unruly, unhelpful and ungrateful. But Oz treated everyone as human beings, whatever the situation, and his attitude was always fair-minded and compassionate. Except now. This grumpy, cynical outlook was something different.

"So, come on, why don't you like him?" Sam asked.

"Who?"

"Tony Deakin."

"I told you before, I don't care one way or the other."

"Yeah, I know, but it's like you don't *want* him to find his daughter."

"Maybe he shouldn't," Oz said flatly.

"Why? I mean if—"

But Oz cut him off. "You read the Misper report, right? She didn't just go missing – she took her stuff and left: ran away. So maybe she doesn't *want* to be found. You thought about that?"

"But if it's her family…"

"What difference does that make?"

It wasn't a question Sam had expected. "It's what families do – look out for each other," he said. "Isn't it?"

"Yours might. I don't know," Oz told him. "I'm a care-home kid – from nine till I was sixteen. No one came looking for me, and I didn't want them to either." He took his eyes off the park gates and faced Sam for a moment. "That's not a sob story – I'm just saying, okay? Playing happy families doesn't work for everyone, that's all."

"Right," Sam said, suddenly aware that he'd got in deeper than he'd really meant to. "Listen, I didn't mean—"

Oz waved it away, looked back to the gates. "I'm just saying," he repeated, flicking the windscreen wiper switch to clear the glass. And this time Sam knew enough to leave it alone, even before the radio interrupted.

"*Sierra units from Sierra One. We're in position. Stand by.*"

"*Sierra Two, received. In position,*" Holly's voice said.

Sam keyed the radio. "Sierra Three, received. Standing by."

17

"She came in last night," Bryan Price told him. "Don't know where she went after that."

"Was she with anyone?" Fuller glanced round, as if he suspected Gemma might still be there, hidden in a corner.

"Nah, she was on her own," Bryan said. "Why – you had a bust-up or something?"

"Yeah, something like that," Fuller said darkly. His hair was dripping from the rain and he pushed it back from his forehead.

"Bloody women," Bryan said and moved to the pumps. "Listen, have a pint. You won't find her in this – it's pissing it down."

Fuller shook his head. "I'll find her," he told him, hard-faced, then he turned and moved off towards the door.

"Where you gonna be, if she comes in?" Bryan called after him.

"Just tell her to phone me," Fuller said. "Or else."

As he pulled the door open and went out, Bryan Price put down the glass in his hand and ignored a man who'd come up for a refill. Instead he went round the corner of the bar and picked up the phone.

Through the strengthening rain Gemma walked quickly,

head down, anxious not to be late as she approached the main road. At the junction she stopped and waited for the traffic lights to change so she could cross. The passing vehicles threw up spray, but her new jeans and trainers were already soaked and her hair hung down in sodden strands round her face.

Being wet didn't matter though – in fact it was better because the rain made her even more certain that Dean wouldn't even consider looking for her out in the park.

Thinking of somewhere to meet – a place that she knew and that Tony Deakin could easily find – had been hard. She didn't want to risk meeting anywhere indoors and she knew she'd feel too exposed standing on a street. But the park would be okay, especially in the rain. She knew the gateways and paths and she'd be able to watch the bandstand from a distance until he arrived. And then, afterwards, she'd be able to get away quickly and just disappear.

That was the plan and in her head she was already rehearsing what she was going to say: just enough detail so he'd believe she was telling the truth, but nothing he might know was untrue. She'd also make him promise that there'd be more money when he'd found Andrea, but it would only be for show. All she needed was the five hundred he'd have with him and then she'd be gone and never come back.

In front of her the vehicles slowed down as the traffic lights changed, and when they stopped Gemma jogged across the road in front of them. Down the hill and only a couple of streets away she could see the still-bare winter trees in the park, and she was already imagining what the future would be like, just as soon as this was done.

When the car ahead of him started forward again Fuller let the van move up too, a short gap between them. As he did so his eye caught the briefest of movements on the other side of the road and for a second he wasn't sure, not completely.

She had different clothes, her hair hung in wet rat-tails and the rain on the windscreen made it hard to see. But when she turned towards the road to the park, then he was sure, even when his view was cut off by a truck. He knew it was her and he pushed the van harder, changing lane as soon as he could. She wouldn't get far.

18.

If anything the rain was heavier than when they'd started and Holly knew she'd got the better end of the deal. Standing in the partial shelter of a maintenance hut she was chilly and damp despite her waterproof jacket, but at least she had some cover. Yvonne was getting the worst of it, just visible about two hundred metres away near the east gate. She was using a small green umbrella and a leafless tree as shelter, pretending to chat on a mobile.

The only good thing about the rain was that it had cleared almost everyone else from the park, which meant that anyone new coming in through the gates stood out a mile. So far though, the only people Holly had seen were a couple of lunchtime joggers and a hassled mother with a toddler in a buggy.

Pushing a hand into her pocket, Holly dug around for the packet of chewing gum she knew was there somewhere, but as she found it a movement at the gate took her attention. A slim, bedraggled figure had just come into the park and although the distance and rain made it hard to see properly Holly was sure the figure was female: shoulder-length wet hair; short jacket; jeans; the right age – possibly.

275

Holly felt the sudden blip of adrenalin and squinted to see better as the girl came three or four steps past the gate, then paused and looked round, as if getting her bearings.

Instinctively Holly stepped back, but not so far as to lose sight of the girl. She was ready to move – to head off as if going somewhere – if the girl came in her direction. That way she could pass her and get a good look at her face.

But even as the girl appeared to make up her mind and started to head into the park, a second figure – male, camo jacket, jeans – came in through the gate at a run.

He was moving so quickly that he seemed to collide with the girl, as if he hadn't expected anyone to be there and couldn't dodge round her in time. But instead of separating, the man and the girl stayed together with no space between them – not in a natural way, but locked together somehow. And then Holly saw the girl tug away, only to be pulled close again before the man spun her round and propelled her back towards the gate.

Whatever was going on between them, Holly could tell it wasn't right – wasn't normal – and she moved quickly away from the hut, striding out. Still nearly two hundred metres away, the man and girl were rounding the gate pillars and disappearing outside as Holly pulled the radio from her pocket.

"Yvonne from Holly. I've just seen a girl and a man come in through my gate. Could have been target one and two but I couldn't see properly."

"*Where are they now? Can you see them?*"

"Negative. It looked like the male forced the girl to leave with him. I'm heading for the gate. Shall I have a look on the road?"

"*Yes yes.*"

Holly picked up the pace, breaking into a run. In her earpiece she heard: "*Holly from Connors. Were they spooked? Did they see you?*"

"Negative, I don't think so," Holly said between breaths. "They were only here for a few seconds."

"*Understood. Try and get eyeball outside and advise.*"

Holly pushed herself as she covered the last fifty metres to the gate, only slowing down when she reached it, then walking through to the pavement beyond, trying to look casual.

To her left she heard an engine revving hard and when she looked a van was pulling away. All she got was a view of its back doors and the index. In case she was wrong she flicked a glance to her right, but there was no one in sight anywhere else along the road.

"DI Connors from Holly – no eyeball. Blue Escort van index Charlie Bravo five one Whiskey X-Ray X-Ray driving off now towards the main road. There's no one else here."

Again she cast round to make sure she couldn't have missed anyone walking away but she knew that she hadn't. It *had* to be the van, and although it was moving away faster now Holly forced herself back into a run as it took the first side road it came to.

"Connors from Holly. Van has turned right right right."

In her earpiece she could hear Connors telling Oz to go mobile, but by the time Holly reached the side street it was too late. The van had disappeared and Holly stopped running and bent double, lungs straining as she tried to get her breath back.

Perhaps twenty seconds later she heard another car coming along the road behind her, being driven hard. She looked up and caught a glimpse of Oz and Sam through the car's windscreen and signalled them into the side road with a wave.

The car took the corner without seeming to slow, skidding on the wet tarmac then punching forward again. In a few seconds it reached the far end of the street and its brake lights went on, but it paused for a moment too long before turning left and then Holly knew that they couldn't see the van and were only guessing at which way it had gone.

Despite the rain Holly opened her jacket to cool off and headed back to the park. By the time she got to the gate Yvonne and the DI were there, waiting.

"What happened?" Connors said.

Holly gestured forward, into the park. "I saw a girl come in through here," she said, replaying what she'd seen in her head. "I couldn't see her properly and she stopped for a few seconds, like she was deciding which way to go. Then a man came in behind her. He was running and I thought he'd bumped into her, but it didn't look right."

"Could you make a positive ID on the girl?" Connors asked. "Was it Gemma Hoskin?"

Holly shook her head. "I don't know. – It could have been but she was too far away to see properly."

"Okay, so then what happened?"

"It looked like the man forced her to go back out to the road so I went after them, but by the time I got here all I saw was the van driving off. I'm sure they were in it though – there's nowhere else they could have gone."

Connors nodded. "The index matches Fuller's van," she told her. "I've put out an all-units to see if anyone can pick it up."

"Oz didn't see it?"

"No. They're having a look round though. They might pick it up."

"Sorry, ma'am."

Connors waved it away. "Not your fault. It wasn't what we expected to happen, that's all."

"So what can we do?"

"Nothing here. We'll collect Ray and Mr Deakin and get back to the cars. If Fuller's taken Gemma Hoskin against her will it changes things. I'm not sure how yet, but this is a bust. – Come on, let's get out of this bloody rain."

And she started back along the path, boot heels clicking briskly on the tarmac.

19

It was only the mattress on the floor of the van that stopped her from being thrown around and hurting herself more. Without windows there was no light, but when the van travelled straight for a short time she was able to feel around on the roof and find the courtesy light she knew to be there. When she flicked the switch it gave out a weak yellow light, but it was enough.

Her left wrist ached with a cold, deep pain and her head throbbed where it had hit the strut on the inside wall of the van. When she touched it through her wet hair she didn't expect to feel the stickiness she found though, and when she looked at her fingers she saw an almost black liquid, like oil, except it was red when she moved her fingers closer to the light.

Seeing the blood, Gemma realised the truth. She'd never seen him so mad before, and he'd never been so quiet: no shouting, no rage; completely silent. He hadn't cared whether he hurt her or how badly – he just forced her to go where he wanted, like she wasn't a person but a thing.

She knew that what she'd done was unforgivable to him now, and it made her cold and afraid in the pit of her stomach. But seeing the blood on her fingers was what made her sure. When he took her out of the van again he was going to kill her.

It all came at once then – the determination and fear and desperation – and she found herself moving as if she was being controlled by somebody else. She crawled to the back doors of the van and took hold of the handle, trying to pull it upwards with her right hand. It was stiff though, refusing to move, and when the van swung round a sharp corner she lost her grip.

Thrown sideways, Gemma used her left hand to brace herself and immediately let out a cry. A white-hot lance of pain shot through her wrist and left her gasping for breath. She knew he must have broken it and for a moment – as the pain washed through her – she wanted to give up and just lie there. What else could she do?

But again it felt like someone else had taken over control of her body and she forced herself to sit up. She shuffled round and took hold of the door handle again with her right hand, tugging and tugging at it – harder and more desperate – until finally she felt and heard something give.

As if released from tension, the door sprang outwards by a finger-width – enough to let in daylight around it – and Gemma felt a surge of hope in her chest. She risked pushing the door open a bit further but when she saw the sickening blur of the road directly beneath her she pulled back, afraid.

Even as she did so the motion of the van changed though – slowing – and the engine note dropped. Gemma forced herself back to the door and again she pushed it open a small distance, willing herself to stay strong as she watched the road surface slowing and slowing below.

She didn't wait for the final lurch of the stop. She thought it was slow enough now so she kicked the door open and pushed herself out. But as soon as her feet touched the ground she knew she'd misjudged it. Like stepping onto a treadmill, the tarmac seemed to whip her legs from under her and she stumbled, went down on one knee and felt gravel rip through her jeans.

Behind the van the road was open and wide and as she struggled to regain her balance she saw there was no other traffic, just the tree-lined road, parked cars along its kerbs. She took all this in with a glance as she pushed herself back to her feet, desperate to move.

She wanted to start running now, but all she could manage was a shambling, drunken stagger – as if her limbs had all forgotten how to work together – and before she had made more than five or six paces she heard the fast-running steps behind her, getting closer.

His hand caught her broken left arm, spinning her round.

"No!" she sobbed. "Don't!"

"Fucking bitch," he said, breath coming hard, then he slapped her and when she sagged and began to collapse he started to half-drag, half-carry her back to the van.

20.

Sam scanned the left-hand side of the road and any side streets they passed, concentrating only on blue vehicles, dismissing all the others. He knew Oz was doing the same thing on his side of the car, keeping the speed down so they could get a good look. Neither of them spoke, but Sam was pretty sure that when Oz broke the silence it would be to give up on the search. After this long, and without any real idea of where Fuller's van might have gone, it was needles and haystacks.

"Six-One-Four from Delta Mike, receiving?"

Sam took his eyes off the road for a moment and keyed the radio. Oz continued to check the roads they were passing.

"Go ahead, Delta Mike."

"Re your all-units for a blue van. Report of an assault on Markham Avenue. IC1 male and female involved, now driven off in a blue van, partial index ends Whiskey X-Ray X-Ray."

Before the woman at Control was halfway through the message Oz was accelerating, going to blues and twos when the traffic ahead looked like slowing. "Tell her we're on it," he said to Sam, pulling out to overtake a taxi.

"Delta Mike, received. Show us on way. Current location Harrison Road. Any updates, over?"

"Informant is a Mrs Banstead. She's outside number 87 – eight seven – Markham Avenue. I've asked her to wait for a unit's arrival."

"All received. Out."

"See if the DI got that," Oz said as soon as Sam signed off. "Tell her our ETA's three minutes."

As they made the turn into Markham Avenue Oz killed the siren but didn't slow down till Sam said: "There."

After a while you got to know when someone was looking out for your arrival and Sam could tell that's what the woman was doing even before she raised her hand to flag them down. She was in her late twenties, standing near the kerb with a pushchair beside her.

Oz brought the car to a stop and they both got out, moving briskly.

"Mrs Banstead?" Oz asked, showing his warrant card. "I'm PC Sitwell, TPO Marsden. Can you tell me what happened?"

"It was a girl," the woman said. "I was walking along here and this van passed me. Then, when it stopped at the junction, this girl just jumped out of the back and started running. It looked a bit odd, you know? But then the driver got out and went after her. He grabbed hold of her and dragged her back to the van."

"He forced her to go?"

"Yes! He pushed her into the front and drove off really fast."

"What colour was the van, do you remember?"

"Blue – dark blue. I only saw part of the number plate. It ended in W X X."

"Okay, that's great," Oz told her. "Did you see which way he went at the junction?"

"Right. That way," she gestured.

Oz turned to Sam. "Tell the DI. He went right on Salisbury Crescent, heading east, okay?"

Sam nodded. "Got it."

"How long ago did this happen?" Oz asked the woman as Sam used the radio.

"Only a few minutes. I called 999 as soon as he drove off. I knew it wasn't right. I mean, you don't expect something like that, do you?"

"No, but you did the right thing to call," Oz said. "Let me just get some contact details from you…"

"All received," Connors said. She was in the front passenger seat next to Yvonne and Holly was in the back. "We're on way to you now. Connors out."

They'd only left Ellsworth Park a couple of minutes ago, intending to check out Fuller's flat in case he went back there, although Holly was pretty sure no one thought that he would. The incident Sam had just reported had changed things again though, and it left little doubt that Dean Fuller had taken Gemma

Hoskin against her will. Suddenly, tracking Fuller down had become a matter of urgency, no longer about cannabis growing but to ensure Gemma Hoskin was safe.

"If he was going north on Markham Avenue he could be heading for the ring road," Connors said. She had an A–Z open on her lap now, tracing a route with her finger.

Yvonne changed gear and put on blues and twos as they approached a roundabout and Holly took hold of the grab bar.

"I don't think he'd go that way," Yvonne said, hardly missing a beat as she swung the car left, then left again. "Markham Avenue's a long way round for the bypass and he did a right on Salisbury Crescent. I reckon he's heading for somewhere in Calow."

"Okay," Connors said, accepting Yvonne's logic. "Do we know if he's got links in the area?"

"I don't think so – bit too upmarket for him."

Holly leaned forward. She'd done a few patrols around Calow the previous month – a pretty well-off area with quiet streets and detached houses.

"Ma'am? DS Woods was telling me about cannabis growers using different residential addresses – I mean, decent houses in quiet areas. So if Fuller was looking after one crop at Frank Chapman's house…"

"He could have another in Calow?"

"It's just an idea," Holly said. "But if he doesn't know we're looking for him and he wants somewhere to lie low for a bit…"

"A lot of the residential roads in Calow run parallel to each other," Yvonne said. "Wouldn't take us long to drive up and down. If he's parked up we might spot the van."

Connors studied the A–Z for a second longer, then nodded and closed it. "Okay, let's have a look."

21

Gemma lay huddled against the wall of the garage where he'd pushed her so hard she hadn't been able to stop herself going down. All over her body different parts hurt, but although there were hot tears running down her cheeks she tried to remain absolutely still, afraid of what he would do if she drew his attention.

She kept her head bowed, but through the tangle of hair across her face she could still see him pacing – each step fast and enraged – three, four, five, then a hard turn which ground grit under his boots, as if he was trying to wear away the floor. He was so angry and distracted that he didn't seem to know what to do next, now that the garage door was bolted shut and there was nowhere left to go.

Gemma couldn't tell how long she half-sat, half-lay with her back to the wall. The bright light and the heat and the smell of the plants made her feel nauseous on top of the pain and discomfort. How long could he just pace up and down like that? How long before something just exploded in his brain and pushed him over the edge?

She knew what he was going to do, but now she also knew it was impossible to escape. No matter what she did, he would always catch her again – again and again – every time. She knew there *was* no escape now and all she could do was—

Suddenly he stopped pacing. He made one extra step and stood over her.

"Get up!"

She lifted her head, tried to brush back her hair. "Baby…" she started to say, imploring, trying to sound like she meant it.

The slap on the side of her head knocked her sideways, so hard that she hardly knew what he was doing when he took hold of her arm and tugged her upwards, forcing her to her feet.

There was a bench next to the wall, cluttered with tools and junk, and when she was almost upright he pushed her against it, yanking a length of electrical cable free from the mess. He forced her left hand behind her, making her sob with pain, and she felt the cable being wrapped round her wrist, pulled tight and knotted…

A surge of pure panic swept over her. In desperation she tried to pull away, to turn. He pushed her harder against the bench and her free hand swept across it, taking hold of the first thing it encountered. And without truly knowing what she was doing then, she finally broke free of his grip and pushed herself around, swinging the hammer as hard as she could – once, then again and again.

22.

They were cruising down the third parallel road in Calow when Holly saw it.

"Over there," she said, and realised that Yvonne had seen it at the same moment because she was already braking. A blue van, parked nose in on the drive of a detached, yellow-brick house.

As Connors twisted round to look, Yvonne swung the car across the road and reversed quickly, blocking the drive. The number plate was right, Holly saw now, and the back door of the van was slightly ajar.

"That's it," Connors said. "Let's take a look. Holly, call for backup." She was already opening her door.

Holly was last out of the car, grabbing her radio as she jogged to keep up with the other two women. The rain was easing off.

"Delta Mike from Seven-Six-Two, urgent assistance required. 27 Winchester Avenue."

Ahead of her Yvonne pulled open the rear door of the van and Connors checked the front. There was nothing. The DI moved quickly to the entrance door of the garage and tugged at the handle. It didn't move. Nor did the side door when she went round to that and jostled the handle.

"Stay back and watch the front," Connors called to Holly as Yvonne caught up with her. "We'll try the house."

Holly nodded as Control came back on the radio: "*Seven-Six-Two, received. What's your situation?*"

"Vehicle registered to suspect Dean Patrick Fuller located," Holly said, moving up closer to the garage. "No sign of occupants. DI Connors and Five-Nine-Two with me on scene. They're trying the house."

"*Delta Mike, Three-One-Seven. Show us on way.*"

It was Oz's voice, but through it Holly's attention was taken by a sharp *snick* from the side door of the garage, like a bolt snapping back.

For a second she thought she might have been mistaken, but when the door started to open inwards she took a step towards it, tensing for whoever was going to come out.

"There's someone here!" she shouted towards the house, where Connors was banging on the door.

And then she saw the girl, holding herself up, but only barely, as she stepped out of the garage.

Gemma Hoskin's face was half hidden by a tangle of wet, blood-matted hair. Her arms hung down lifelessly by her sides and one hand trailed a length of electric cable, tied to her wrist. Her other hand grasped the handle of a hammer, but it fell with a clatter when she began to pitch forward.

Holly moved quickly to catch the girl before she hit the ground and struggled for a moment under her unconscious dead weight. Then Yvonne was beside her and together they dragged Gemma away from the doorway, let her down gently, turning her so that she was in the recovery position.

"Delta Mike from DI Connors, we need an ambulance to our location please. Asap. Unconscious female, looks like an assault."

"She's breathing," Yvonne said. "There's a pulse."

"Stay with her. – Holly."

Holly stood up and moved to the garage door beside Connors as the DI flicked out her asp and used it to push the door wider.

"Police!" she said. "Show yourself now."

There was nothing, but Holly caught the same cannabis smell she knew from Frank Chapman's garage. And then she saw the blood, trickling hesitantly across the smooth concrete floor in a rivulet of red.

Connors must have seen it too, because she stepped inside, her asp half raised, and took two quick paces to turn and look for the source of the blood. Behind her Holly tensed and crossed the threshold, ready to act if there was any movement or threat, but when she saw the DI's gaze drop to the ground she followed it and saw there wasn't going to be any danger.

On the floor near a workbench Dean Fuller's body lay in an unnatural pose, legs crooked, one arm outstretched. The upper part of his body had fallen on a number of small cannabis plants, breaking up several neat rows of pots, but leaving dozens more undisturbed. His face was pressed against the concrete and the blood they'd seen had pooled around it before leaking away towards the door.

Neither Holly nor Connors moved for a moment, but finally Connors lowered her asp, then picked her way carefully to the body and reached down to feel for a pulse.

Perhaps because the harsh overhead lights lent an almost surgical starkness to the scene – as if it had been set up for a movie – Holly felt no emotion: no desire to look away, no revulsion at the blood or the wounds. She knew what Connors was doing was only a formality and it was confirmed when the DI straightened up again after only a few seconds.

"He's dead," she said flatly. She gave the body one more appraising look, then stepped back, carefully retracing her steps.

"You okay?" she asked Holly.

"Yeah, fine," Holly nodded.

"Okay, let's get outside and preserve the scene."

Holly stepped out into the drizzle and saw that Gemma Hoskin was conscious again, with Yvonne still kneeling beside her. Then, from the road, Holly heard car doors slam and a few seconds later Sam and Oz arrived, running. In the distance there was the sound of an ambulance siren, getting closer.

23.

Gemma Hoskin was in shock, anyone could see that. As she sat on the cubicle trolley her eyes had a glazed look and when she answered questions from the young doctor it was only in monosyllables, her voice dull and lifeless.

She wasn't under arrest – not yet, at least – and although Holly and Yvonne were there to make sure she didn't try to run off, Holly knew there was no chance of that. Gemma Hoskin looked about as close to defeated as it was possible to be.

By the time the doctor had finished examining Gemma's injuries DS Woods had arrived with a female DC called Lorraine Pelman. The DC was plump and in her late thirties – the sort of woman an injured girl might feel comfortable with, and Holly was sure that was no coincidence.

"How is she?" Woods asked as he came over to Holly and Yvonne. He kept his voice down and looked Gemma over as he spoke.

"She's got a nasty cut on her head," Yvonne told him. "Possible broken wrist and she's been knocked about too."

"Any doubt she did it?"

"Don't think so," Yvonne said. "She was the only one in

there and she came out with a hammer in her hand."

"Right."

As he said it Holly's mobile started to ring and when she looked at the screen she hesitated, then glanced to Woods. "Sorry, Sarge. I think I should take this."

Woods nodded, okaying it, and Holly moved away towards the waiting area as she accepted the call.

"Hi, Taz," she said, making it light and friendly.

"Listen, I found out his name," Taz said without preamble. Her voice was modulating slightly so Holly knew she was walking as she talked. "I mean, the guy I saw this morning," Taz went on. "The one from the pictures: The Bandit. Danny told me to call you as soon as I found out. His name's Liam."

For a moment Holly hoped she might have misheard. "Liam? – L.I.A.M?" she asked.

"Yeah, that's it."

By a set of swing doors Holly paused and turned away from the passers-by. "Do you know his last name?"

"No, just Liam, that's all I could get. But Danny said that'd be all right. He said that'd be enough."

"Yeah, yeah, it is," Holly said, trying not to let the tightness in her chest make the words sound unnatural. "It's really good."

"So you'll tell Danny, right? Cos there's other stuff, too – stuff I've seen, yeah? But I need to meet you."

"I'll tell him as soon as I can," Holly said. "It probably won't be till later though, okay?"

"Okay. Tell him to call me then, yeah?"

"Yeah. Yeah, I will. Thanks, that's really great."

"Okay. I gotta go."

When the connection went dead Holly stood without moving for a moment as she realised that the slender doubts she'd been keeping alive had just been dispelled. That one word had done it.

"All right?"

"Huh?" She turned quickly at Yvonne's voice. "Oh. Yeah."

"Okay, come on then. We've finished here: DS Woods is taking it."

And as Yvonne started towards the exit Holly put her phone away and tried to work out what to do now.

By the time they got back to the nick fifteen minutes later she thought she knew, and when Yvonne was called away to give Inspector Williamson an update Holly turned down the corridor towards the Duty Sergeant's office.

The door was open and inside Sergeant Eddie Stafford was taking papers out of a printer. He looked up when Holly knocked on the door, then beckoned her in before moving back around his desk to sit down.

"You just back from the Vic?" he asked.

"Yeah." Holly nodded.

"I don't know – two deaths in two days? You'll be getting a reputation."

The way he said it, Holly could tell he was making it sound

flippant so he could judge her reaction. She knew she should come back with something to show it wasn't a problem, like *Yes, Sarge, people are just dying to meet me*. But she also knew she wasn't in the right frame of mind to carry it off, and besides, maybe it wouldn't be a bad idea if he *did* think she was finding things a bit difficult.

"Yeah, I'm just lucky I suppose," she said without any conviction.

The reply was enough to make Stafford narrow his eyes and frown. "So what did you need?" he asked, more serious now.

"It's a favour," Holly said. "My mum just called me and there's a bit of a problem at home. She's not feeling well and my brother's going to be back from school soon, so she could do with some help... I know it's not— I mean, I wouldn't normally ask, but if I could clock off a bit early..."

To her surprise, Stafford nodded before she'd finished the sentence. "If you need to be there, you'd better go. A family emergency counts as a valid reason to leave early, so get yourself gone. How're you going to get there?"

"I thought I'd better get a taxi."

"Fine. Go and get your stuff, I'll call it – should be out the front by the time you're ready, okay?"

"Yes, Sarge. Thanks."

As she moved to leave the office she felt bad about lying to him. Stafford was probably the most decent copper in the building, but she knew she didn't have any choice.

"Holly—?"

She looked back. "Yes, Sarge?"

"If you need to be there tomorrow as well, let me know, okay?"

"I don't think I will," Holly said. "But thanks."

24.

The minicab pulled up outside just as Holly left the station through the front entrance and when Holly told the driver where she wanted to go he took a minute to put the postcode into his satnav before setting off. He didn't say much after that and Holly was glad of the silence. She didn't feel like making small talk; all she wanted was to get there.

No, not true.

The last thing she wanted was to get there, because then she'd have to tell her mum what she knew: that Liam hadn't changed at all; that he was lying to her and that soon he was going to be in trouble again.

And the trouble wouldn't end there. Because not only had Liam lied to Lisa and Archie, he'd also made a liar out of Holly as well.

From the moment she'd seen his face on the CCTV of the warehouse raid she'd been lying, just by keeping quiet. As soon as she'd seen the CCTV she should have spoken up and told Danny Simmons the truth. She should have said *I know him. His name's Liam, Liam Mason.*

But she hadn't. Instead she'd pretended to herself that she might be wrong because she'd been afraid of the inevitable questions Danny would ask: *how* did she know Liam...? How *long* had she known him...? What was her relationship with him...was she aware...didn't she know...?

And then, as sure as a falling brick hits the ground, all the things she'd wanted to keep to herself would be out there in the open: that she knew Liam was a criminal; that he used to live with them and that for years she'd covered her ears when he got drunk, trying to block out the sounds she knew would come when he slapped her mum around.

She should have spoken up, but she hadn't and now it was too late. When Liam was arrested, as he would be once Danny Simmons had talked to Taz, it would all come out and everyone would realise that just by trying to keep it a secret Holly had proved herself unfit and unsuitable to ever be a copper, no matter how much it meant to her.

Suddenly it was all too much to hold in at the same time and Holly leaned forward quickly, her voice urgent and desperate over the cab driver's shoulder.

"Can you stop? Stop the car, please!"

She saw the driver glance in the mirror and caught a glimpse of her own pallid face there too. Then the car was braking, pulling in by the kerb, and Holly already had the door part way open by the time it came to a stop.

She managed to scramble out and made it three steps across the pavement before she bent over and threw up on the grass verge.

* * *

Finally, when it was over, she spat a couple of times, then straightened up and took some deep breaths before moving back to the cab.

"You feeling okay now?" the driver asked. He hadn't left the car, but just sat there and waited, eyes turned away.

"Yeah," Holly said. "Sorry. Dodgy burger for lunch."

"There's a twenty-five pound cleaning charge if you're sick in the car, okay?"

"Yeah," Holly said. "It's okay. I'm all right now."

She dug in her pocket for chewing gum to take away the taste, then pulled the door closed.

The driver watched her suspiciously for a few seconds longer, then turned to face forward and put the car into gear. Neither of them spoke again until they reached Collington and Holly told him where to pull in as she looked for the fare.

On the pavement she waited till the cab drove away, then started towards the low-rise block where her mum's flat was on the first floor. Part of her still wanted to change her mind and just leave it, walk away and go back to the Section House. After all, there was still a chance that no one would make a connection between Liam and her – *if* she said nothing, if *Liam* said nothing, *if* her luck held…

But she knew it wouldn't. Liam would know she'd kept quiet, and that meant he'd always be able to hold it over her – as a threat, as a way of getting what he wanted. *Do this or I tell them.*

No, there was nothing else she could do now, only go forward and face whatever came in the end.

* * *

As she climbed the stairs to the first-floor landing Holly looked at her watch and realised that Lisa probably wouldn't be home yet. Archie would be finishing school about now but it would take them a while to get back – maybe enough time to make a cup of tea to strengthen her resolve.

As she passed the window of the first flat in the row she kept her eyes forward and walked briskly, but before she reached her mum's door she heard a movement behind her and knew she hadn't escaped.

From the neighbouring flat Mrs Brodie – a stick-like woman in her late forties with black, heavily dyed hair – had come out. There weren't many people who made it along the walkway without Mrs Brodie clocking them and noting their business.

"Oh, hello, love – it's you, is it?" the woman called out. "Back again already? They don't keep you very busy at that police station, do they?"

"We caught all today's criminals so we finished early," Holly told her.

She pushed her key into the lock and turned it to open the door. Mrs Brodie wasn't put off though, and she came two or three steps along the landing, closing her cardigan over her thin chest.

"Oh, right," she said, missing or ignoring Holly's sarcasm. "Still, must be nice for your mum to get a bit of privacy when you *are* away, eh? Now she's got a new man in her life, I mean."

She gave Holly a knowing wink. "She's still a good-looking girl, your mum."

"Sorry, I don't know what you mean," Holly said, not in the mood to play games.

"Ooh, don't you?" Mrs Brodie made an exaggerated play of the exclamation. "Well maybe I shouldn't have said anything then. – No, but you *do* know," she went on. "I saw you and him yesterday, out here talking before you went off."

When she said that Holly realised who she was talking about. She shook her head. "No, that was Archie's dad," she told the woman. "My mum and him aren't together any more. He just comes round to see Archie sometimes."

"Really?" Mrs Brodie arched an eyebrow. "Archie's been off school today then, has he? Cos I saw him – what's his name – his dad?"

She broke off and deliberately waited for Holly to fill in the blank.

"Liam," she said.

"Ah, right – Liam. – Well, like I said, I saw him here this morning. Went in for a bit, then went off again about ten minutes later. I remember cos I thought it was odd, Lisa being out at work and all. But then I thought—"

"Wait," Holly said, cutting her off. "Liam was here today?"

"Yes, like I said, about half eleven – just for ten minutes. – Oh dear, I hope nothing's wrong."

Holly could see that the woman was hoping just the opposite, but she stopped herself from saying the first thing that came into her head and instead gave her a falsely sweet smile. "No, I'm sure it isn't," she said. "He was probably just dropping some stuff off for Archie. – I'll see you later, okay? Bye."

And before Mrs Brodie could come up with anything else to say Holly stepped into the flat, closing the door behind her.

Inside she stopped and just stood there. For a moment she listened to the silence, then called out: "Hi, it's me! Anyone home?"

There was no answer, no sound, which was what she'd expected. She shrugged off her coat, dropping it over the back of the sofa. The sitting room looked no different to the previous day – a few scattered toys and one of Archie's sweatshirts draped on the arm of a chair. But it *felt* different, knowing that Liam had been here when no one else was, like he'd left a lingering smell. And because Holly was sure she knew what he had been doing, it made her feel sick – not sick in her stomach this time, but in her chest: a tight, angry thing. How *dare* he!

To be certain though – for the proof – she had to go and look, so she moved then, briskly and with purpose, past the kitchen-diner and along the hall past the bedrooms.

She didn't bother to look at any of those places because she knew they wouldn't have interested Liam. People like him – like Liam especially – didn't change their habits, so she knew exactly where he would have gone: the one place he could go whenever he came to the flat on the pretence of seeing Archie;

the only place he could lock the door and be alone for five minutes without anyone wondering why.

Holly knew all this because once – when she'd been a lot younger and they'd lived in their previous flat – Liam hadn't bothered to lock or even close the bathroom door. He'd thought he was alone but Holly had seen him, kneeling down beside the bath in virtually the same position she took up now, awkward and uncomfortable on the hard wooden floor.

A strip of chromed metal secured the bath's side panels where they met at the corner and using the edge of a penny it took her less than two minutes to wind out the screws that held it in place. The end panel sprang free then, and when she put a hand into the gap it created she immediately felt the smooth surface of a polythene bag. She drew it out carefully, and after a brief look at its contents she started to refix the panels the way they had been.

25

She was eleven again, sitting on the bedroom floor, waiting for the silence to end with the sound of the front door banging closed. It hadn't been her mum and Archie she was waiting for then. It was always Liam – waiting to see what sort of mood he was in and trying to gauge how long it would be before the shouting started or something was thrown, usually a bottle or glass.

She didn't blame her mum; she never had, although she knew Lisa didn't believe that. Her mum always thought it was her fault – for not being strong enough, for not being able to cope – but Holly had always known the truth. There was only one person to blame and that was Liam Mason.

It had been worse in the last few weeks before he'd finally left for good. Archie was only a year old then, but it made no difference to Liam. Liam was the man of the house and in his eyes his needs should always come first, even if it was midnight and he was coming in drunk from the pub.

When Liam walked in he expected everyone to stop what they were doing, no matter what. Sleeping or eating or changing a nappy, none of that mattered: Liam was back, king of the bloody castle, make no mistake. His word was the law, and the punishment for not obeying, for not moving quickly enough, was always the same.

The one thing – one very small thing – that Holly might have offered in mitigation for Liam Mason was the fact that he'd never laid a hand on her or Archie – only ever her mum. And she felt guilty about that – guilty for the fact that Lisa took the slaps and punches and she didn't.

Sometimes – if Holly had tried to step in, to protest, to protect her mum – Liam had raised his hand to her, threatening, making her wince and shy away. But the threatened blow had never landed and Holly had never been able to work out why. But as she thought about that now she knew the answer. Liam hadn't hit her because he didn't need to. In the moment when she braced herself for the blow, Liam knew he'd won. Holly was scared and powerless then, just like Lisa, and that, more than anything else, was what Liam Mason wanted.

Beyond the bedroom she heard the sound of the key in the front door and then the rise of two voices – her mum's and Archie's. Holly came out of her thoughts; no longer eleven, no longer powerless and no longer scared.

She picked up the mug of tea that had gone cold beside her and got to her feet, calling out as she did so to tell them she was there.

26

In the sitting room Archie was watching cartoons. They could hear the sounds of crashes and bangs but neither of them wanted him to turn the volume down because the sound covered what they were saying.

Lisa was standing beside the dining table with her back to the window. She held had a hardly-touched cup of coffee in both hands.

"It might not be him though. You said the pictures weren't clear."

"It's him," Holly said flatly. "Mum, he's *using* you – using this place. *Look*. This was hidden under the bath."

She held up the plastic ziplock bag, the incontrovertible proof. At a rough estimate there was about 200g of what she was sure was cocaine, divided up into half a dozen individual sealed sachets. In a separate bag there were also about fifty Ecstasy tabs, each impressed with the outline of a flower.

Her mum looked at it for a moment, disbelievingly. She shook her head. "But why would he—"

"Because he's on parole!" Holly cut in. "He knows they could search his rooms, but if it's here it's safe, isn't it? He just takes what he wants – what he can sell – whenever he comes to see Archie. And if you're not here he lets himself in."

"But he hasn't got a key. I didn't give him one. I wouldn't."

"Mum, Jesus! How hard would it be for him to nick the spare, get it copied? Mrs Brodie *saw* him coming in." She paused, shook her head. "Look, why are we even *arguing* about it? This proves it!" Holly shook the plastic bag. "This and the warehouse robbery. He's going back inside, as soon as CID know."

"Are you going to tell them?" There was a note of trepidation in her voice.

"I don't have to," Holly said. "Someone else has identified him: an informant. I should have told Danny Simmons already but he'll find out even if I don't."

"Are you sure? If—"

"Yes!" Holly couldn't keep the frustration out of her voice. "I *told* you this would happen. I told you he was never going to change, and he hasn't."

She hadn't wanted to say *I told you so*, and when she saw her mum's face fall she felt even worse about it. But she wanted to get it through to her mother that there was no going back on this, no way to pretend it wasn't happening. Her mum had to see things the way they really were, and if that meant saying *I told you...*

"So what are you going to do?" Lisa said then.

"First, get rid of this." Holly picked up the plastic bag from the table and headed out of the room.

By the time Lisa came to stand in the doorway Holly was using a pair of scissors to cut open each individual sachet of white powder before shaking the contents into the toilet bowl.

"Don't you need it?" Lisa said, sounding worried. "Isn't it evidence?"

"I can't hand it in," Holly said. "I'd have to say where it came from and no one's going to believe I found it on the street."

"But when Liam—"

"I'll deal with that."

Holly turned so her mum would know this was important. "Mum, listen, he can't come here again, okay? He can't come to see Archie, he can't take him out. He's going to be nicked – any time – and if Archie's with him... He just shouldn't be, okay? – Okay?"

Lisa hesitated, then nodded.

Holly took the last bag – the one holding the Ecstasy tabs – and emptied it into the toilet bowl, then she flushed it. When the water stopped running there was nothing left and she moved to the sink, running hot water from the tap into each plastic bag, rinsing them all thoroughly.

Her mum watched in silence. It was as if she no longer recognised her daughter – or the brisk, calculated efficiency of her actions – and there seemed to be a sadness in her face, as though she realised that things had changed for good.

"Are you— Can I do anything?" she said in the end.

Holly looked up from the sink. "I need a carrier bag."

When Lisa came back Holly had finished. She dropped each wet plastic bag into the carrier, then tied it firmly with the handles. She was pretty sure there would be no trace of the drugs left, but she wanted to be certain that even if the sachets were found they couldn't be linked to the flat, to her mum or herself.

"I'm going to get rid of this," she said. "Five minutes."

Outside Holly held the carrier bag under her coat as she passed Mrs Brodie's flat. The woman was on the landing, cleaning her windows – the cleanest in Collington – but because she was already talking to another neighbour Holly managed to get past with just a nod.

She went down the stairs at the end of the landing, then round to the back of the block where the large communal dustbins were kept. She lifted the lid of the furthest one and threw the carrier bag to the back. It was done.

Except that it wasn't. But calling Danny Simmons would have to wait, at least for a little while, until she worked out what she was going to say.

She was almost back at the stairs when the sound of a car door closing made her look round – no reason why – and then she saw Liam.

For a moment she hesitated, then she stiffened her back and strode out across the parking area towards him.

He was pocketing his keys as she approached and when he saw her he smiled, half-raised a hand in greeting.

"Hiya," he said, right as rain, normal as anything.

Holly didn't return the smile. "Did you forget something?" she said.

"Sorry, what?"

"When you were here this morning."

He frowned. "I don't know what you mean."

"Yeah, you do. You were seen."

"Listen, I don't know what you're talking about," he said, smile fading.

"Yeah? Well never mind, you can go away again now."

"Look, I just thought I'd bring this." He held up a plastic box. "It's another game for the Wii. I thought Archie'd like it."

Holly shook her head. "He doesn't need it," she said. "And that stuff – the stuff under the bath – it's gone. You should've thought of somewhere different to stash it."

He studied her for a moment, as if he was trying to weigh up whether this was a bluff. Then, suspiciously, he said: "What do you mean, 'gone'? Where is it?"

Instead of answering, Holly just gave him a look, then turned and started away. She'd gone three paces before she heard his feet behind her, then felt his hand on her arm. She stopped, spun on her heel and threw off his hand.

"Don't fucking touch me," she said.

"Or what?" His face was angry now, just like she remembered. "You gonna arrest me? You going to tell all the other coppers about it? – *Where's the stuff?*"

Holly stood her ground, jaw set. Then she laughed. It was deliberate, goading, because she wanted a reaction. She wanted to *see* him react – to *make* him react – because that was the only way she'd really know that she'd got the better of him.

"Down the toilet," she said. "Flushed away. – Happy now?"

She only half-saw it coming, and by then it was too late. The punch – not a slap, but a fisted punch – hit her from the side, connecting with her cheekbone, then with her nose, so hard it swung her round, made her stumble backwards. It was only the fact that she bumped into a parked car that kept her on her feet, leaning against it as its alarm started to go off.

By the time she'd recovered herself, blinked her eyes free of tears enough to see properly, he was already heading for the stairs. And despite the blood from her nose, the pain in her cheek, she went after him, determined he wasn't going to go anywhere near the flat.

"Liam!"

He stopped and turned round, hand half-raised for another blow. But Holly didn't stop. Instead she charged right up to him, grabbing his shoulders as if she was about to hug him. Only it wasn't a hug and she brought up her knee as hard as she could so it connected with his crotch. Then, when she heard and felt the explosive "Ooof" sound he made, she did it again before stepping back to watch him double up and fall to the ground.

27.

The IRV must have been in the area already because it had arrived before Liam could stand on his own. Even by the time he'd been arrested he still couldn't walk properly and he'd limped to the patrol car with his hands cuffed in front of him.

Holly didn't know the Collington coppers, but once they'd seen her ID and she'd told them what had happened they were pretty decent. Why not? She was in the Job and she was the victim, that much was clear from the blood down her front and the swelling under her eye.

It was Mrs Brodie who'd seen it and called the police, Holly found out later. She'd also hurried along to Lisa's flat to make sure her neighbour didn't miss the drama, although by the time Lisa had run down to the car park it was all over and the IRV was there.

For Holly the worst thing was her mum's horrified expression when she got close enough to see the blood and the bruising. Holly thought Lisa was going to cry, but then she stiffened her shoulders and came forward to gather Holly into a hug.

"Don't Mum, you'll get it all over you," Holly protested, meaning the blood on her jacket.

She tried to step back but her mum held her closer. "Oh, sweetie, I'm so sorry," she said. "It's all my fault."

"No." Holly shook her head then repeated the word more

firmly. "No, it isn't. It's his." She looked towards Liam Mason, over her mother's shoulder, then turned away and finally put her arms round Lisa.

"*I'm* sorry," she said. "For before, the stuff I said... I never thought it was your fault. I *knew* it wasn't. I was just so— So mad about what he'd done. I shouldn't have been like that though. I never meant it."

Lisa studied her daughter's face, then she drew her closer, as tight as she could, and Holly did the same, needing that more than anything.

TUESDAY

Sergeant Stafford had left a message on her phone telling her not to come in until eleven, and then not unless she felt up to it. But although Holly knew the large, swollen lump and the sickly-green black eye above it gave her every reason to call in sick, she didn't. She wanted to face whatever was coming and get it over. At least then she would know how bad it was going to be.

So at five to eleven she entered the nick and got changed in the silent locker room: no stab vest or utility belt, just uniform shirt, tie and trousers – Station Duty wear.

Once she'd changed she went to find Stafford, but she was surprised by the reactions she got from the other officers she passed in the corridors. Almost without exception, they smiled or winked or said something chirpy, like "*Nice one*", or "*Eye-eye*". And it made her feel a little – just a little – less out on her own.

Stafford was in the Duty Office and he waved her in and told her to close the door before motioning her to a seat. He took his own chair out from behind the desk and came to sit opposite her.

"How're you feeling?" he asked first, assessing her eye.

"I'm fine," Holly told him. "It only hurts when I smile."

"Okay, I'll keep it serious," he said. "That was a joke, by the way, but you don't have to smile. This is just you and me having a chat – completely informal, okay?"

"Yes, Sarge."

"Okay. So, the good news is that Liam Mason's been returned to Telbridge Prison for breaking the terms of his parole. He's also been charged with assault on the police for hitting you and he's under further investigation for the Shenford warehouse raid. You know about that case from working with Danny Simmons, yes?"

"Yes, Sarge."

"Right. – Have you talked to Danny about it since yesterday?"

"No, I haven't seen him."

"Hmm," Stafford said thoughtfully. "Well I think you'd better see if you can find him – just so things are straight. And Chief Inspector Harlow wants to see you."

"Now?"

Stafford shook his head. "He's at County this morning – budget meeting. After lunch. In the meantime, find Danny Simmons and sort out any paperwork you've got pending, okay?"

"Yes, Sarge."

"Where's Holly?" Taz asked. She didn't like the fact that the female copper Danny had brought with him was old enough to be her mum. The woman had a kind of do-goody look about her, like she was going to ask if you'd had enough to eat, got money for the bus and a clean hankie – in other words, treat you like a kid instead of like you knew what you were doing.

"She couldn't come today," Danny said. "Don't worry about that for now. She'll be here next time. Let's talk about this guy Liam."

He tapped the laptop keyboard and brought up an arrest photo of Liam Mason. "Is this the man you saw yesterday – the one with Tommy Vickers and Drew Alford?"

"Yeah," Taz nodded. "That's him."

"Was there anyone else with them – anyone with Alford?"

"No, just the three of them," Taz said without the shadow of a lie.

"So how did you find out his name – Liam Mason's name?"

"I saw Drew later," Taz said. "I've been chatting him up. Not that way – you know, like you told me: keeping in with him. He told me."

"Right," Danny Simmons said. "Okay."

"He's the right guy though, yeah?" Taz said of the photo. "I mean he's the one from the CCTV. That's him."

"Yeah, we think so," Danny said. "You did well to find out. It was a great tip-off."

"So will you nick him?"

"We already have. It was for something else but we'll be questioning him about the warehouse raid now we've got him."

"And there's a reward, right?"

"Yeah, there's a reward. We'll get to that in a bit."

"Cool," Taz said, pleased and showing it. "Cos there's some other stuff I need to tell you an' all – about Drew and Tommy Vickers, stuff I've seen them doing…"

DI Connors was in her office, but when she saw Holly enter CID she rapped on the window with a pen and waved for her to come in.

"Hello, BB," she said, standing up and coming round the desk as Holly opened the door. "Christ, that's a nice shiner. Did Collington get evidence photos?"

"Yes, ma'am." Self-consciously, Holly half-raised a hand to the swelling, then stopped herself. "Sorry, what's BB?"

"Ball Breaker," Connors said dryly. "You'd better get used to it cos I think it might stick. I heard your man's going to need an operation – *if* they can find them. Apparently the doctors think they ended up somewhere north of his belly button."

"I don't know. They might have," Holly said.

Connors chuckled. "Nice to think he's got a couple of lumps in his throat. – So, has anyone told you where we're up to on Frank Chapman, Dean Fuller and Gemma Hoskin?"

"No, I've only just got in."

"Well, Gemma's admitted killing Fuller – in self-defence. She's also confirmed that Fuller was growing the cannabis you found at Frank Chapman's place."

"Did Fuller kill Frank?"

"Gemma doesn't know, but she did hear Fuller and Mr Chapman arguing on Saturday night, which fits with the time of death. I think we'll be on pretty safe ground to say that Fuller *did* kill Mr Chapman, but it'll be up to the Coroner to decide whether it was an accident or deliberate – not that it makes any difference now."

"So it's sorted," Holly said.

"Yeah. – Which just leaves our falsetto friend, Liam Mason, and the Shenford raid – right?"

"Ma'am—" Holly started, but Connors cut across her.

"Have you spoken to Danny since last night?"

"No. I was coming to find him. Sergeant Stafford said I should."

Connors nodded and her tone became more serious. She said: "Danny's out at the moment, but I've talked to him. – Sit down for a minute."

She gestured Holly to an armchair and when she sat down Connors said: "This is unofficial, okay? Strictly speaking you should hear it from Chief Inspector Harlow, but I want to make sure we've all got our ducks in a row – do you know what I mean?"

Holly shook her head. "No – I mean, I'm not sure. I'm supposed to see Chief Inspector Harlow after lunch."

Connors pursed her lips, as if she'd hoped the answer would be different, then she sat down in the other chair, facing Holly.

"Off the record, I've been reliably informed that Liam Mason's made a complaint against you."

"A complaint?" Holly said. It was the one thing she hadn't expected.

"For assault and for planting evidence."

"What evidence?"

"A hundred Ecstasy tabs found when he was nicked. Apparently he's claiming you tried to give them to him and when he wouldn't take them you kneed him in the balls."

"No, that's rubbish," Holly said immediately. "I kneed him because he'd hit me and I wanted to detain him. I didn't even know he'd got drugs on him."

"He's claiming you planted them because you wanted to stop him seeing your mother and brother."

For a moment Holly didn't say anything, but she knew it was exactly what she should have expected from Liam.

"Tell me about Mason," the DI said. "How do you know him?"

"He's— He used to live with us, with my mum."

"When?"

"About four years ago – until Archie was a year old."

"He's Archie's father?"

"Yes."

Connors nodded, as if that made sense. "So, *did* you want to stop him going round to your mum's flat?"

"Yes," Holly said, the truth.

"Why?"

"Because—" Holly hesitated, but then she gave up trying to guard her words, to disguise the truth. "Because he used to hit her, when they were together. And because he's scum. Archie doesn't need a dad like that. He doesn't need him at all."

"Did your mum report the assaults?"

"I don't think so. The police never came."

Connors considered that, then she said: "Mason sounds like a great father figure. I'm not sure I'd blame you if you did try to get him sent away."

"I didn't, ma'am," Holly said emphatically. "I—"

She was going to say *I didn't need to* but stopped herself. "If he had drugs on him it was because he brought them with him. I didn't put them there."

Connors drew a slow breath, then nodded. "Good. I believe you – mostly because I don't think you're that stupid. So, let's move on. Danny's briefed me about the identification of Liam Mason on the Shenford warehouse raid. I'll tell you how I think it stands and then you can say if that matches your take on it, okay?"

"Yes, ma'am."

Connors stood up and paced a little – the way she usually gathered her thoughts. "Okay, as I understand it, on Saturday your informant, Taz Powell, was shown CCTV footage of the raid and asked if she could help identify one of the men in it. Yes?"

"Yes."

"Then yesterday Taz phoned you and said she'd found out that the man on the CCTV was Liam Mason."

"It wasn't—" Holly started to say.

"Wait," Connors cut her off, then continued her train of thought. "Because you know Mason from your personal life you challenged him when you saw him in Collington and he assaulted you. Mason was arrested and as soon as you could you contacted Danny to tell him what had happened."

The DI paused, then looked directly at Holly. "Have I got that right? You couldn't have identified Mason any sooner because you didn't see the CCTV from the warehouse when it was shown to Taz Powell. Correct?"

Holly took a moment, then drew a breath. "Ma'am—"

"Good," Connors said. "That's what I thought. Danny doesn't usually get things like that wrong and anything else would just make life more complicated."

For a second or two – although it seemed longer – Holly didn't reply. She knew that the DI was giving her a way out – a way to explain away the fact that she hadn't identified Liam as soon as she'd had the chance or even the suspicion – but she also knew that she didn't want to cover things up any more.

"I don't want to make things more complicated," she said. "But it isn't that simple."

"I know. It never is," Connors said, as if she'd expected it. "Christ knows, it's never simple when the Job bumps into your personal life – and it happens to everyone some time. The question you have to ask yourself is, would anything you could say now mean that Liam Mason shouldn't be back in prison or investigated for the Shenford robbery?"

Holly thought about it, then shook her head. "No, ma'am."

"Right. So we'll stick with the simple version. I like keeping things simple – it helps the men around here. Okay?"

"Yes, ma'am."

"Good. And now you can bugger off and let me get on."

In the Observation Room Sam Marsden watched the monitors as DS Woods took Gemma Hoskin slowly and painstakingly back through the sequence of events that led up to her arrest on suspicion of murder. A duty brief sat beside the girl and there was a social worker off to one side as an appropriate adult. The social worker had been brought in when Gemma had finally revealed her true age as sixteen, rather than the eighteen she'd always claimed when previously arrested for prostitution.

This was the second interview. Last night's had been relatively short, ending fairly soon after Gemma had admitted hitting Dean Fuller with a hammer in the garage at 27 Winchester Avenue. Although Gemma couldn't remember how many times she'd hit him, Sam knew the PM report said three. Cause of death: blunt force trauma consistent with the hammer retrieved from the scene.

The whole case seemed cut and dried. Gemma was denying nothing. Her voice was flat and emotionless when she spoke and her shoulders sagged. Unthinkingly, she picked at the cuticles of her nails, occasionally lifting a finger to her mouth to worry at the skin.

"So you planned to get away from Dean by taking money from Tony Deakin, is that right?" DS Woods asked.

Gemma nodded. "Yeah."

"You told Mr Deakin that you knew where his daughter was."

Gemma gave another flat "Yeah".

"*Do* you know where Andrea Deakin is?"

For a moment Gemma appeared not to have heard him, but then she shook her head. "I just needed the cash," she said, tired and lifelessly. "To get to London. That's why I said I did."

"But it wasn't true."

"No."

"Right," Woods said. "So let's talk about what happened when Dean found you at the park…"

In the Observation Room Oz Sitwell shifted beside Sam. "Come on, that's all we needed to hear," he said.

Sam nodded. It was.

"Are you *sure* she doesn't know?" Tony Deakin said.

"Yes. I'm sorry," Oz told him. "She just wanted the cash to get away from her pimp. She was just stringing you along."

Tony Deakin sat very still and Sam could tell that he was finally accepting that it was true and that there was nothing more he could do – at least nothing here.

"What'll happen to her?" Deakin asked then. "I mean, look, I don't want to press charges or anything – over the money. I don't want her to get in any trouble, so…"

He looked at Oz, then at Sam, and Sam realised the man didn't know about what had happened at the garage, or that Gemma Hoskin had been arrested for murder.

"It's okay," Oz said. "You don't need to worry about it. There won't be any charges from that."

"Oh. Right. Good," Tony Deakin said, and it seemed that his relief was genuine. "So, is that it then?"

Oz nodded. "As far as we're concerned, yes."

"Right." Deakin nodded.

"What will you do now?" Sam asked, not just as something to fill the silence.

Deakin shrugged. "Keep on looking. That's what I set out to do. This doesn't change it. I just want to find Andrea, or at least let her know I'm trying." He looked at Oz. "I will get some new flyers printed though – I mean, that don't say there's a reward."

"Might be wise," Oz said and stood up.

He opened the door of the front interview room and the three of them went out into reception. As Deakin fastened his coat, Oz said: "Have you talked to anyone at the Charlestown House Project?"

"No, I don't know it," Deakin said.

"They've got a drop-in centre on Old Dock Road. Quite a few homeless teenagers use it. Might be worth a look. The manager's name is Dianne Sommers. She's pretty good and she should be able to tell you where else you could try. Tell her to call me if you need to."

"Thank you, I'll talk to her."

"Good luck, Mr Deakin."

He shook Deakin's hand when it was offered and then Sam did the same.

"I hope you find her," he said.

He didn't say anything more to Oz when they went through the door into the back of the station. He knew better.

Holly saw Gemma Hoskin in the corridor as the girl was led out of the interview room. They'd make a good pair, Holly thought – her and Gemma, matched up with black eyes and bruises. It was different men who'd hit them but they were both the same type of men. The only real difference was that Gemma Hoskin had used a hammer to fight back, with the result that Dean Fuller wouldn't ever assault or abuse anyone ever again.

As Gemma was taken back towards Custody, Holly turned the corner and made her way up the stairs to the first floor. Outside the doors to the senior officers' corridor she paused and straightened her collar, then she stiffened her shoulders and went through. When the receptionist looked up from her keyboard Holly said: "TPO Blades to see Chief Inspector Harlow."

"The allegations against you are serious," Chief Inspector Harlow said. "You realise that?"

"Yes, sir." The sinking feeling in Holly's stomach had levelled out into a dull kind of resignation by now.

Harlow was a big man behind a big desk. He had three

silver pips on the epaulettes of his uniform shirt and matching streaks of silver in his hair at the temples.

He said: "I've spoken to Sergeant Stafford about your progress here and I've reviewed the statement you made to the officers at Collington yesterday evening. I'm also aware that Liam Mason was on parole and is currently the subject of an ongoing enquiry by our CID."

He paused, thought for a moment, then put his papers aside. "As far as the allegation that you assaulted Mr Mason is concerned, I'm satisfied that you acted in self-defence and that your actions were justified and proportionate to the situation, so there'll be no further action on that."

"Thank you, sir," Holly said, allowing no emotion into her voice.

Harlow nodded. "But as to the other allegation – the planting of evidence – it's less clear-cut. The fact that it involves— That Liam Mason had a personal relationship with you via your mother, makes it more complicated. – Was he living with your family when you applied for the TPO scheme?"

"No, sir, he was in prison and I hadn't seen him – *we* hadn't seen him – for a couple of years before that."

"Hmm. Okay. – Even so, with an allegation of corruption, which is what this amounts to, I have to involve the Directorate of Professional Standards. That's not to say I believe the allegation, but the DPS has to make sure it's properly investigated, and in many ways it's in your best interest that it has a full and proper airing. Do you understand?"

"Yes, sir," Holly said, her voice tightly controlled.

"So while that investigation is in progress you'll be removed from operational duty, starting now."

For a moment Holly just let it sink in. Then she said: "How long will that be for, sir?"

Chief Inspector Harlow shook his head. "To be honest, this situation – one involving an allegation against a TPO – hasn't arisen before, so it's hard to say. However, you'll remain on your training allowance and I'll see if there's a way you can usefully use the time at the training academy, okay?"

"Yes, sir."

"Okay, thank you, Holly. That's all for now."

In the locker room Holly changed back into civvies, then collected a few personal things she didn't want to leave behind. Yvonne remained quiet until she did that, then she said: "Don't take all your stuff – you're coming back. This is just extra holiday with pay."

"Yeah," Holly said. "Pity it's still March, otherwise I could work on a tan."

Then she asked the question uppermost in her mind: "What do you think will happen if Liam keeps on saying I was trying to frame him?"

Yvonne shook her head. "Listen, you're going to get this again and again – we all do. You nick someone and they try to get out of it by slinging accusations around: *I was framed; I was assaulted; she had it in for me*... We all know it's bollocks, but it goes with the Job."

"So what happens?" Holly repeated.

Yvonne's expression became firmer. "Listen, no one's going to believe him – they just have to go through the motions. And you have to ride it out – okay?"

Holly nodded, but it was more confident than she felt. "Yeah. – Yeah, sure."

She closed her locker, fastened the padlock and picked up her holdall.

It was raining when she left the station and started towards the Section House to collect her overnight bag. It was still raining two hours later when she boarded the bus for Collington, but Holly Blades didn't notice.

She stared out of the window but saw nothing beyond the grey-silver glass. Instead she thought back over everything she'd been through in the last few days and wondered if it had really been worth it.

But as the bus finally pulled out of the depot and the rain started to make long thin lines down the window, she knew that it had been. Whatever happened now, there'd be no more secrets and lies. Liam Mason could no longer cast his shadow over any part of her life. That was enough.

Two days after receiving information from Taz Powell, CID and uniform officers from Morningstar Road station raided a flat in Cloudsley House on the Cadogan Estate. It was found to be empty, although traces of Class B drugs were discovered, as well as cardboard boxes which were later connected to stolen goods. No arrests were made.

Apart from Dean Fuller, no other suspect was linked to the cannabis-growing operations at Frank Chapman's house and at 27 Winchester Avenue. Intelligence sources indicated that Thomas Vickers had supplied or paid for the equipment found at the properties, but this could not be corroborated. The owner of the second house – Edward Soper – pleaded guilty to allowing his premises to be used for the cultivation of cannabis. He claimed that he had only ever dealt with Dean Fuller and had been paid £1500 for the use of the garage. Soper was sentenced to eighteen months, suspended for three years. He was also fined £1500.

After considering all the evidence, the Crown Prosecution Service decided it was not in the public interest to bring charges against Gemma Hoskin relating to the death of Dean Fuller. The fact that she believed herself to be in immediate danger when she killed Fuller was deemed sufficient to justify her claim that she had acted in self-defence.

Gemma was assisted in finding accommodation by Weston Social Services and was supported while she remained on bail. A month after being informed that no charges would be brought against her, Gemma enrolled on an NVQ course in Beauty Therapy at Weston College. She has had no further contact with the police or with her family.

Liam Mason was returned to Telbridge Prison to continue his previous sentence and in October he was brought to trial for his part in the Shenford warehouse raid. He refused to name his accomplices and was found guilty by a majority verdict. He was sentenced to six years, ordered to run concurrently with the remainder of his existing sentence. He was told he would have to serve at least three more years before becoming eligible for parole.

Tony Deakin did not locate his daughter in Weston and returned home to Cardiff two weeks later. He and his wife have since been contacted by Andrea, who said she was well but did not wish to return home. Andrea Deakin has been removed from the Missing Persons database.

DON'T MISS...

VICTIM: TEENAGE FEMALE, 14 YEARS OLD.
UNCONSCIOUS. HEAD INJURY. LACERATION TO ARM.
STRUCK BY LORRY.

Why was Ashleigh Jarvis running so fast that she didn't see
the lorry? Why was she so scared? And why was she barefoot
on a cold winter's night?

It's Holly Blades' first case and she wants to know the truth.
But how much is she willing to risk to get at the *real* facts?

ISBN: 9781409547280
ALSO AVAILABLE AS AN EBOOK
EPUB: 9781409547297 KINDLE: 9781409547303

www.streetdutycasenotes.com
www.usborne.com/fiction